ONCE YOU
HAVE FLOWN

Amy Redford

Amy Redford

PublishAmerica
Baltimore

ISBN: 1-4241-4468-X (softcover)
ISBN: 978-1-4489-1070-0 (hardcover)
PUBLISHED BY PUBLISHAMERICA, LLLP
www.publishamerica.com
Baltimore

Printed in the United States of America

To Lindsay, my parents, Linda, Laura and Matt

ACKNOWLEDGMENTS

I would like to thank Andrea Criss for her editing/story assistance and Lola Davis-Jones for her suggestions and knowledge about the history/ geography of North Carolina. I also would like to send a special thanks to the 'Page Avenue Desperados' for their encouragement to write about friendships and to Billy Rickard for giving me wings to fly in his airplane.

Once you have flown, you will walk the earth with your eyes turned skyward; for there you have been, there you long to return.

—Da Vinci

CHAPTER 1

Ruby's auburn hair was blowing wildly as she headed south towards the Cape Hatteras Lighthouse. She knew Highway 12 by heart rounding curves through the scenic dunes that were peppered with sea oats. She could feel the intense heat from the afternoon sun causing her to perspire and feel sticky. Looking up through her open sunroof, she saw the blazing fireball against the blue July sky. The heat index had to be up in the hundreds she thought to herself, using a towel to wipe off her sweat.

Closing the windows in her olive Safari jeep, she turned on the air conditioner. *Maybe I should have put on a stronger sunscreen.* She frowned observing her pink skin. She aimed the vents towards her face. 'Oh yes, much better,' Ruby smiled welcoming the coolness. She passed empty vehicles parked along the road. *At least there are some surfers out there cooling off and hopefully catching a few good waves.*

Ruby was making great time until she approached a procession of tourist driving large campers and various colored pickup trucks adorned with fishing poles. They were crawling at a snail's pace. The tall sand dunes snaked along the road making it difficult to pass the convoy on the narrow, two-lane road. She was anxious to reach her destination but she knew she had to have patience for the remaining ten miles. The gap was going to be slow and long.

The radio station she was listening to began to fade. Ruby inserted a CD and began tapping her hands to the rhythm of Tina Turner's hit, "Simply the Best," as she sang along with the world famous diva. During the saxophone solo in the song, she pictured the musician giving his heart and soul to the music. Ruby longed to see her musician surfing the waves of the Atlantic or flying his Cessna in the clear sky overhead. She took a sip of her bottled water and continued driving to Frisco, North Carolina.

Several new businesses had replaced old ones and a few additional shops revealed themselves in Avon and Buxton. She would have to wait for a rainy day to explore the beach stores and intriguing art galleries. As she passed the front of The Red Drum Pottery in Frisco she read a sign advertising a bluegrass/jazz group. The performance would be held on Wednesday. Ruby loved all types of music, especially jazz. She made a mental note repeating, 'Wednesday, 7:30' out loud to make it official in her mind.

The last few miles seemed like decades until she made the familiar left onto Seaside Drive. She could hardly see the house from the uneven paved road. Massive new homes now occupied the previously empty lots. Ruby turned the corner and it quietly came into view.

The house was situated east facing the ocean. The two story fifty-year old cottage was built when the island was much wider and protected by gigantic sand dunes. Now the ocean could be seen from the ground level. Ruby waved to it as if it were a person. It looked much smaller compared to the recently built cottages, but it stood proudly with its history and longevity.

Ruby parked her jeep and examined the structure for any damages. The exterior of the house was terribly weather-worn. The wood siding had become a faded gray with paint peeling off of the maroon trim. She noticed some of the roof tiles were missing and a downstairs window had a hole, the size of a baseball. It had been at least two years since the house had been revamped and it looked like it needed another facelift. She would have to hire a carpenter to make the necessary repairs.

Ruby grabbed her drink and headed up the outside steps to the main part of the house. She could smell the salty breeze as she looked over the banister at the water. It was a sight for sore eyes.

She fumbled for the keys inside her bag and unlocked the padlock to the screened porch. It hadn't changed much since childhood. It had a comfortable wooden rocker with faded flowered cushions and a glass covered coffee table that displayed an old map of Hatteras Island. A round wooden picnic table occupied the far end, surrounded by three round shaped benches. It was a great place to eat and piece together jigsaw puzzles. The outdoor carpet was beige in color which helped to hide the sand trailed in by the beach lovers. Ruby quickly opened the windows to air out the hot, musty odor. It was like an oven inside. Sweat continued to trickle down her face.

In the kitchen Ruby hurriedly located the fuse box. She flipped on the main switch and went down the hall to turn on the AC control. It would take a while for the coolness to overcome the heat. At least there was a mild breeze blowing through the porch screens.

She plugged in her cell phone and turned on a CD to make the house seem more alive. Ruby retrieved the remaining groceries and bags before making up her king sized bed. She was soaked from the humidity and exhausted from the long drive. She wet her towel again with cold water and went to cool off on the porch. She sat in the rocking chair and used the wetness to wipe off the perspiration. She finished another bottle of water and leaned back in the chair. It was then she noticed the plane hanging above the couch in the living room. Ruby had painted the picture years before and recalled the day she had taken it to sell at the international art show in Vienna. She sold all of her work that day except for the plane. She had several offers for the painting, but Ruby couldn't part with it. She thought how perfect it looked on the beach wall. She longed for a ride....and to see the pilot...

* * *

It was barely dawn as Ruby climbed out of bed the next morning and slipped on her Lisbon t-shirt and jean shorts. She automatically flipped on the coffee button to make her favorite gourmet, vanilla-flavored brew. Ruby opened the sliding glass door and stepped into her pale blue flip-flops that had seen better days. She put on her sunglasses and Maui cap before heading to the beach.

Ruby kicked off her shoes and left them by the wooden fence. She walked along the water's edge watching her footprints sink into the wet sand. The sun was shining and the breeze was just beginning to stir. Ruby walked about a mile and ran up a tall sand dune to see the airplanes chained at Billy Mitchell's Airport. She remembered the numerous times she had landed and taken off from the miniature airstrip. She closed her eyes for a moment in reflection. Then like a stallion she charged toward the waves. She needed to cool off and focus on her long awaited rejuvenation that she knew would take place on this magical island. The water was cold and refreshing, taking her breath away. She swam over and under the waves like a dolphin feeling the force of the undertow thrusting against her body. Exhausted, she laughed staggering back to the edge like a drunk, falling into holes she couldn't see under the ocean floor. She grabbed her hair and slicked it back wringing the excess water. She twisted her shirt and watched the water trickle down her legs.

Back at the house, Ruby showered outside, washing away the salt and sand. She lathered up the fragrant shampoo and washed her hair letting the sudsy bubbles coat her body. The shower was open at the top and Ruby could feel the breeze blowing down on her. It was the feeling of freedom that she simply adored.

She quickly dressed and headed to the upper deck breathing the salty air again and welcoming the offshore winds. There were two Adirondack chairs and a table waiting for her on the platform. She chose the rocking chair and sat down carefully while gripping a fresh cup of coffee in one hand and balancing a bagel, book and reading glasses in the other. She carefully placed the items on the table and took her camera off of her shoulder. She removed the lens cover and snapped a few pictures of surfers and sea gulls. She had brought many rolls of film so that she could capture subjects and landscapes of the Outer Banks. Later she would interpret the photographs on canvas.

Having breakfast outside in Frisco made her feel spoiled. She had eaten in many cafes and restaurants all over the world but this spot was her number one. The island held her soul.

She finished her bagel and continued to sip her coffee. She propped her feet up on the railing and scoped out the scenery. She could see the Frisco Pier with a handful of anxious fishermen casting their lines…waiting to catch blues, trout, or whatever the ocean had to offer. Ruby could picture them at the end of the day in a local tavern sharing their "fish stories" with a mug of beer in one hand and bellowing laughter accompanying their tall tales.

In the distance several fishing trawlers were bobbing up and down with the busy ocean waves and a few tourists were gathering shells in front of the cottage. Ruby could hear drips of water splashing on the pavement under the deck where water had become trapped and settled. Unless it rained again, it would soon dry up and evaporate when the sun warmed up. Sea gulls were making noises as they glided through the sky over the water looking for their morning meal.

Tucking her shoulder length hair into her baseball hat, she finished her coffee. She thought about what she wanted to accomplish during her stay. She had paints, several canvasses, a typewriter, and, of course, her camera.

Ruby leaned back in the rocking chair feeling the sun's warmth. She closed her eyes as it hypnotized her. She rocked back and forth lulling herself to sleep listening to the creaking of her chair. She was trying to figure out what the date was and then she remembered… Today would have been her twentieth wedding anniversary. So many years had gone by since her divorce and she thought about how much her life had changed.

Suddenly Ruby heard a small plane taking off from the airport. She recognized it as the local green and orange Cessna tourists could hire to see the Outer Banks. When the weather cooperated, the pilot was always flying somewhere. She longed to be inside the plane and looking at the island through his eyes. The hum of his motor, the warm sun, and the rocking seemed to pull her through a heavy cloud. It was taking her back to her wedding day and the days gone by…

* * *

The organist began playing "Here Comes the Bride" while everyone stood up to honor Ruby. Her father was at her side quickly wiping away a tear with a brush of his hand. He was ready to be his daughter's escort down the flower-pedaled aisle. John Fraser was a tall, good-looking man with dark features. The gray tux he wore showed off his recent tan from his vacation at Frisco where he was born and raised as the son of a Scotch-Irish fisherman. He didn't realize how difficult it was to give away his little girl even though he thought Troy was a great person for Ruby. He admired Troy's drive and ambition giving him comfort.

Ruby was instantly blinded by the flicker of a flash from the photographer she hired. She turned and smiled at her father seeing a blue dot in the middle of his forehead. When the color went away she instantly became aware of all the eyes looking at her.

"Are you ready, Ruby?" asked her dad.

She nodded hesitantly.

Together, they locked arms and started their slow practiced walk.

Ruby felt like a princess. She had always dreamed of this day but now that she was the center of attention she was having second thoughts. She had been so happy the day she selected her gown. It had a small train with pearls embroidered around the edges. Her oval neckline also revealed a thin strand of pearls accenting her diamond teardrop necklace. Now, she was thankful to have the short veil hiding her emotions that were building up inside of her. She acknowledged her guest as she made her way down the aisle while her vision remained blurred. She had applied a light green eye shadow to match her almond shaped eyes. She envisioned the shadow and black mascara making watery streaks over her rosy cheeks. Ruby's mother had brushed her hair up in a knot and accented it with baby's breath. Her stomach seemed to match the knot on her head. She wished she had thought to tuck a tissue in her sleeve. *No one warned me about the crying. Isn't this supposed to be a happy occasion?*

The July weather proved to be quite hot inside the church even though the air conditioner was on. Ruby could feel her sweaty palms and heart pulsing as she walked towards her best friend. She momentarily had a private conversation with her conscience voice that peppered her with questions. *"What are you doing? What do you really know about this guy? Ruby, you're only twenty-one years old! Do you really love him? You've only known each other for one year. Is that long enough to marry someone?"* She was experiencing 'cold feet', but it was too late to run for it.

"It's OK honey, you'll be fine," her dad whispered sensing her nervousness and supporting her weak state. "I love you, Ruby. You look beautiful, and I'm so proud of you. You will always be my special little girl."

"Thanks, Dad," she whispered back, "I love you too."

After her father said those words, Ruby started thinking about her family and leaving home. John Fraser owned a small furniture store in downtown Raleigh and her mother, Sally, worked part time as a hairdresser at a nearby beauty salon. They were strict parents and had worked hard to raise their family. Ruby was the oldest of five children. The girls were two years apart. Diane and Elizabeth (nicknamed Lizzy) had blond hair and blue eyes like their mother. The twin brothers, Liam and Brad, were ten years younger than Lizzy favoring her father's side of the family with dark hair and eyes.

Ruby came back to reality when she saw her future husband anxiously waiting at the altar with a big grin on his face. He looked incredibly handsome in his light gray tuxedo with his blond hair and sea blue eyes. Ruby soon felt relieved with Troy's calmness. Her dad patted her arm as they stood in front of the minister.

"Who gives this bride away?"

"Her mother and I do."

John Fraser turned to kiss Ruby's cheek through her veil and he gave her hand to Troy.

Troy and Ruby repeated their vows.

"I, Ruby Leigh Fraser, take thee, Troy Alexander Slader, to be my lawful wedded husband 'til death do us part."

"I, Troy Alexander Slader, take thee, Ruby Leigh Fraser, to be my lawful wedded wife 'til death do us part."

"The rings please," said Rev. McDonald motioning Ruby's twin brothers to come forward. Diane, the Maid of Honor, took her bouquet and they exchanged rings. Lizzy had a firm grip on the twins after they delivered the rings so they wouldn't get into trouble. No one messed with Elizabeth, especially the twins.

"You may now kiss the bride."

Troy lifted her veil and kissed her quickly.

"Ladies and Gentlemen, let me introduce to you to, Mr. and Mrs. Troy Alexander Slader." Everyone clapped. Linking arms, they briskly walked out of the sanctuary while the "Wedding March" played loudly. When the church had emptied, the wedding party met the photographer to take pictures of the special occasion.

"I love you, Mrs. Slader," said Troy kissing Ruby in-between the photo shoots. "I could sure use a drink! It's hotter than Hell!" he swore wiping his sweaty face with his hand.

When they arrived at the reception they could hear the band playing and several couples were already dancing. The band members were good friends of Troy's and their music was a wedding gift. The newlyweds were told to form a line by Ruby's aunt who was Mistress of Ceremony. The party was a sit down dinner buffet with an open bar that seemed to be very crowded.

"Would you like a drink, Mrs. Slader?" asked Troy, smiling at her.

"Yeah, honey, thanks. You may as well give me a double of what you're having because it'll probably be a long time before we make it over to the bar again," Ruby said realizing how dry her throat felt. "I think I need some water first. I'll meet you at our table," Ruby said turning around as someone tapped her on the shoulder.

"Hi Bridge," Ruby said hugging her cousin from Asheville. "I'm sorry I haven't had much time to visit with you. I'm sure you remember what your wedding day was like. Were you as out of it as I've been?"

"Of course, I was probably worse. Don't worry, Ruby. We're having a great time even though I had to get up so early this morning. We had to get here an hour before you walked down the aisle. I think I did pretty well considering I had to miss rehearsal yesterday because of work. Anyway, I'm still trying to wake up." explained Bridgett looking up at her husband, John. She continued, "We left at four this morning. You know what I'm like at that time of day?"

"Yeah, you should've had the pleasure of waking her up," said John shaking his head and frowning. Bridgett punched him on the arm and then gave him a kiss.

Anyone could tell they were obviously still on their honeymoon.

"That color looks great on you," Ruby said admiring the bridesmaid dress she had picked out. "I hope you'll be able to use it for other occasions, as well," Ruby added touching the material of her sleeve.

"I'm sure there'll be something coming up at the end of the summer," Bridgett remarked putting her arm around Ruby.

"Yeah, remember when we'd drive around the Asheville mountain roads talking about life and boys and listening to loud bluegrass and country music. Now here we are five years later, old married women," Ruby laughed reaching out for the glass Troy handed her.

"Hi, you two. How'd you like the ring show?" said Troy clicking their glasses and then taking a huge gulp of his drink.

"It was almost as grand as ours," said John. "But you don't have a bluegrass band! You know us mountain boys like banjos and fiddles," he complained pointing to the band with his full glass.

"That's true, but ours is free!" boasted Troy.

"Do you think it's time to sit down and eat?" Ruby asked changing the subject and looking around as to what they were supposed to do next.

"Mom and everyone are over there at that table," said Bridgett looking over in their direction. "I'm going to get another drink. I'm so hot. You must be roasting in that wedding dress, Ruby."

"You're right, Bridge. I'm really hot and I need to get off of my feet before I fall over. Let's go find our places at the table."

Ruby's aunt rescued them from well wishes and whisked them to the wedding table. They happily sat down. Diane brought Ruby's plate to her and Elizabeth had fixed Troy's.

"Thanks, girls. You're lifesavers. Remind me to do this for you when you get married," Troy said hugging Lizzy and nodding to Diane.

"I don't plan on getting married," replied Lizzy seriously. "I'm not sure my husband could handle me!"

"I can see your point," Troy nodded agreeing with her.

"Well, I'm planning to marry," said Diane dreamily. "But first I want to live in New York and perform on Broadway. Maybe I'll marry a famous movie star."

"Maybe you can meet up with Bronco Billy for your sister here," laughed Troy.

"I'm sure he's too tame for her," retorted Diane smiling. "I think she'll need someone more like a football tackler from the NFL."

"Any one of the Oakland Raiders works for me," beamed Lizzy.

"Don't forget to sing my song later, Diane, when we start dancing. Maybe there's a talent scout out there waiting to discover you this very minute."

"OK, I haven't forgotten. But just to give you a warning," Diane said quietly.

"Lizzy wants to play the drums with Troy's friends. She and the twins have a special performance for the newlyweds. You know no one messes with Lizzy when she has her mind on something. You might want to put that veil back over your face!"

Ruby took a sip of her drink and decided not to think about Lizzy and her shenanigans.

"Girls, hurry and fix something to eat. They're filling up the champagne flutes and I'm sure you're both starving," Ruby said taking a bite of her chicken.

The sisters quickly left to fill their plates.

Troy's father started to clink his glass for silence. "I'd like to be the first to toast this wonderful couple. To the bride and groom. May they live happily ever after."

Tom, one of the band members, used the microphone to toast next. He held up his free hand to make Dr. Spock's Vulcan sign, "Everyone has to make the sign...It's the latest since the peace sign," he remarked with laughter. "Seriously, I only wish I'd met Ruby first!" Another uproar of laughter filled the room. "OK, my last remark for the evening." Everyone clapped.

"May you live long and prosper."

"May you always keep laughter and love in your hearts." said Ruby's father holding his glass up high. "Your mother and I have been very happy all these years and we hope you and Troy will be too."

Troy stood up taking Ruby's hand to join him. "I'd like to thank everyone for the toast and well wishes. I have to say I'm a lucky man today. I thank you all for attending this special day with Ruby and me and for all those expensive gifts. Just to let you know, if things don't work out for us, I want you to know I'm still keeping them. No refunds."

Everyone laughed.

With the toasts complete, the newlyweds were being signaled to cut the cake. Ruby threatened Troy with his life if he shoveled the cake all over her face. He was an angel except for the icing he placed on her nose. Ruby took a napkin and wiped off the excess. She didn't get a chance to rebel because a voice demanded their attention.

One of the band members announced: "Ladies and Gentlemen, we have several guest musicians and performers in our midst tonight. It gives me great pleasure first to introduce the Fraser Twins, Brad and

Liam, accompanied by the beautiful sister, Lizzy, on drums. This is a little number you may all recognize."

Lizzy sat behind the drums and tapped out the rhythm of "Great Balls of Fire" with the assistance of the band. Liam and Brad had slicked their hair back and pretended to play on cardboard pianos like Jerry Lee Lewis, the singer and songwriter of the famous number. The twins were actually good singers, but it was the hairdos that helped with the performance. Lizzy shook her blond hair wildly as she continued to beat the drums to the popular tune. She had acquired a headband and red tennis shoes that protruded under her dainty bridesmaid gown. She was defiantly the tomboy in the family. By the end of the song the boys had danced on top, under, and beside the real piano.

They were a huge success. Whistles and yells were heard when the song was over.

"That's a hard act to follow, but I think Diane can pull this one off if anyone can."

"This song goes out to Troy and Ruby," said Diane holding the microphone close to her lips.

The band started to play, "You Look Wonderful Tonight."

"They're playing our song. Are you ready to dance, Mrs. Slader?" asked Troy reaching for Ruby's hand. He walked her out to the center of the dance floor. Everyone soon joined them.

"I love you, Mr. Troy Alexander Slader. I can't wait until we can go to the hotel and take a nap." Ruby said sarcastically.

"Oh, you won't get any sleep tonight, Mrs. Slader. Didn't anyone ever tell you about the honeymoon?" he whispered in her ear. "I'm going to keep you up all night. You won't even think about sleep. I'm going to be the best husband to you and I will love you forever," he added kissing the back of her neck making goose bumps cover her arm. Ruby was ready to leave right then.

CHAPTER 2

The newlyweds found an apartment in the vicinity of North Carolina State where they had originally met and were attending school. Troy worked as a bartender two nights a week and Saturdays. Sometimes he wouldn't finish cleaning until the wee hours of the morning. He was taking an overload of courses each semester. Ruby admired the ambitious goals he had set for himself. Troy was hungry for money and being accepted socially by the upper class was important to him. He wanted to be the best at everything, no matter what the cost. On his time off between work and school, Troy lifted weights and worked out. He challenged opponents at local basketball courts at the city park and liked to show off his muscular physique to flirty girls when they walked by.

Ruby was employed at a photo shop and attended night school studying media and film. She had always been interested in special effects and being behind the lens of a camera. Photography was her hobby and she particularly focused on subjects using black and white film. She liked the shadows and detail it seemed to add to her prints. Her boss allowed Ruby to develop her own pictures at a discount.

During Troy's absence, Ruby decorated their apartment. She had an eye for interior design and assembled the items with great care and taste.

Most of their furniture was hand-me-downs from relatives and didn't really match, but was comfortable. Troy's grandparents had given the couple an old couch from their attic. It revealed a worn, dark brown covering and it had acquired a terrible musty smell. Ruby had never taken an upholstering class before, but she decided to attempt it. She purchased a light blue fabric with small yellow and purple flowers dotted on the material. She also bought a staple gun, nails, and a thick sewing needle. After three days she finally finished. The odor soon disappeared once the original covering had been removed. Ruby was quite proud of the results. It had a few flaws, but it looked new on the outside especially with the covered pillows she made to give it that Southern Living touch.

Ruby machine quilted a peach and green bedspread and matching drapes by using discarded material she found in her mom's closet for their oak bed. Her parents had given them an aged, white rug that now looked gray and dirty. No matter how much Ruby tried to vacuum or shampoo it, it still looked the same. Ruby was determined to change the color. She purchased some forest green dye, taking a day off from her job to complete the project. Using a bucket, scrub brush, and rubber kitchen gloves, she started to work. She emptied the dye into the watered bucket and scrubbed on her hands and knees for several hours bringing the dirty rug to life.

Troy complained about having to walk around with green feet for a week! But they had a beautiful new rug when it finally dried, even with a few small white spots where she couldn't lift the heavy bed. As long as Ruby didn't rearrange the furniture, no one would ever know, especially Troy.

Ruby was decorating their first Christmas tree when Troy walked into the living room with something wiggling in his arms. "Ruby, I have a Christmas present for you," he shared excitedly. "It's a little bit early, but the shop will be closed tomorrow," he continued rubbing some brown ears.

"A puppy," she exclaimed in delight. "A collie, Oh how adorable. Is it a he or she?"

"It's a she and I thought 'she' could keep you company while I'm away so much. What do you think? Do you like her?"

"Of course, Troy. What a sweetheart. You are so thoughtful. What shall we call her?" she said kissing him on the lips.

"I'm leaving that up to you, honey."

"How about Sadie? Oh, she is so cute," Ruby said taking the puppy into her arms and examining her. She rubbed her nose.

"I think Sadie is a perfect name. Just like my Ruby."

Ruby didn't realize it at the time, but the puppy would become her new companion. After the Christmas holidays, Troy rarely was home. When he woke up on Sundays he was off to the library to study for a test or to write a paper. It became a way of life. She knew it had to be this way for a few years until Troy finished school. But Ruby also knew the honeymoon was over.

Troy graduated with honors receiving a degree in Political Science and French. He spoke the language fluently and was interested in pursuing a career eventually in International Law. He knew that if he could speak French, he would have a good chance of securing a high paying job, maybe even overseas.

When Troy was accepted to Law School, Ruby decided to put her remaining two year education on hold and channel her energy on helping him achieve his goals first. After all, they were a team and had the rest of their lives to spend together. She would go back to school later.

* * *

Troy and Ruby attended the weekend orientation of the Georgetown University Law School in July. The room was full of anxious Want-to-Be Lawyers. One of the elderly law professors welcomed the new rookies and announced that if there were any married couples in the room, not to expect to be so after three years. Ruby took offense to her comment.

How's that for an introduction into law school? Even if it is a true statement for some cases, I don't think it's necessary to condemn my happy marriage. Of course, Ruby didn't want to believe it. She and Troy had the perfect marriage or at least it would be once they had both completed their degrees. Even though sometimes it felt like the light at the end of the tunnel would never be reached.

Ruby was hesitant at first about moving to Washington, D.C. She had heard how terrible the traffic was and how fast paced the large city moved. But the history and beauty of the capital embraced her. She soon fell in love with the excitement and flamboyancy it had to offer.

She and Troy stayed at a small hotel on the outside of the city, near the metro. Ruby ventured out alone to the Smithsonian when Troy was engaged with additional orientation meetings. She found a small one bedroom apartment listed in the newspaper. It was located in a high-rise apartment complex on the twelfth floor near King Street in Alexandria, Virginia. The rent included the use of a community pool and had a washer and dryer access in the basement. In addition, there were two assigned parking spaces in the underground garage. A nearby grocery was within walking distance, as well as, a small park for hiking.

Before the move, Ruby found a nice family with two small boys that lived out in the country to adopt Sadie. She knew it was only fair to her four-legged friend to give her a home with love and a yard to play in. It was an emotional time for Ruby, but it was soon evident that she would miss Sadie the most.

During their first fall months in Alexandria, Troy was home most nights and weekends. He usually appeared by the time Ruby had dinner ready to eat and they would talk for hours sharing their daily activities. They enjoyed most of their meals on the balcony when the weather was warm. Ruby had decorated it by planting flowers in several green window boxes and placing fresh herbs by the sliding glass door. The plants welcomed the east sun. Ruby loved the view and being high above the trees. It seemed like everything was falling into place. But trouble was around the corner for the couple, as the law professor had predicted…

Ruby actually met "the girlfriend" her first day of work at the university as the sport manager's secretary. Ruby walked up behind them while they were both laughing, standing in line at Dan's Deli in front of the student center. Ruby's first impression of her was that she was short, stocky, unattractive, and had a loud, obnoxious laugh. She had shoulder length brown hair and eyes. She was wearing a pair of jean shorts and a snug, pink tank top, revealing her protruding cleavage. Her polished lip gloss seemed to match her small top.

"Ruby, where did you come from?" asked Troy surprised to see her.

"I have half an hour for lunch before I go back to work. How long is your break?" she questioned avoiding eye contact with his friend.

"We have an hour. Oh, by the way, Ruby, this is Marla Hutchinson. Marla, this is my wife, Ruby."

"I didn't realize you were married, Troy," said Marla with a toothy smile that turned into a lower disappointed smirk.

"You weren't very observant, Marla. Here's my ring," he defended himself holding up his left hand. Troy had a possessive arm around Ruby while they waited in line and he kissed her several times in front of Marla. He hardly ever did that in public.

"Where are you from, Marla," Ruby asked irritated with her false pretense.

"I grew up in New Jersey, east coast," she replied in a thick northern accent. "I just love Washington, don't you?

"Yes, it is wonderful," Ruby answered agreeing with her. "Are you married, Marla?"

"Not yet, but I have a fiancé, Pierre Truso. He lives in Paris and goes to the university there to study business. We went to undergraduate school together. I have to wait until the semester ends before I can visit him on my break. We're planning to marry when I finish law school. Troy has offered to give me French lessons for a small fee, I might add."

"French lessons?" Ruby asked. "I don't know when Troy will find the time to study law and teach. I do want to be able to see him once in a while, you know, Marla," Ruby added with disapproval.

"Honey, you know we could use the extra money and I could use the practice with my French," he said. "You know practice makes perfect," he retorted in French.

Marla nodded to Troy in agreement. She then removed a gloss case from her purse and applied it on her lips with her middle finger. Before putting the lipstick back in her purse, she licked her finger slowly making sure Troy watched.

Ruby was appalled at the obscene gesture. She did not like this Marla Hutchinson. She wished she already lived in Paris and didn't go to school with her husband.

"It's time to order," Ruby said reaching the counter and changing the subject.

When the threesome sat down to eat at a picnic table, Marla sat opposite Troy and Ruby.

"Marla wants to be in a study group I'm organizing, as well as, two of her roommates," Troy informed Ruby taking a sip of his water. "I think we'll make a great team."

"Yes, I think our first meeting should be tonight," suggested Marla looking up at Troy with a flirtatious smile.

Ruby was aware of the chemistry that was taking place between the two when they made eye contact. "How often will you have this team meeting?" Ruby inquired trying to remain calm.

"We must meet at least twice a week maybe more depending on the class assignments. It's advised by the professors to have these meetings so we can help one another learn the massive case loads that we must memorize for Torts, etc. The nice thing about our group will be that Marla and her roommates live only a few blocks from school and we can study in the library or at their place."

"Will I get to meet your other roommates soon?" asked Ruby, anxious to see what they were like.

"They'll be at the freshman picnic on Saturday. They're great girls," bragged Marla. "We're already *very* close."

"Well, I must leave. Nice meeting you Marla. Good luck with the group. You must stop by sometime to visit us in Alexandria. Troy, I love you. See you at home later," said Ruby kissing him goodbye.

Reluctantly, Ruby returned to her office. At the time, she just brushed off the memory of them together when she walked away. But the scene was so vivid now. She remembered she left them laughing and visiting under the old shaded oak tree with the warm wind blowing Marla's hair...

Being the sole "poor couple" in Troy's class, it became too overwhelming for him. Most of his friends were from the New England states and they were from very wealthy families. Most of the Georgetown students were driving BMWs, Mercedes, Audis, and Porsche's. All brand new, Ruby noticed. An old blue Ford truck was their main transportation. The vehicle was as solid as a rock, but hard as nails to shift and the clutch was a real workout on the thighs! Troy had traded in their 1976 Mustang for this tank. Troy joked and laughed about the truck with his classmates but Ruby could tell deep inside that it really bothered him.

To add to their financial burdens, Ruby became pregnant shortly after her first meeting with Marla. Sarah Maude Slader was born on a hot, humid August day in Georgetown University Hospital. Ruby had a long labor but was able to have a natural delivery. Troy had stayed with Ruby during Sarah's birth. She knew he still loved her.

Sarah was the prettiest baby she had ever seen, even though she was bald and wrinkly. The nurse wrapped her in a hospital blanket and placed her in Ruby's arms. Troy took rolls of film and acted as a proud father should. A huge, bouquet of yellow daisies were placed on the table by her bed with a note from Troy. He was handing out cigars to everyone. Ruby understood the tremendous pressure he had with school. He attended summer classes and had exams at the end of every week. She prayed this new bundle of joy would help with the tension that seemed to always be present and building.

To Ruby's dismay, Marla also came to the hospital with a gift for Sarah. She offered to baby-sit for the new parents on any future, special occasion. Ruby felt her generosity was given for selfish reasons and to win points with Troy. It was obvious that he was infatuated with her. Ruby noticed he seemed to undress Marla with his eyes as her clothes lately had become tighter, revealing a sexier figure.

She must be working out. Why can't she just go to France and marry this fiancé, she always claims she has. It's funny that she never mentions him anymore. Marla reminds me of the evil step sister in Cinderella.

But she had to keep her thoughts to herself because Troy would always defend Marla and take her side. They had had this argument quite a lot lately.

Sarah was a demanding child that had become allergic to milk. The experts called it *colic*. It caused her tiny little system to react with pain causing frustrations for Ruby because she didn't know how to calm her constant crying. It was especially difficult to keep Sarah content when Troy had to study. He would throw his books down on the dining room table and pack up without saying a word. Usually he didn't return until the next night. Troy was around less and less because of exams and classes, or so Ruby thought. Sometimes he would bring home chocolate chip cookies and brownies that he said Marla had made especially for her. When Ruby confronted Troy with the idea of Marla liking him again, he told her she was crazy. "There will never be another you," he would always say with a smile.

Ruby wanted things to be the way they used to be. She tried to make special dinners, wear sexy nightgowns, use candles and play soft music. Nothing seemed to spark Troy from his studying or wanting to go out late at night to play basketball with the neighborhood brothers to get some exercise. The nights they did manage to have sex were long and miserable. It seemed like Ruby had become a robot instead of a lover and companion. Many times, Troy couldn't perform, which she later learned was from the drugs he was addicted to. She started to lose interest in making love with him and focusing on Sarah's needs, reading and needlepoint. She would go to bed before he would come home and pretend to be asleep when she wasn't. Ruby wondered how long this would keep going on. Ruby finally started eating before he got home and slowly but surely, she went to bed alone.

It was almost Christmas and Ruby was looking forward to attending the annual law school party. She had purchased a black evening gown on sale and had bought imitation diamond dangles to wear. She looked at her reflection in the mirror and saw an attractive woman. Ruby had curled her shoulder length hair and pulled hair up on both sides with barrettes to show off her earrings. She had an attractive figure under her clinging black dress. She was proud of losing the extra pounds she had gained before Sarah's birth. She thought she looked pretty good for being a twenty-four year old mom.

The dinner/dance was in the Crystal City Hyatt. The room was beautifully decorated and low lighted chandeliers hung down from the high ceilings. They sat at a table with several other married couples Troy knew from school. Troy looked incredibly handsome in his dark suit. Ruby brought her camera so they could get some photos to send to relatives for the holidays.

The dinner was a buffet and absolutely wonderful. The silver trays were decorated with poinsettia flowers placed in-between the finger foods and a large Christmas tree was centered in the middle of the dessert table. Around the main course entrees were small advent wreaths decorated with white, lit candles and miniature blue, red, and gold Christmas balls. Ruby would have loved it if they only had hamburgers. She had a night off.

The band played all the popular tunes and it was their night. They danced most of the numbers. Then Troy started asking some of the other girls in his class to dance. Ruby noticed Marla was sitting there waiting for him to come over. Marla couldn't keep her eyes off of him.

She had a date, but left him to dance with Troy. Ruby wondered if this was the famous fiancé. She couldn't believe he left her by herself at the table. She became quite upset and went to the ladies room to wipe away her tears. When she returned, the band announced they were going to play their last number, 'You Look Wonderful Tonight'. Ruby looked everywhere for Troy. She finally saw him already on the dance floor…she didn't even have to guess with whom.

Ruby tapped him on the shoulder and said, "This is our dance, Troy."

He said angrily, "I'm dancing with Marla. We'll catch the next dance. Go sit down. This is our Christmas Party."

"It's my party too, Troy. This was *our* song," Ruby said feeling her voice crack. Ruby managed to say angrily, "I never want to dance to it ever again."

Marla had that toothy grin on her face that had become her trademark. She teasingly backed away from Troy so he could dance with Ruby, but before Marla could say anything to her, Ruby had turned and gone to claim her coat at the counter. Tears trickled down her face. If she had had enough money for a cab she would have taken it. Instead she waited in the car. Troy didn't show up until an hour later. "Don't even start with me, Ruby. I had a great time and I don't want you ruining it for me." He slammed the car door and drove home without saying another word.

Ruby never attended another law school Christmas party. Neither did Troy.

* * *

Troy's graduation came and went. Ruby left her job at the university and began working for a Senator on Capital Hill during the Reagan Administration. Sarah was placed in the Senate Day Care and rode to work with her mom. Ruby could visit her on her lunch breaks and read to Sarah's friends. She liked having her close. Every day Sarah looked more like her father. She was a beautiful two years old with curly blond hair and bright blue eyes. She was a happy and sensitive child. She would rather play with other children than be left alone. On her days off, Ruby dressed her up and took pictures in different outfits relatives had sent in the mail. She would enlarge the best poses and give them away as gifts.

Ruby managed to buy a second hand car with the substantial pay increase at the Senate. It was a white Honda hatchback. Ruby liked it because it was small, good on gas, and easy to park. She kept extra food and diapers in the car with her because traffic jams were not uncommon.

Troy was employed by a small law firm in Roslyn. He appeared content with the position and responsibility that he had been given. When he was home though, he played with Sarah and seemed to love having a child however, their relationship had remained strained. Ruby was hoping the new job would give him a better outlook on life. It did, but not in a healthy way.

Ruby worked diligently in her office on Constitution Avenue. She had to admit that she was attracted to several single guys her age at the Senate. They were smart, already well established in their careers, good looking, and had money. *What was there not to look at?* She needed to feel attractive, because Troy didn't make her feel that way often. He began to mentally destroy her confidence. He complained that the house was never clean enough, she shouldn't stay on the phone so much, her clothes didn't match and her hair was too long or too short.

Several times the guys from work would ask her to lunch and at first she would decline. But after their persistence, she found herself saying *yes* to one.

His name was Matt Connery. He was from California and had graduated from UCLA. He drove a small red MG and lived in Georgetown. He always dressed in an expensive suit and looked incredibly handsome in whatever he wore. Matt had jet black hair and brown eyes that usually peered through a pair of wire rimmed glasses. He was an attorney for the senator and Ruby was his personal secretary. Matt was a perfectionist and many times drove her crazy when she had to retype something. Ruby liked kidding around with him and enjoyed his friendship, especially when she wasn't irritated with his picky corrections.

"Ruby, I'm going out to lunch. Why don't you come too? You've been working on that stack of papers all morning and you need to eat," said Matt placing his palms on her desk looking down at her. "I know a great place where we can eat and have a little conversation. We need to celebrate your eighth month in our office." he added before she could say a word.

"Why are you keeping track of how many months I've worked here? Are you going to replace me?" Ruby said making a face. "I don't even know how long I've been here myself," she replied holding up one hand and shrugging her shoulders.

Matt continued to stare at her not saying a word.

"OK," she said giving in. Ruby happily left the work on her desk. "Let me powder my nose and I'll meet you in front of your office."

She applied peach lipstick and looked at her reflection in the mirror. Using a scrunchy she pulled her hair up in a knot. Her hair was a little longer than her shoulders. The light peach blouse made Ruby's eyes have a soft glow and she thought her figure looked attractive in her suit. The weather had begun to get cold so she put on her black jacket and wool hat.

Matt was waiting for her. He smiled and they chatted all the way to the restaurant. Ruby felt at ease with him, away from the stress and busy schedules that needed attention. The day was sunny and the leaves showed reflections of the fall colors. They walked past a beautiful garden surrounding a fountain. There was a statue in the center of it with children playing. Water came out of the pitcher one boy held in his hand. Yellow and orange mums had been planted around the fountain. Each season the city changed the flowers to adapt to the weather. The spring had had colorful tulips and cherry blossom trees. The summer held marigolds and geraniums of all colors. It was a nice place to sit and read on one of the benches, as she had done during the first months of her employment. *I will have to bring Sarah here some day.*

He escorted her to a small French restaurant near the office.

"Have you been here before, Ruby?" asked Matt after they were seated in a cozy corner by the window and given menus by the waiter.

"No, but I've heard the other girls from the office talk about how wonderful their salads are. What do you recommend?" Ruby questioned him smiling.

"I also like their salads. I don't like to eat too much during the day because I get tired. You know how much work we have to do, so no time for napping." he laughed. "I really like their French onion soup. Please order what you wish, this is my treat," Matt said as he looked into her eyes, while placing the napkin in his lap.

The waiter took their orders. They discussed the decorations of the restaurant and other *good* places to eat near the office while they waited for their lunch. The soup and salads arrived with Perrier for both of them. The salads was elegantly displayed with orange and purple flowers sprinkled on top. *What a perfect picture to paint!*

"The salads look too pretty to eat. I've never tasted flowers before," Ruby smiled putting a purple one in her mouth.

"I kind of like the orange ones myself," he laughed. "Personally, I can't really taste the difference in either of them," he admitted with a grin.

"Thank you, Matt, for inviting me here today. It's good to get away from everyday life once in a while."

"How do you like working in our office? I know it gets a little hectic at times, especially when the senate is in session," said Matt spooning the hot tasty soup into his mouth.

"Yes, I find it challenging and stimulating, even though you irritate me sometimes with your tedious editing marks." Ruby said smiling at him. "I really like the office staff and Sarah is right next door," she replied. "I never knew there were shops below the senate and house buildings or restaurants. DC is such a beautiful city to live and work in. How long have you worked here?"

"This is my fifth year. I worked in LA for two years before moving the DC."

"Where do you live?" Ruby asked curiously.

"I live on K Street in a small townhouse. It's close to many shops and the city life that I like. Although most people will tell you that I'm married to my work."

"Do you have a girlfriend?" she boldly asked blushing from her question.

He took off his glasses and put them in his pocket. "No, I did live with a girl until last year about this time. We dated for a year. She decided to keep our apartment so that's when I moved into the townhouse." He said finishing his last bite of salad. "She's a bank accountant and very independent. She travels a lot, which with my schedule worked well, but she met someone else with more money and that was it."

Ruby could sense in his voice that he must have cared a great deal for her.

"I'm sort of dating around. There are several young ladies that I'm stringing along," he laughed with a twinkle in his eyes.

"Yes, I could see you breaking all those hearts at one time. I hope you give them an easier time than you do me in the office," she said jokingly. Ruby took another sip of her water and inquired curiously, "Tell me about your family. I know so little about you really." Ruby noticed that he seemed deep in thought. "I'm sorry Matt, I didn't mean to get too personal." she exclaimed. "It is none of my business."

"Why should you be sorry? I enjoy talking to you, Ruby. I know that whatever we say or do is between lawyer and client. Right? If we're going to work together, we must know each other's dark secrets," he said winking at her.

"Do I have to pay you for your legal advice counselor?" she said jokingly. "I'm afraid to disappoint you but I'm broke. However, very few people get to know my dark secrets. But if you are willing to divulge yours, you can be assured that I'll never tell."

"Don't worry, I have my methods of extracting information from my clients, especially the pretty ones," he said placing his folded napkin on the table.

"Ha. So you are throwing in compliments as one of your tactics?"

"I can see you're going to be a little more difficult," he beamed. "Well, to start with, tell me about you and your husband? I never hear you talk about him. Does he still exist?" he asked as if in a courtroom.

He nodded a *yes* to the waiter when he asked if he would like to see a dessert menu.

"What a good question. Does he still exist?" she echoed his words nodding her head as if to say *yes* and *no*. "If I get dessert, I could be persuaded to tell you more," Ruby said looking at all the dessert choices smiling.

"What would you like to order?" asked Matt motioning the waiter to come over.

"I'd like the Napoleon thanks and a Cappuccino."

"I'd like the fruit tart and a Cappuccino, as well," said Matt handing the menus back to the waiter.

Ruby took a sip of water and then said, "I fell in love with Troy once, but things have been a little strained lately. Sarah has become my sunshine. She showers me with hugs and kisses. I need that," she said seriously. "Troy isn't home much and I can't tell if he's happy with his new law job. The firm is small and they run a tight ship. I make more money than Troy and I know he resents it. Especially after finishing school recently and working so hard," she added looking down as the coffee was placed before her.

Matt reached for Ruby's hand. "Let me know if there's anything you need or if I can help," he said sincerely.

She let him hold her hand for a minute. It was a strong hand, one that she needed desperately. The waiter brought the desserts and he released his grip. "Thanks," she said.

Ruby could feel her heart racing. *Was it my imagination or was his racing also? Did he just make a pass at me? I've noticed several times in the past few months when I've retyped some of the speeches he wrote for the Senator, he stands over my shoulder as I type. It makes me feel a little nervous but I like him standing close. It's been such a long since I've paid attention to any other man except Troy.*

"Oh, these look delicious. Do you want to try mine?" she asked taking her knife and cutting her Napoleon in two. Before he could answer, she put her half on his plate. "It's too late to argue, Mr. Connery."

He did the same for Ruby without saying a word, which was unusual for him. "I think I like yours the best," he said taking a bite of the Napoleon and chasing it down with a sip of the coffee glancing at his watch.

"We'd better go. I don't know where the time has gone," Matt commented pulling his wallet out of his back pocket.

Matt asked for the bill and paid it, tipping the waiter graciously. He helped Ruby put on her coat. The walk back was fun. They teased each other about being so serious at work, and about eating flowers for lunch. It was so nice to go out and be treated like a lady again.

As they entered the Russell Building, Matt turned and stopped in the doorway.

"I won't see you for the rest of the week because I'm off to a meeting for the Senator until Monday in New York. I hope you get caught up on your work by then. Don't worry, when I'm back I'll make sure your desk isn't too bare," he teased laughing.

"I look forward to the silence and uninterrupted work this week," Ruby said smiling and making her hands go together as if praying. "Thank you for the lunch and have a nice trip."

Ruby started walking towards her office when she heard Matt say "Before I go, just one important question," he said pointing his finger at her. "Why did you put your hair up for our lunch date? I like it better down, Ruby." He disappeared through the door before she could say another word. Several people were in the hallway listening to his remark, but Ruby didn't recognize any of them.

She sat at her desk and smiled. She felt like she had been reborn.

CHAPTER 3

Troy seemed to be envious of Ruby's job and the new friends she had met at the Senate. He was upset that she had her own checking account with the senate credit union and gave him only a certain portion of her salary. He didn't like not having his thumb on their finances. In retaliation he began to buy things he wanted and charged them on their joint credit cards.

One night he came home drunk and answered the phone. Ruby could tell he was angry with a collection agent on the other end of the phone.

"Look, Mr. Arnold. I sent in the payment last week. It's not my fault your company has a screwed up billing system. You should get it fixed and leave us innocent paying customers alone. You're harassing me at my house over a bill that I have already paid." Troy practically yelled into the phone slamming it down.

"What was all that about?" Ruby asked innocently.

"I paid that credit card bill last week. This stupid ass said he doesn't have any record of it," said Troy going over to his desk to search for his check book.

He started writing a check. He stuffed it into an envelope and licked it. "There," he said angrily squeezing it between his fingers. "Put this in the mail tomorrow on your way to work," he ordered walking over to Ruby and tossing it on the couch.

"So he was telling the truth? You hadn't paid it? What's it for anyway? What did you buy?" she asked inquiringly.

It was this behavior that Ruby began noticing some personality changes in Troy. He was edgy with her constantly. He wasn't as attentive to Sarah, hardly ever picking her up while she pleaded for him to lift her.

"It was just some small things I needed for my new office. I can write them off for taxes this year. Why are you questioning me too? It's none of your business what I buy," he yelled on the defensive.

Ruby followed him into the bedroom and said angrily, "Look, I work too. Aren't we a team anymore? I don't buy anything unless I tell you about it. But that's not the first collection agent I have talked with recently," she added nervously sensing the anger in his eyes as he stared a hole through her.

"I don't like not knowing what's going on with our bills," she continued when he turned around ignoring her and looking for something in the closet. "What's going on with our money? We make more money than we did while you were in school. I haven't bought anything for myself in such a long time. I don't even like to go shopping anymore. It's frustrating for me to see beautiful clothes in the windows and all I can do is look. I'm still young. I want some new things every once in a while too. It seems like we don't have anything to show for these credit card bills that have been piling up. I just want to be part of what you are purchasing. Maybe we can put ourselves on a budget. I'm your wife, remember? I want to help."

Angrily, he found what he was looking for on the top shelf in the closet. Suddenly he whipped around and waved a gun in the air. Ruby had never seen it before. She didn't even know he owned one. He pointed the tip at the ceiling. "I should just blow my brains out with this. I work so hard and you don't even appreciate it. We have a daughter that I didn't really want and look at all the bills that she accumulates. I'm a lawyer, Damn it! I have to purchase expensive suits that are high quality in order to meet with my clients. You don't need to wear lots of outfits just to be a secretary! Why don't you try to do something with your life? Then you could make a decent salary." He threw the gun down on the bed.

Ruby was scared. She didn't know him. She was afraid of him for the first time in her life. *Why was he so angry? Why did he owe money? They were both working now and had two incomes instead of one.* She should have been smart enough to read all the signals of his guilt and cunning actions. Ruby was blinded by her love for him.

Tears began to well up in her eyes. *I'm just a secretary! He's jealous of me making more money and only having a secretary position with no degree. What's wrong with him?*

"How could I afford to go to school, and work, and raise a child? You're never home early enough to pick up Sarah from school much less drop her off in the mornings. It seems to me the only responsibility you have is to take care of yourself. I do everything else. Troy, please put the gun away—it's making me nervous, and I don't like them anyway," Ruby said trying not to let him see how scared she was but she knew her voice was giving it away.

He reached for the gun and threw it back in the closet. "I'm out of here," he said disgustedly. He slammed the bedroom door as he left, and Sarah started to cry. Ruby went into her bedroom and picked her up. She needed to feel her small life next to her chest and hug her. She was her lifesaver. Ruby found her strength and courage in Sarah.

After she put Sarah to bed, Ruby went to Troy's desk and started rummaging through his papers. She tried not to mess them up because she knew he would know. She found bills that were charged to the max and noticed that several suits had been purchased recently, (of course for four hundred dollars a piece), two silk ties, and several shirts. He also charged two pairs of shoes. She found some of the bills for electricity and the phone. Suddenly she noticed that one charge was for over one thousand dollars. Ruby looked through the items purchased. There was only one item and it was for a pearl necklace! Christmas was coming up in two months and her birthday was in January. Perhaps it was for one of those special occasions. She didn't have any proof of anything so she had to keep everything quiet.

Troy came home early the next day and announced, "I have a new post office box in Arlington. My business mail can be delivered there. I just wanted you to know about it. I also wanted you to know that they're sending me to California at the end of the week. I won't be home until Tuesday."

"Don't you think I should know the number of your post office box and have a key to it in case something happens to you?" Ruby asked wondering why it was necessary to have another place for mail.

"No, they have the key in the office if they need to get in it," he answered matter-of-factly.

"Well, are you excited about your trip?" she asked changing the subject. "I wish my job would send me to a warm beach."

"Yeah, I'll start packing my things tonight. I need some time away from you for a few nights before I leave. I want some time alone, you understand, don't you, Ruby." he said not even looking at her. He turned to go to the bedroom. She could hear him packing his bags. It only took him about five minutes and then he was gone.

Ruby's job was her salvation—she should correct that and say Matt was her salvation. When he returned from his meeting the following Monday, there was a red rose on her desk. A small card beside it said in Matt's handwriting, "Ruby". Beside the rose, her desk had remnants of his presence...So many files and letters to type and mail before the day was over. She guessed these were the thorns that went with the rose. HA

Ruby went to see Sarah during lunch and she read her classmates a "Dr. Seuss" book. She sat in Ruby's lap while she read the story. Sarah looked adorable dressed in a pink corduroy jumper and a stripped turtleneck. Ruby had braided her hair into one long pigtail and attached a pink bow.

"Read it again, mommy," she said when Ruby closed the book. She hated to leave Sarah but she had to return to work.

"I can't honey, but I'll read it tonight. OK?" Ruby promised hugging and kissing her goodbye. "I want you to take your nap, and I'll be back here before you know it."

Her teacher, Miss Riley, thanked her for reading to the children.

"I'll try to come in every Monday and Wednesday if that will be convenient. It really depends on my boss. Sometimes he gives me too much work and I have to skip my lunch. But I'll try to keep to the schedule as best I can." she said putting on her coat and waving goodbye to everyone.

As she left, her mind was racing with so many things about Troy and what her life was becoming. She was so wrapped up in her own thoughts that she ended up in Matt's arms.

"We've got to stop meeting like this! Did you miss me dear?" he said hugging her.

"Never, I wish you'd leave again so my desk wouldn't be so cluttered. I actually could see the wood on top of my desk for the first time since I've been here," Ruby said with a smirk backing away from his clutches.

"Well, you have to admit, the rose does give it a little color," he remarked shyly. "How have you been really?" he asked concerned.

"I don't have much time left for my lunch. I'm afraid it would take me forever to give you the details. Anyway it would bore you, but thanks for the offer," she said touching his shoulder.

"What are your plans for the weekend? Are you and Troy going anywhere?" he inquired.

"As a matter of fact, Troy will be out of town for a week. He's flying to California of all places. I don't know what he's going there for but I'm assuming work," Ruby answered. "I guess Sarah and I will go for a hike in the woods and maybe over to see an old friend of mine whose husband is stationed at Fort Belvoir. I haven't seen her in years."

"Well, that is sad news. I want to fly to Asheville's Lake Lure this weekend. I thought I'd ask you and Sarah if you'd like to come too?"

asked Matt. "I have a small, rustic cabin on the lake and could use the company. I think Sarah would enjoy flying and maybe we can even do a little fishing. There won't be many pretty fall days like this before winter sets in"

"Thanks Matt, but I can't afford a ticket. You have a good time and you can bring me some fish, but make sure they're big and filleted. I don't want any puny ones. And if you can't catch them, at least buy some and put them on ice. I need to hear a good fish story" Ruby said looking up at him.

It was then their eyes met. Ruby wanted to hug him again. She needed someone to lean on. A tear began to trickle down her cheek but she wiped it away quickly before he could see it.

"Ruby, I'll bring you the biggest damn fish this side of the Potomac," he said bragging.

"I won't settle for anything less!" she said laughing. God, why could he always bring her back up so easily? She used to love to laugh. Ruby needed to learn how again.

They parted ways back to their individual offices and Matt continued on to another meeting with the Appropriation's Committee. He had to brief the Senator on new Middle East developments and Ruby needed to finish typing his notes.

The next day another rose was on her desk. This time there was no card. The girls in the office were starting to tease her now. Three different voices exclaimed one right after the other.

"You have a mystery man."

"No one has seen the secret admirer."

"Do you know who it is?"

"I haven't a clue." Ruby responded innocently. "My husband will be so jealous. Perhaps it's from him." she said coolly rolling her eyes.

They all said, "Right!" together.

They knew Troy hardly ever called the office and no one had ever met him. Maybe they thought she just wore the marriage band for looks.

Mary carried an envelope in her hand as she approached Ruby. "OK. What have you done to Matt? He usually is the Nightmare from Elm's Street when it comes to having his work done perfectly and on time. You must have caught his attention somehow. He's even smiling when he comes to work," said Mary with a little twinkle in her eye, whispering in Ruby's ear so the others couldn't hear.

Mary was a wonderful friend. She was the one female friend Ruby had confided in since she had started to work at the Senate. She was the Senator's personal friend and secretary. She had known his family for years and worked for him forever. She was originally from Portland, Oregon. She had jet black hair and beautiful dark eyes. She had a second husband that traveled quite a bit and a teenage son who lived in Alaska with his dad. She was a few years older than Ruby. Sometimes they would meet and go to lunch together.

"I'm sure I don't know what you mean Mary, but I do try to smile and act politely when he comes in here to check my work," Ruby answered looking away. "Maybe we need to meet for lunch one day this week and discuss his issues."

"Let me know when." She winked at Ruby and left the room with her envelope.

The phone rang and Matt's voice was on the other end.

"Hi Ruby," he said. "Listen, I've been thinking about that big fish I promised you and I think it will take two, maybe three people to work together to reel in that sucker. I want you to reconsider my offer about joining me."

"I told you I don't have enough money for tickets," she whispered in the phone so the others couldn't hear her conversation.

"Personally, I think you need some time away from here for a while and maybe you can relax a little. The costs won't be a problem. The plane belongs to me. It is a small yellow Cessna. I keep it parked at Dulles Airport. I've been flying since I was sixteen. You can trust me," he said. "Just call me *BOND, JAMES BOND*."

"Listen Bond, I never knew you could fly," Ruby said trying not to laugh too loud. "Well, let me think about it. I'll let you know in the morning," she said hanging up the phone. She stared at the stack of papers on her desk before starting to type again.

That night was quiet in the apartment. Ruby made a pizza, a salad, and some brownies for dinner. She and Sarah had to wash clothes down in the basement. There were some carts on rollers that Sarah liked pushing around as they waited for their clothes to wash and dry. Ruby had some paper and crayons to keep her entertained. Ruby saw some neighbors and spoke casually, making small talk.

Ruby frequently called their apartment complex the United Nations because they had quite a few ethnic groups from all over the world as their next door neighbors. She thought it was wonderful to meet people that were international because she had never been outside the United States. However, there weren't any open windows in the halls for the smoke and odors to escape the twelve story building. Smells would often linger for days. Sometimes they were good smells and sometimes they weren't.

Ruby checked the answering machine. She listened to several hang-up tones with no messages. She deleted them. The phone rang as she was drawing a bath for Sarah. She turned the spigot off to answer. It was her friend, Alexis. Ruby was planning to visit Alexis at Fort Belvoir but she asked her if she could change the date until the next weekend. They would meet the following Saturday.

"Mom, hurry I'm cold," said Sarah climbing out of the tub.

"Are you my freezing chicken?" Ruby said laughing drying her off. She dressed Sarah in her Strawberry Shortcake gown and Bert and Ernie bedroom shoes. They sat in a rocking chair together and watched the Disney Channel. Sarah fell asleep in her lap and Ruby tucked her in bed. Then she climbed into her own bed and curled up into a ball before she cried like a baby. Troy did not call from California—or from anywhere for that matter.

The next day Ruby's eyes were swollen, but she felt better than she had in a long time. She had decided to go with Matt to the mountains. It would be fun and it gave Ruby something to look forward to.

When she walked into her office there were two large red roses and one small peach one. The note said: Bond, James Bond. Ruby couldn't stop laughing. What a character. Who would have ever thought this tyrant lawyer had anything under that tough skin?

CHAPTER 4

The plane looked like it belonged in a circular ride at an amusement park. It was small but incredibly cute. It was yellow with a few decorative blue markings. There were black numbers on the tail and on the side of the plane was a small sticker of James Bond. Ruby couldn't help but laugh and point to it.

"So now you believe I am who I say I am. The Matt Connery is just a disguise not to reveal my true identity," he said putting on his sunglasses and posing as if he were a secret spy. Then he chuckled and said, "You can both sit in the back seat if you want, Ruby. Sarah might be more comfortable with you there. What do you think?" asked Matt placing his hand on her shoulder.

"You're so thoughtful, Mr. Bond. I find it hard to believe all that gossip Money Penny has shared with us. But you do have a way with the girls," she said sarcastically getting into the back seat. Ruby helped Sarah who had her favorite pink and purple security blanket in her lap with her belt.

"Mommy, are we really going up in the sky?" she asked excited.

"Yes, honey. You can help me count the stars. It'll be dark while we're flying. Maybe coming home we can see it during the daytime," she explained.

"Here, Ruby. Take these headphones so we can talk during the flight. The engine is unbelievably noisy. Unless you have these headphones on, you can't hear anything."

Ruby had never been in a little plane, but she loved flying commercial planes to visit her relatives in Florida. It was a perfect evening for the flight. The stars were bright, and it wasn't too cold. Ruby had packed small bags for Sarah and herself. She didn't know what exactly to pack for this rustic cabin weekend. Matt said they were going fishing, so she brought what a woman usually brings with a small child, everything but the kitchen sink.

He made his correspondence with the air traffic controllers in the tower as they approached the Dulles runway. They had a ten minute wait for some of the bigger jets to land. He checked his equipment and revved his engine. They sped down the lined road and were off. It was just like being in the movie, "Out of Africa." They flew with a full moon out of the right side of the airplane and stars leading them to their destination.

"Are you OK back there? You haven't said a word since you got in the plane," said Matt over the headphones.

"Yes, I'm thrilled about leaving DC for a while, and I just love flying. I wish I could see it during daylight."

"We'll take a spin in her tomorrow. We should be there in a couple of hours. The wind is behind us. It will be a smooth flight I believe. Are you warm enough?" he asked turning his head.

"Yep, you just keep your eyes on the sky road. I don't want you to be too distracted," Ruby said pointing her finger out in front of him.

He grabbed it and gave it a light pull. "It's not polite to point. Didn't you learn that in school?" he said teasing her. "If you get thirsty or want a snack, look in the bag under my seat. Compliments of Bond Airways."

"Thanks," Ruby said opening the bag and passing out the snacks to the pilot and passengers.

The rest of the flight was held in silence. Ruby rested her head back against the seat and closed her eyes. She didn't realize how tired she was. It took about one and a half hours to get there but Ruby must have fallen asleep because it seemed like minutes before they were getting ready to land. No big jets here. In fact it was quiet and peaceful. Little farm houses and cabins looked like dotted lights in the distance.

"Time to land. Make sure you have your seats in the upright position," said the captain with a chuckle, since there weren't any other positions but upright in the back seats.

Matt had radioed ahead to have someone turn on the landing lights. Ruby could see them below as they slowed down. He circled the airport and then softly floated down to the small runway. He passed several other planes parked in the lot before stopping.

"I have a Bronco that I store here for convenience. It's really hard to get a taxi in the country, especially late at night. One of the farm boys keeps an eye on it for me. I give him a little money every time I come here. Nice kid. You and Sarah stay here for a minute until I can get you to the car. It's cold out here," Matt said hopping out of the plane. He anchored it down with the cemented chains. He made all the necessary preparations for the safety of his plane and then walked to his car. He started the engine and adjusted the heat knobs.

Matt came around and picked Sarah up and Ruby climbed out following them to the Bronco. He was right. The temperature was a lot colder here than in Washington. She was freezing.

Matt unlocked the jeep and placed their bags in the back. It took a few minutes for the cold air blowing out of the vents to heat up. Sarah snuggled up to her and went back to sleep. Ruby knew she had had a busy week too.

"It's only a ten minute drive from here. I want to stop at the store to buy a few groceries. I don't remember what items I left here last July. Do you need anything for you or Sarah?"

"I'd like some orange juice and pop tarts for breakfast. Also, could you get me some Tabs?"

"You got it," he said smiling.

He pulled into the Quick-Stop and carried two full brown bags to the car. He was a pretty fast shopper. They drove another mile and turned down a dirt road. It twisted up a small hill and then a two story cabin could be seen behind some trees. The mailbox read: Connery

"I guess you have to keep your Bond name a secret here in the mountains," she whispered sarcastically. "Looks like a well hidden retreat. I can't wait to tour the inside."

Matt turned off the ignition and left the parking lights on so he could see. He switched on the outside and inside entrance lights, as well as the heat.

"Come on in," he motioned from the front door. "It'll take a while to warm up the cabin. I'll build a fire. I always stack wood in the fireplace.

"Mommy, are we there yet?" asked Sarah in a whinny voice. "I need the bathroom."

Ruby carried Sarah and her overnight bag to the front door and entered the main hallway. Directly in front of her was a wooden staircase that led to the upstairs.

"Bathroom's to the right," said Matt, as if reading her thoughts while kneeling over the wood and striking a match to let the newspapers catch. "It'll be going soon."

The bathroom was painted a dark blue with maroon rugs and towels to accent the walls. It was clean, but freezing.

"You and Sarah can sleep upstairs in the first bedroom on the left. Don't worry about your bags. I'll bring those up after it warms up in here a little. Would you like something to drink? I can put on a pot of water to make some hot tea. I thought it would help with the cold or would you rather have champagne?" said Matt putting some groceries away.

"Hot tea sounds like a winner for me, thanks Matt."

"Mommy, I want some juice. And I'm hungry. Can I have a pop tart?" asked Sarah making a frowning face.

"Yes, I'll fix you a little snack and read you a story by the fireplace. OK?" Ruby said pouring juice into a small plastic cup that she brought. It had a tight fitting lid and Ruby was glad to have it just in case Sarah had an accident. Matt's place looked so immaculate. She should have known.

As Ruby glanced around the room it had a warm and cozy atmosphere. The fire had already started to give off some warmth and Matt had lit some extra candles. It almost looked like Christmas with the white candles reflecting off the white walls. The living room had a cathedral ceiling and fan that was graced with a blue and white porcelain square light cover. The wooden floors were semi-covered with a blue and green oriental rug. An 'L shaped' dark blue couch fit around the fireplace and an old Bentwood Rocking Chair sat beside the couch. It had blue plaid cushions and a tapestry pillow placed almost perfectly in the center of the chair. The walls had several lake and mountain scenes painted on canvas. One picture had a small boy holding up a fishing pole full of trout. He had a big grin on his face. After looking at it closer, Ruby knew it was Matt. What a cute boy, she thought. And so proud of his catch.

"I'm going out to the car to get the luggage. Be back in a minute," said Matt opening the door and shutting it quickly keeping out the cold.

"Sarah, are you finished with your snack?"

"Yes, mom, I want you to read now and I want my blanket," Sarah said as she grabbed it off of the chair and put her thumb in her mouth.

Matt walked in carrying the bags heading up the stairs. "It's really cold out there! Brrr!" Ruby located Dr. Seuss, Left Foot, Right Foot. She had already dressed Sarah in pajamas before leaving DC knowing it would be late when they arrived at the lake. 'I'm getting smart in my old age,' she thought to herself.

They sat in the rocking chair by the fire, and Ruby rocked back and forth using her propped foot on the hearth to push with, reading Sarah's story. She was soon asleep.

"Matt, can you pull down the covers to her bed? Or do you think its warm enough up there?" Ruby whispered.

He nodded and said, "It's done. I read your thoughts. It's quite toasty. I think she will be very comfortable. "Do you want me to carry her up?" he said softly. Before she could answer he reached his arms around Sarah and went up the steps.

Ruby followed them. They kept the bedroom light off and used the hall lights to see. From what Ruby observed in the low lights the walls were white and a handmade pink and green quilt covered a double bed. The frame was brass and on both sides were two oak nightstands. There was also a dresser. A small nightlight was plugged in the socket beside the bed. It was enough light for Sarah in case she woke up. Ruby pulled a chair against the bed so Sarah wouldn't accidentally roll out. Matt turned and walked out of the room. Ruby kissed Sarah's cheek. She happily went down the stairs to see Matt.

CHAPTER 5

Matt removed the whistling kettle and made tea. He placed fresh flowers in a blue glass vase on the counter. He lit a white candle that flickered to the soft guitar music playing in the tape deck.

Ruby sat in the rocking chair warming her hands by the fire. "Do you need any help?" she asked lazily rocking back and forth.

"No thanks. I think I have it," he replied carrying the mugs in his hands. "Be careful, it's hot," he said handing her the cup.

"I love your place, Matt. Do you visit here often?" she asked accepting the tea.

"Not as often as I'd like. I appreciate the solitude, unless there is a beautiful woman to talk to," he smiled, "And, of course, I DO love to fish."

Ruby blew steam across the top of her mug and then took a sip. "I think perhaps you've had many years of practice. I noticed the picture of you when you were a small boy on the table over there," she replied, looking in the direction of the photograph. "You looked really proud of your catch. I know Sarah will be thrilled tomorrow even if she only has a slight tug on her line."

"We have a busy day tomorrow starting at dawn. We probably

shouldn't stay up too late because the sun will be up before you know it. But before we go to bed, I want you to dream about a fish contest. The person with the largest fish gets to enjoy watching the other person cook. What do you think?"

"You're on, Matt. Don't worry, I'll be ready. My goal is to catch the biggest fish. I'm on vacation, so I'm determined not to cook! I'm very competitive, you know."

"I've observed that about you at work. I'm looking forward to the contest." They clinked mugs and laughed. She placed her empty mug in the sink and wished him a goodnight before she went to bed.

* * *

Ruby and Sarah had the best night's sleep in Matt's peaceful guest bedroom on Lake Lure. They snuggled together with Sarah's blanket between them.

Matt tapped on the door quietly, but the girls were already awake. Ruby was in the middle of telling Sarah how to catch a fish.

"Hi," Sarah said as he opened the door. "Are we going fishing now, Matt?" she asked pushing the covers away.

"Yes, my little friend we are. Dress warmly. It's really cold outside but it's going to be a nice and sunny day," he said with a smile closing the door.

Ruby thought Matt looked incredibly handsome in his brown and blue plaid shirt and blue jeans. He could probably wear a brown paper sack and still look gorgeous.

Ruby threw on her robe and opened the door. "Matt," she said watching him walk down the stairs. He turned and smiled at her.

"Can Sarah come down and eat with you? I'll dress her first. I want to take a quick shower."

"Sure beautiful. Nice hair. I haven't seen you in that style before."

Ruby realized her hair was going in a hundred directions, mostly up. She took one hand and tried to smooth it down. "It's the latest."

"I can see how that would be popular."

"I'll remember to wear it this way more often," she smirked running her hand over her hair again.

Ruby dressed Sarah in a blue turtleneck and her pink overall jeans she had inherited from a first cousin. She braided her hair Indian-style with blue bows at the end of each. Sarah wanted to put on her own socks and shoes. Ruby was glad she had the Velcro kind. It was so much easier instead of dealing with shoe laces, although Sarah always put her shoes on the opposite foot. Ruby corrected the situation and sent her downstairs to eat breakfast with Matt.

"Take your time, Ruby." Matt turned on the cartoons for Sarah. "Breakfast will be ready in one minute, young lady," said Matt as he poured her orange juice and removed a toasted pop tart. He carried it over to the coffee table and let her eat on the couch. She was so engrossed in the cartoons, he could have left and she would never have known. "You're welcome," he said walking back into the kitchen.

Ruby dressed in jeans and a maroon turtleneck placing a wool vest over it for additional warmth. She braided her hair, which wasn't long, down her back and used a scrunchy to hold it in place.

Matt had left a bagel and a cup of coffee for her on the counter. Ruby spread strawberry cream cheese on top and licked her fingers. She added milk and sugar to her coffee. She carried her breakfast over to the hearth and sat by the fire to eat. Ruby watched cartoons with Sarah while Matt packed the car with fishing gear, a cooler, and a bag of small snacks. He started the car and turned on the heater.

Matt entered the house and teased, "Come on girls, we don't want to keep the fish waiting, do we?"

They put on coats. Their gloves were in their pockets.

Matt fit a light blue baseball cap over his head. 'Maui' was embroidered in purple letters on the front of his hat. He turned off the TV and locked the door behind them.

They sped off down the end of the road and turned right, winding along another dirt road leading to the lake. A row boat was tied to a small dock.

"I'll bet that's yours, Bond," Ruby said tormenting him.

"Well, I hate to break it to you, but I accidentally destroyed all of my other speed boats and yachts chasing the bad guys. Now I'm down to a small plane and an old row boat. I don't even have an engine on her," he explained shaking his head. "It's hard to get good help nowadays since 'Q' has retired," he added scornfully. "That's why I have to work two jobs!"

"I guess I need to quit complaining about my workload then."

"I just want you to appreciate me. Is the guilt trip working?"

"I'll think about it."

"Good. Now can you carry these down to the boat, Ruby? And Sarah, you have the most important job. You have to carry the bucket for the fish we catch. I'll bring the rest."

Matt gave them both life jackets to put on. Ruby stepped into the boat with Matt's assistance and then he handed Sarah to her. They sat in the front of the boat and tried to balance it as Matt climbed in, rocking the boat on purpose. He started laughing.

"Thanks, Matt. One of these days you're going to fall in and then I'll throw you an anchor!" Ruby said trying to steady the boat again.

"Mommy, that was fun. Can we do it again, Matt?"

"See what you started? No, honey, sit down before we scare all the fish away." Ruby said trying to get her to return to her seat.

Sarah leaned her body from side to side trying to make the boat rock some more. "Are we really going to catch some fish?" she said pointing to the fishing poles.

"Yes, Sarah. I have to row us to the middle of the lake and then we'll toss in our lines. I heard there is a particularly smart fish out here named Marty. Let me know if you see him jumping. You have to look really hard," said Matt looking out towards the middle of the lake.

Matt shoved off with one of the oars and began rowing. The mountains were breathtaking with the fall leaves peaking with their robust colors. Several other fishing boats were out and they looked a little concerned when they saw Sarah. But Ruby waved to them and then whispered in her ear, "You have to be very quiet so that the fish don't know you're here. Then they'll swim around the boat and bite the hook. Our job is to reel them in by turning the handle. Keep looking for Marty."

Matt lowered the anchor and started to bait the hooks. He let Sarah and Ruby share a pole. Ruby had fished many times before at Frisco so she felt comfortable and relaxed with the rod in her hand. She cast her line, thinking to herself about catching the most fish. The contest had begun. She waited patiently with Sarah. *I do not want to have to cook tonight.*

Matt winked at her as he cast his line. She smiled when their eyes met. It was like a lightning bolt and fireworks at the same time.

Suddenly, the girl's line started to pull. Ruby jerked it and let Sarah help her reel in the fish. Ruby had to remind her to keep her voice down or the fish would jump off the hook. Sarah was very cooperative and excited, especially when she caught the first fish. It was a nice size and Matt put it in the bucket she had carried. In a two hour period, they had accumulated a dozen trout for their dinner.

Matt passed out sandwiches in the boat and they drank Tabs. The sun felt warm on Ruby's face. Matt handed her a straw hat that he pulled out of one of his bags and said thoughtfully, "I brought this along just in case you needed it."

"Thanks, Matt. I forgot mine back at the house," Ruby said placing the hat over her head. It was nice to have the sun out of her eyes but still feel its energy. She had forgotten her sunglasses too. 'I guess this is a true sign that I am really relaxed,' she thought.

As they made their way back to shore Ruby noticed how athletic Matt was. He rowed with such strong, muscular strokes, and he never seemed to be out of breath, or panting for that matter.

"You sure row this boat as if it's as light as a feather, Bond. I guess you have to keep in shape for all those dangerous assignments and women drooling at your feet."

"Yes, I work out at the gym three times a week so I can be prepared to destroy all enemies. The women just love it when I flex my muscles. I love that part of my job," he replied enjoying the sarcasm.

"So Matt, tell me about your family. I know you're from California and you went to UCLA. And I know you're a good pilot and a ruthless, perfectionist lawyer. But under all that thick skin there's a nice guy. You had to have a good upbringing for all of those qualities. I only trust two lawyers and they are both blood relatives. One is my cousin, Martin, who lives about an hour from here. The other one is a cousin, Harrison, from Ohio. And now I consider you a third addition to my list."

He understood the bad reputation lawyers had. He nodded his head. "I'm glad you have some good lawyers in your family that are honest and can be trusted. I appreciate your feeling comfortable to include me in your list. But you have to say that because I'm your boss," he said proudly.

"You're right. You seem to have me all figured out! I could always use a raise," she retorted.

"We'll have to see about that," he pondered, stroking his chin as if in thought. "Now where were we? Or yes, you asked about my family. You'd like them and I know they'd like you. I'm the eldest of two brothers that live in LA and are both doctors, Tristan and Brian. Tristan is married and is an OB/GYN. Brian is a radiologist and single. My dad's an engineer for NASA and hoping to retire in the next two years." he said taking his shoes off and putting his feet up on the end of the boat.

"My mother died when I was ten. My dad never remarried. It was a very difficult time for me and my family, as you can imagine. You remind me a lot of my mom, probably because she had the same color red hair and beautiful green eyes. She was an elementary teacher.

"How did she die?" Ruby asked sadly.

"She had ovarian cancer. That's one reason why Tristan became an OB doc. He wants to try to save other women from such a horrible death."

"I can't imagine losing anyone you love so much. I feel incredibly lucky," She said quietly.

"So when were you in Maui?" Ruby asked pointing to his cap.

"My dad used to take us boys there on vacation every year during Christmas after mom died. The holiday season was his hardest time without her. We'd rent a small condo for the week of Christmas and New Years. We'd always go to a small island church for the midnight Christmas Eve Service. It was so great to be sitting outside wearing shorts and watching an island dancer perform a native dance to honor the birth of the Christ child. We'd scuba dive with dad searching for tropical fish, turtles, corral, and whales that Maui had to offer.

Now that we're grown boys, our work schedules don't always allow us to be there together. We are, however, talking about meeting there this Christmas. I booked four rooms at the Maui Hilton Hotel so we can each have our own private rooms and plan for outings around the island," said Matt.

"I guess you could say in a way, that Maui is kind of my home at Christmas. I definitely have a "Bond" with the island. Sometimes I rent a plane and fly. You should see the view from above. Some day if you're lucky, I might take you there myself," he said winking pulling up along side the dock and tying the ropes around the poles. "I could be your personal pilot."

"I'd love to go there some day. I've only seen pictures in magazines and Hawaii 5-0. 'Book um, Dan-O'" she said seriously imitating the police chief on the show.

"I know I'll get there someday. I've always wanted to have a job where I could travel around the world," Ruby replied stepping out of the boat. "I suppose you could be my personal pilot. Maybe you could even teach me to fly."

"We'll talk about that later," he said with a grin.

Matt lifted Sarah on to the dock and Ruby walked her to the Marina to buy some M&Ms and to use the restroom. They returned shortly to help Matt with the gear and bucket of fish.

"It seems you won the contest, Matt, but I must insist on you cleaning them. I don't think I have the stomach for it."

"It's a deal."

Matt drove them back to the cabin. Ruby could see it much better in the daytime. It looked more inviting with the sun shinning through the protective trees. It had a log cabin exterior and a cute front porch with a swing and rocking chair. A round wooden table was placed under the kitchen window with a brick clay pot holding red geraniums. A brown straw mat was placed in front of the entrance to wipe feet before entering the cabin. A Norfolk Island pine stood in the corner behind the swing and was planted in a large blue clay pot.

"I'll clean these fish a little later," said Matt starting another fire. Ruby picked up a book and began reading to Sarah. Matt came over and sat on the other side of her to listen, as well.

"I have a story I want to read to Sarah too," he said sliding it out from under the couch. It was a small book that looked like it had seen better days. He explained that it was his when he was a little boy. It was called, Marty the Smarty. "My mom use to read it to me when I was your age, Sarah."

Sarah listened carefully to the story and when it was finished said, "Can you read it again, Matt?"

"OK, but remember next time we go fishing, maybe you can spot Marty. I don't think he was out there today," said Matt shaking his head.

"He must have been playing with his friends," said Sarah seriously.

"Yes, you must be right," said Matt trying not to laugh.

Matt's hand brushed Ruby's hair as she laid her head on a pillow to listen to it a second time.

"I think we should take a little airplane ride. The leaves are really pretty and you can enjoy the pilot's view of the lake. Are you girls up for a little tour?"

"Mommy, can we go, can we?" asked Sarah jumping up and down.

"Sure, let's go," Ruby said running upstairs to grab her sunglasses, camera, and Sarah's blanket.

The plane was waiting for them as they walked up and climbed into the back seat fastening their seatbelts. Take off was smooth. Up and up they lifted over the lake with the sun shimmering diamonds on it. Ruby started snapping pictures through her glass window. She even took some of Matt from the back seat showing all the panels with his instruments, buttons, and switches. She reached her hand to touch Matt's shoulder. He placed his hand on top of hers.

"Thanks, Matt. This is so beautiful," Rudy said looking out of the window. "I'll give you the prints if my pictures are any good. Can I get one of you on the ground when we land?" Ruby asked speaking into the microphone.

"Sure, maybe I can get the store owner to take one of all three of us. Would that be OK with you?" he said. "Oh look, there's Andy McDowell's summer house? Do you see it?"

"Wow, it's so big. Who else has a house down there? Anyone I know?"

"No, I think she's the only Hollywood celebrity. But once the word gets around, I'm sure you'll see many more big homes springing up."

They flew up and down the lake circling a few other new homes being built. They passed the marina with all the pontoons and paddle boats tied up for vacationing renters. Several boats were being used by tourist enjoying the crisp fall day. Sarah loved looking out the window and seeing the boats.

When they landed, Matt climbed out and held out his hand to help Ruby. He hugged her. "How was your ride, Ruby?"

"I have to admit I'm in love with flying," she replied patting the airplane wing. "Maybe you can give me some lessons."

"That could be arranged," he said thoughtfully. "We'll talk about that later."

Ruby knew she only had one more day before she would soon be back in reality and would have to wake up from this fabulous dream.

"And how was your ride, young lady?" asked Matt lifting Sarah out of the back seat.

"I want to go again. Can we, Matt?" she said tugging on his jacket.

"Well, we'll get to go again tomorrow. How will that be?"

"OK," she said climbing into the Bronco.

Back at the cabin Matt carried the bucket outside to clean the fish. Ruby covered three baked potatoes with foil and put them in the fireplace. She also made a toss salad.

"Don't forget the carrots!" said Matt seriously toting the filleted fish and placing the pan on the counter. "I never eat salads without carrots! Besides they remind me of your hair," he added jokingly.

"You're such a pest, Matt. Don't worry. You'll have one in your salad." she said smirking.

She put the tallest, whole carrot in his salad, unpeeled, sticking straight up in the middle. She braided the leafy green top and made a silly face with a black marker she found in the kitchen drawer. She was proud of her creation.

Ruby helped fry the trout in batter and she set the table for three. She found some matches and lit candles on the table. She took one of the flowers from the coffee table and placed it in the center. She opened a napkin and placed some bread in the basket she located in a cabinet and set it on the table. She grabbed the butter out of the refrigerator and put it next to the bread. Matt put on a Louie Armstrong tape.

The fish were delicious and the potatoes were perfectly baked. Luckily, the foil made them cook evenly. Of course, Matt ate his carrot without even flinching, top and all. "Great Salad," he said rubbing his stomach to show he cleaned his bowl. Sarah ate all of her fish and wanted more.

"Would anyone like ice cream for dessert?" asked Matt going to the freezer and pulling out some mint chocolate chip ice cream and cones.

"I do, Matt," said Sarah running over to him to give him a hug. He hugged her right back and kissed the top of her head.

They each had an ice cream cone. It didn't take long before Sarah had the ice cream all over her mouth and hands, not to mention her clothes. She licked her lips and cone as it melted and oozed out of the pointed end of her waffled cone. Ruby found the washcloth and cleaned her up.

"Matt, will you read me Marty the Smarty?" she asked going to retrieve it under the couch. "You see. I found it," she smiled and waved it over her head.

Ruby cleared the table and washed the dishes. She had forgotten how good mint chocolate chip was. Matt rose to give her a hand in the kitchen.

"Let me help your mom with the dishes and then I'll read it to you, Sarah. Do you want to watch TV until we're done?" asked Matt walking over to turn off the music and turn on the TV.

"OK, but hurry up," she said grabbing her blanket.

"Mommy, there isn't any color. Can you fix it?" asked Sarah pointing to the TV.

Ruby checked out the situation and flipped through several channels but the only clear channel showed an old black and white western. There was a woman riding a horse being chased by what looked like some bandits.

Matt walked in and said tapping her on the shoulder, "I thought you were helping me in the kitchen."

Ruby caught a glimpse of the masked man and said to Matt seriously, "I know that guy. I've seen this movie before. He used to be the man of my childhood dreams. What a hunk!"

Suddenly, Zorro appeared with his black mask and distracted the bad guys.

"So you like men in tights, wearing a mask?" he said teasingly.

"This is great. I haven't seen Zorro in such a long time. Matt, come on in and watch. Leave the dishes. I'll be there in a minute."

Ruby was engrossed with the chase scene. Once Zorro lost the bad guys, he found the damsel in distress and rescued her. Ruby didn't realize that she was watching the movie longer than she had meant to.

Matt finished the dishes. He smiled and said shaking his head, "Anything to get out of work. Don't worry, I'll make up for it on Monday. You better rest, you'll need it."

Ruby looked down at Sarah while she sucked her thumb. She liked Zorro too. "Mommy, what's coming on next?"

"Why don't you draw Matt a picture of the fish you caught?" Ruby said sprinting up the stairs to collect her crayons and paper.

Sarah started to draw and was humming to the music. She drew all three of them in the boat and a big fish on her fishing pole. Matt and Ruby had smaller fish on their poles. Of course, her fish was smiling with big teeth. Theirs hardly had a grin.

The next picture she drew was his plane or at least that is what she said it was. For being three, Ruby could only identify scribbles on the paper, but Sarah could easily tell her what everything was.

"OK girls. I need your help for a song. Do you want to be my mockingbirds?" asked Matt retrieving his guitar from the corner of the room

"Matt, what's a mockingbird?" asked Sarah.

"Well, it's a bird that likes to say everything you say. For example, if I sang: 'Twinkle, twinkle, little star' you would sing, 'Twinkle, twinkle, little star' after me. Do you think you can try this song with your mom? Here are the words, Ruby."

"I'm always amazed at your incredible hidden talents, Matt. OK. Carly Simon and company are ready for you. Sarah you can sing with me. Let's be mockingbirds. Are you ready?"

"OK, mom,"

Matt started to strum the song 'Mockingbird' and the girls followed his lead. They sang several songs and ended it with 'Mockingbird' again. They laughed when they messed up. But actually both were able to sing on key and had a great time.

It was getting late when Ruby took Sarah upstairs to bed. When she returned, Matt was gone. She pulled the rocking chair up in front of the fire. Louie's famous song "Wonderful World" had just started to play. She thought about Troy and wondered where and what he was doing. The memories began to haunt her again. She heard the player stop and rewind. Her eyes were still shut. Was she dreaming? Then the song started over. She suddenly felt a hand on her shoulder and Matt was motioning her to get up and dance. She put her arms around him and placed her head against his chest. He stopped and took his hands cupping her face. "Don't worry, Ruby. I just want to dance with you. I know you have a lot on your mind. I don't mean to complicate your life. It's just that I'm glad you're here and I like being with you and Sarah. Let's just let the chips fall where they may," he whispered in her ear as the song finished.

He brought out a bottle of red wine and two glasses, placing them on the table. He poured the wine handing Ruby a glass. Then he sat down facing her.

"Do you have other favorite places you like to go to besides here?" Ruby asked curiously.

"Well, you guessed it. This log cabin, my plane because I can go anywhere, and I suppose if you count Maui at Christmas, I have three. Matt paused for a moment then asked, "Would you believe at one time I'd thought about being a forest ranger?"

"I could see you doing that," Ruby replied nodding her head.

"When I tire of working for the Senator, who knows, I may end up a boy scout some day. Maybe buy a place out west. I guess I better get busy and start making a lot more money so I can buy several retreats to take pretty girls," he added laughing. "What about you, Ruby? Where do you like to relax?"

"Frisco, in the Carolinas," I answered automatically. "My parents have a small rustic cottage on the beach called Frisco Sandbox. My dad actually grew up there as a boy. My grandfather was a charter sea captain and I remember him telling some great fishing tales, almost as truthful as yours."

"Ha. Well, with fishing in your genes, you should be an expert in catching and cleaning them."

"I knew I shouldn't have revealed that small piece of family history. I thought you'd use it against me."

"Don't worry, your secret is safe with me," he grinned. "Now tell me more about his place." He poured more wine into the glasses.

"Growing up we spent many summer vacations there with my

grandparents. I have such fond memories in that cottage. Sadly, they passed away several years ago leaving the property to dad, their only child. It's closed up during the winter months because my family is too busy with work and school right now. Of course, my brothers still vacation with my parents, but my sisters and I each take turns using it when we can. I usually end up with my vacation sometime in July."

Ruby took a sip of her wine. She leaned her head back running her hand through her hair. "To me, the best part of the house is the top deck. I can enjoy the view and hear the ocean surf. I can read in the Adirondack Chairs and sometimes paint. I can see the fishing pier and watch surfers catch their big waves. They have a small airport, Billy Mitchell Airport. We're in their flight pattern. Have you ever been there?" Ruby inquired.

"Yeah," he nodded. "I flew along the coast once to Ocracoke Island two years ago and landed my plane. I went to the beach for a few hours, ate at a local restaurant, and then flew back to DC. I can see why you like it there so much. It's a peaceful, quite place to relax and enjoy the sun. I had a big week approaching with the Senate, and I'd flown there to get away for the day," said Matt recalling the beauty of the ocean. "I know you don't believe it, but I also surf. I did a lot of it growing up in California."

"I can see you are a beach boy and I'm sure you're good at it too," Ruby smiled taking a sip of her wine. "But are you really serious about becoming a forest ranger, Matt?" Ruby chuckled. "You don't look like the type of lawyer that would get too dirty."

"You'd be surprised at how easily I could adjust to that life. I've been reading a lot of articles about Jackson Hole, Wyoming. I've never been there, but from what I've heard, the scenery is something to behold," he said staring at the fire. "Could you ever live in a place like that?" he asked looking at Ruby again.

"I've never really thought about moving out west, but I love to travel and meet people. And I do like the outdoors. I guess it would be worth looking into, if you're serious about changing your career. But personally, I think you like your position and the excitement of working with the Senator too much. I could actually see you becoming a Bond character in real life. You have such a sense of adventure and never seem to stay in one place for very long," she added feeling his arm muscles. "Besides, I won't have anyone to give me a hard time at work if you leave and become a boy scout."

"Would you really miss me or are you just trying to stay in my good graces, hoping I won't give you too many files on your desk on Monday?" he mused.

"I will miss you terribly, Matt. I can't imagine life in DC without you. You've saved my life and given me a reason to like myself again," Ruby said shyly looking into his beautiful brown eyes. "But my reasons are selfish. You need to look to your future and decide what you enjoy the best. I know flying is one of them. Perhaps you could work for a rescue team up in the mountains. I'm sure they could use a good pilot. Who better to have than Matt Connery," she said raising her left palm up.

They sat quietly by the fire finishing the bottle of wine and listening to the music. She leaned her head into his chest. She wanted this night to be forever. She was actually happy and she didn't think it was all from the wine.

"Oh, I didn't realize how late it is. It's time for bed. What time do you want us up in the morning?" Ruby said brushing her red hair behind her ears and standing up.

"Let's sleep in until around nine. We should be at the airport no later than ten. How does that sound? I'm sure you have some things to do before Monday, right?" he asked holding his arms out for a hug goodnight. "Oh by the way, I want you to keep this," he said taking off his Maui cap and placing it on her head.

"Goodnight, Matt," she said touching the cap with her right hand. "Thanks again for the wonderful weekend and for the cap. I shall treasure it always," Ruby said kissing him on the cheek.

"Goodnight, Ruby."

She heard him change the tape to Elton John singing 'Someone

Saved My Life Tonight, Sugar Bear…You really had me roped and tied, Ordered About, Hypnotized, Sweet Jesus whispered in my ears…You're a Butterfly, and Butterflies are free to fly, fly away…Bye-Bye."…The words echoed in Ruby's mind as she thought about Matt. She wanted to be that butterfly flying high up in the sky like his plane giving her a new perspective on life.

CHAPTER 6

Troy returned late on Sunday night around midnight. He tiptoed into Sarah's room and kissed her goodnight. He was dressed in a jogging outfit that Ruby hadn't seen before. She also noticed his new sneakers that he was unlacing while sitting on the bed next to her. She wondered what charge card he had used to purchase them.

"Ruby, first I want to tell you I'm sorry for the way I've acted recently. I haven't been myself and I think it's because I've been unhappy," he said holding her hand. "But I've made you unhappy too because of my own frustrations," he added leaning over on his elbow, quickly kissing her on the lips. "I've missed you and Sarah so much. Did you miss me?"

Ruby nodded her head, not really awake and comprehending the apology. Her thoughts were still on the new clothes and shoes!

"I have some good news. I think they may want to offer me a job next fall, maybe even sooner. The firm wants to expand their office in San Diego and need at least ten new attorneys by this time next year. What do you think?" asked Troy smiling. It was the first time she had seen him enthusiastic about anything in such a long time.

"Well," Ruby said sitting up in bed sleepily propping up her pillow so she could lean against it, "What's the salary?"

"They've offered me $20,000 starting out which, as you know, is more than I make now and a 5-10% increase each year in salary, based on clientele."

"Wow, how wonderful, honey. I've always wanted to visit California and now it seems like a possibility we might move there. How exciting. I've heard it's a fantastic place to live. I love warm weather and the beach. I'm sure Sarah would love it too," she said squeezing his hand. "We'll talk about it tomorrow when I'm more awake. Hurry and come to bed. I want to hold you for a while before I have to get up early to type a speech for the Senator. He's heading to New York and needs it by noon."

"Ruby, I'm too wired to sleep. I need a drink. I'll see you tomorrow," Troy replied and kissed the top of her head before walking into the living room and turning on the TV. She could hear him popping the top of a beer. He fell asleep on the sofa.

How could he just walk away after being gone for a whole week when he said he missed me? Actually, she was relieved when he left. She was getting use to the empty bed. It finally dawned on Ruby what had just transpired. She didn't want to move and leave D.C. This was her home. *California?* Her mind was a whirlwind of confusion. She closed her eyes and started to smile thinking of Matt. Ruby was falling in love with another man. She dreamed about flying away to Jackson Hole, Wyoming in a small Cessna with a 007 emblem on the side.

***

The next few weeks were hectic at the Senate. Matt had meetings with the Senator or had to fly around the U.S. attending other meetings with organizations and companies regarding governmental matters. He left amusing notes on her desk when he was around, and of course, the letters to be typed and retyped. It had been three weeks since their trip to the mountains. Ruby had to deliver some papers to his office and walked in to set them on his desk. She didn't see him at first. He was behind the door hanging up his coat. He grabbed her arm and gave her a big hug with the files in her arms. He held her close and kissed her on top of her head before closing the door.

"I've missed harassing you so much. How's Sarah? How's my Mockingbird?" he asked taking the files out of her arms and placing them on his desk. He had on his typical dark suit and a handsome red, white, and blue tie.

"Your Mockingbird has been too busy to sing. I know I have a desk buried somewhere in my office. You must be tired after writing all those letters and proposals, Matt. Don't you get a vacation soon? Don't you think you should go catch some fish or something?" she asked shyly laughing, trying to look away.

He took his hands and touched her face turning it towards him. Ruby looked through his wire rims and could feel her heart pounding. He kissed her. It felt so natural and she wanted him to.

"I want to take you to lunch today. Will you be free around one?" he asked smiling. "We need to catch up on us."

"Yes, I can go with you. I'll meet you outside by the front door," she said quickly opening the door and waving.

Ruby had worn her old brown midi-wool skirt and cream-colored blouse that matched it with a tweed brown jacket she had bought on sale over the weekend. She had also purchased some low brown pumps through a catalog that made her outfit complete. Those were the first items she had actually bought for herself in over a year. She figured if Troy could buy new clothes, so could she. Her hair was up in the usual scrunchy. She kept it that way when she met Matt outside.

"Let's have Chinese. I'm in the mood to use some chopsticks. How about you?" said Matt taking two fingers and demonstrating scissor actions.

There was a marble fountain in the entrance with colorful flowers floating in the basin. A waitress seated them at a table by the back corner window. It was the last table available, which Ruby later found out Matt had reserved. A red candle was lit in the center of the table. Matt surprised her with a red rose he placed beside her plate after she sat down. He had hidden it inside his jacket. "I've got to keep my favorite singer happy. I'd be lost without her."

She smiled and thanked him.

They both ordered two different chicken dishes and decided to share. Hot tea had been brought to the table.

"First, tell me how Sarah's doing?" Matt inquired placing his napkin in his lap.

"She's fine. I've been reading to her friends twice a week. She's growing up so fast every day. She asks about you often."

"I'll have to stop by and see her at the daycare when things slow down. Now tell me what's happening with you and Troy," asked Matt concerned and serious pouring the hot tea into the red china tea cups.

"He interviewed for a job in San Diego. If he gets it, which according to him he will, we may be moving as soon as August or before. I haven't seen him this excited about anything for such a long time. He's anxious about leaving D.C. and getting a new start with this firm. He thinks he'll be able to someday become a partner. That's one of his dreams, of course. Isn't that the big dream of most lawyers?" Ruby looked at Matt smiling. "We're supposed to go to his parent's house for Thanksgiving in a couple of days to share his news."

"But truth be known, Matt, I'd rather go fishing and flying around Asheville Mountain Lake." Ruby said pausing for a sip of the hot tea. She looked up at Matt. "Tell me what you're thinking and feeling. Is it just me?"

"You already know that I have strong feelings for you, Ruby. I know the situation is not good, with you being married, and me being your boss. I've tried to keep myself busy—to give us both breathing room but I long to hold you and be with you. I miss your singing and your red hair all mashed when you get up in the morning." He added jokingly. "And you have a wonderful little girl that I simply adore."

Matt looked up as the waitress brought the chicken dishes and placed them on the table.

"Thank you. This looks great," Matt commented. She asked if they needed anything else. Matt nodded his head, no.

"I brought the pictures I took of our fishing trip. After we eat I'll share them with you. I captured some great shots out of your airplane and some of you with your fishing pole. But my favorite is the one the store keeper took of all three of us in front of your yacht, Mr. Bond," she mused lifting the tasty chicken dish up with her chopsticks.

"I can't wait to see them. Say, you're pretty good using those sticks," said Matt taking a bite of chicken off of her plate. "I think I like yours the best. Next time I'll get this," he pointed to Ruby's with his chopsticks. "It's a little spicy, but not too hot."

"Don't act so surprised about my talents, Matt," Ruby said looking at him raising her eyebrows.

"So when can we go flying again?"

"Maybe after Thanksgiving. I think Troy will have some more weekend business trips out to California." Ruby took the pictures out of her purse and handed them to Matt.

He began flipping through the stack. "Nice work. When did you take photography lessons?" asked Matt. "Wow, these are so clear from the air. What shutter speed did you use?"

"I took several classes in college, but my dad taught me how to 'frame' a picture. I give him the most credit for my talent. I feel like I've been taking pictures all my life. I love to photograph Sarah and send her pictures to relatives. It's cheaper for me to do it and I get to have fun dressing her up and using different props. I think I used 200 for these."

"I want copies of these. Can I take the negatives?" inquired Matt. "I think I might enlarge a few. I love the ones of you two young ladies fishing and the view of the cabin."

"These are all for you. I can't let Troy discover them."

"We better get going. It's almost 2:30 and the girls will be asking where I am. Thanks for lunch but it's my turn to treat," Ruby said getting out her wallet.

"No deal, Ruby. You'll never pay for anything while you're with me," said Matt persistently. He picked up the check and deposited money for the bill and a generous tip for the waitress.

Ruby slid the rose under her coat to take back to the office. They said their "goodbyes" and went back to work.

Matt called long distance the day before Thanksgiving to wish Ruby a nice holiday and to say he would see her sometime in December. He reminded her to get lots of rest because he was working on correspondence letters and the Senator had several speeches she needed to type. Their conversation was general and very business like. She wanted to reveal how much she truly missed him, but it wasn't fair. If that were the case, why was she still with Troy?

They traveled to Greenville to see Troy's family for Thanksgiving. Some of the other relatives from his mother's side came from Idaho and they had quite a large crowd of nineteen. The food was wonderful. Troy's dad was an excellent cook, and he smoked the turkey on his new smoker grill outside in the cold. He had covered it with lots of grease and marinades to keep it moist while it cooked slowly. Everyone else brought casserole dishes and various desserts. Troy's mom loved chocolate cake so Ruby made one just for her. Sarah played with her cousins, Eva and Sam. They were two and three years older than her, but they got along well.

Ruby's family had gone to New York to help Diane and her husband, Paul, move into their new apartment. They had married the year before, but decided to elope because they wanted to save money. They were both aspiring young musical actors and were pursuing their talents on Broadway. They were celebrating their daughter, Lilly's, first birthday. Ruby regretted having to miss being with them, but that was one of the sacrifices a married couple had to make, alternating holidays with each other's families.

She longed to phone Diane and talk to her about Troy, but she had enough going on in her life. It would have to wait.

Thanksgiving was hardly over when Christmas ornaments were being displayed all over D.C. The popular State Christmas trees were decorated with paraphernalia representing each state. The city was beautiful that time of year.

The Senator's office and Troy's firm had scheduled their Christmas parties on the same night, so Ruby ended up attending the law office party. She didn't want to go to hers because of Matt. She didn't want to face him while she was with Troy.

Jenny, a sweet fifteen year old blond that lived next door to their apartment, babysat Sarah. They had become good friends. Sarah liked playing dress up with her and putting on make-up. She must have gotten that from her Aunt Diane.

Troy was chummy with several of the secretaries in the office. Ruby noticed one young blond, Sally, was extremely attentive and vice-versa. Troy left Ruby alone while he went over to flirt with her. It would have bothered Ruby before, but not now. She was glad he wasn't by her side. Ruby mingled with several of his male colleagues and put on some of her Scarlett O'Hara charm. She knew her black evening dress looked great and she used it to her advantage. Ruby could see Troy watching her from a distance. Matt had given her back some of the confidence she had lost. Troy sensed her new persona and didn't like it.

When Ruby went to work on Monday a note was taped to her phone. It said *Ruby, I need to see you. Can we meet after work or maybe this weekend? Matt*

As she sat down and tried to get organized her phone rang. It was him.

"Did you get my note?" asked Matt.

"Yes, where are you?" she asked looking around the room to make sure none of the other girls were paying attention to the conversation.

"I'm in L.A. My dad isn't well and I've been here all weekend. They're going to operate on him so I don't think I'll be able to see you this week. I wrote the note before I had received the message about dad."

"Is there anything I can do for you, Matt? How sick is your dad?" Ruby inquired knowing how family oriented he was and how upset he must be.

"They're operating on him this morning at 8. It's only 5 now. I haven't slept much and I'm a little jet lagged. There are some files on my desk that need to be typed and edited by you and put on the Senator's desk before you leave today. I'll keep in touch. Thanks for being there and finishing my work. I hope to see you by Friday," said Matt hanging up with a click in her ear.

Ruby went into his office and started to sort through his papers. She found the ones that needed to be typed for the Senator's signature. When she picked up the files, a piece of paper fell to the floor. It was from Jackson Hole, Wyoming. It was a letter expressing interest in Matt working for their fire and rescue team. There was some information on real estate homes, apartments, and land. *Was Matt seriously thinking about quitting the Senate and becoming a rescue pilot?*

Ruby learned from the girls in the office that the Christmas party was a lot of fun. They had rented a huge room at the Hyatt and had a sit down dinner. When Ruby asked who everyone was with, they told her Matt was with a blond lawyer. She was a friend that the Senator had asked him to escort. They said Matt turned on his charm but only danced with her several times. It seemed that most of the time she was alone because Matt was playing his saxophone with the band. They said he was an unbelievably talented musician. No one knew he even played the sax. Unfortunately, he had received a phone call in the middle of the jazz concert and had to leave. Tom, another attorney and his wife took the girl home. They later learned that his father had collapsed at work and he was called by his brother to come to California.

Matt phoned the following week and said he was in New York. The Senator was there and they had some contracts to work on. He said his father had had open heart surgery and it had been successful. His family was still hoping to meet in Maui if he recovered in time. Otherwise, they would all meet in L.A. with their dad and celebrate in their home for the first time since his mom had died. He sounded tired. Ruby wished she could have been with him.

Troy had been unbearable since his party. He was staying out late again and returned with his usual depressed, 'poor-pitiful-me' state. Ruby hadn't seen him for the past two days. Troy only left messages on the answering machine during the day when she wasn't home.

Ruby was home with Sarah when he unexpectedly came home early.

"What are you doing here?" he asked irritated.

"I might ask you the same thing. I missed work because Sarah had been running a high fever and I had to take her to the doctor. She was given some antibiotics and told to rest. I just hope I'm not going to get it too," Ruby answered rocking her. She brushed the top of her head. Troy's eyes were red and he seemed drugged.

"You should have told me she was ill. You don't include me in anything with her anymore," he hissed through his teeth.

"And where was I supposed to reach you? You've been away most of the week. I'm assuming on business trips. You don't leave any numbers. Where should I try to call you? I leave messages at your job but never get an answer," Ruby spoke back trying not to get hysterical.

"You have all the numbers you need. I just came in to grab a few items and I'll let you and Sarah comfort each other. I can't afford to get sick right now. I have a big case I'm working on and I need to go back to the office," he added rummaging through the bedroom and throwing things around. He came back into the living room and stood over them looking down at Sarah.

"Honey, I'll bring you some ice cream tonight when I get home," he told her when she looked up at him with her sick eyes. She smiled and then closed her eyes. He waved and was gone.

He never did bring the ice cream but Ruby wasn't counting on him to. She knew Sarah wouldn't forget, so she slipped downstairs while Sarah was napping and bought a pint in the store. Ruby told her it was from her dad and that he brought it on his lunch break. If Troy only knew how many times she covered his promises.

Christmas was just around the corner and Ruby had to buy presents for Sarah. Troy had left for the weekend, nothing unusual. He said he was being sent to Chicago until Wednesday. Ruby asked Jenny if she could watch Sarah for a few hours on Saturday so she could shop. She said she would be glad to. Jenny was studying for exams and could use the extra money to buy her family gifts.

Ruby drove out to Tyson's Corner and finally found a parking space. She stepped out of the car and started walking towards the mall. Suddenly she realized she had locked her keys inside and panicked. She didn't have any cash for a locksmith and began to feel alone and desperate. She knew Sarah's presents would have to take a backseat to the stupid keys. She was mad at herself for being such a dizzy redhead.

"Can I offer you my services? You look like a damsel in distress," Matt asked putting his arms around her.

"How did you know where I was? Are you following me?"

"Bond always knows where you are. It's my job to keep an eye on you so you don't try to escape and have me retrain another secretary," he replied. "Stay here I'll be right back."

He left and shortly returned. "I've called a locksmith and he should be here any minute."

"I'm so glad you're here. I can't believe you're back. I thought you were still traveling. Where have you been, Matt?" Ruby asked curiously.

"I've been trying to catch up on laundry and cleaning my house. I flew into DC late last night."

A white truck pulled up and Matt went over to talk to a dark haired driver. The locksmith opened her car in a matter of seconds.

Matt paid him and the truck pulled away.

"Thanks, Matt. I can repay you on Friday," Ruby said embarrassed by the situation.

"I'm glad I found you. It must be fate. Please don't think about the money. Anyway while I'm here we should do some shopping. Do you still have any spare time?"

"Yes, Sarah's with a sitter and I need to purchase a few gifts for her. I'd love the company."

The mall was crowded. "Let's go into the children's clothing shop first. I want to buy Sarah a new dress. Would that be OK?" asked Matt making Ruby smile again, as she nodded, *Yes.*

He picked out a beautiful light green pinafore with a white apron. Ruby knew it would look adorable on her. He also bought her a small white shoulder purse and a book.

Next, he took Ruby to one of the department stores. He had selected several things and said she should try them on. She modeled them and he looked pleased. When Ruby was in the dressing room, he had gone to the racks and picked up the same sizes and had purchased them. He bought her a black blazer, a purse to match, and a blue dress.

"Merry Christmas, Ruby. I appreciate all the work you do for me at the office. You deserve these and much more."

"Matt, I don't know what to say. I didn't want you to buy me anything." Ruby said surprised by the package he carried.

But Matt just smiled and said, "I think we need to find a place to eat. I know a great place to get a fish dinner."

CHAPTER 7

Ruby followed Matt to his townhouse in Georgetown and parked on the side street. She opened the trunk of her car and put the packages inside closing it quickly. Matt waited for her and they walked up the steps to the red brick townhouse with dark green trim.

"I hope I didn't leave it too messy," said Matt looking around when he walked inside.

"You know I can't stay if it is."

He quickly grabbed her keys. "It's too late now, you're my prisoner."

"OK. I'm in. Now what?"

"You can leave your shoes over here and I'll get you some thicker socks to cover your feet. You can hang up your coat here," he said opening a closet. "Don't move. I'll be right back." Matt left to get her socks.

Ruby noticed a beautiful painting in the main hallway of a woman with auburn hair in a red evening gown. She was standing in front of a grand piano with a glass of champagne in her hand. Her hair was brushed up into a net outlined with a gold border. She had a white dangling pearl earring. Her green eyes seemed to follow Ruby as she walked by to take off her shoes and placed her coat in the closet.

"This is an exquisite portrait. What a beautiful woman," Ruby commented. She felt like she was looking into a mirror.

"That's my mom's portrait painted shortly before she became ill. It's my favorite picture of her. She played that piano and had taken ballet when she was a teenager. The ballerinas in the background were she and her sister. Dad has the original in his bedroom, but I hired the same artist to repaint one for me several years ago. You've probably noticed you look a lot like her. It's quite remarkable really. Not only do you have her same features, but you also have similar mannerisms," Matt smiled looking up at her. He handed her the socks and helped hold her steady as she covered one foot. Before she finished putting on the last sock, he intentionally made her tip off balance and laughed as he caught her before she fell on her backside.

"You can be such a gentleman at times, Matt. The other times you're a pain!" Ruby said letting go of his grip and leaning against the wall for more stability.

"Come in and make yourself comfortable. I'll fix us a glass of wine and start preparing your dinner. I know you don't have much time before you need to get back to Sarah," said Matt disappearing to find the opener.

The living room floor was covered with thick peach carpet continuing up the circular steps at the far end of the room. The white cathedral ceilings had two skylights angled towards the kitchen giving the room more openness about it. The masculine leather couch and recliner complimented the room that surrounded an enclosed red brick fireplace. Wood was neatly stacked to one side. On each side of the fire place were tall bookshelves lined with law books neatly placed in an order of some sort. In the corner sat a saxophone case and a Martin Guitar. She could picture a new band forming. Ruby smiled to herself.

His teak desk had a few papers scattered and several files were stacked on the floor beside his chair. The tiffany desk lamp was still on and she could see where he'd been working. A black phone was in the corner and a photograph was framed in the center of his desk. An IBM word processor and a tape recorder were on a wooden stand to the right.

The kitchen walls were painted cream with yellow flowered tiles placed evenly over the stove and counter. The window overlooked a tiny backyard and had light yellow curtains opening in the center to let in the light. A hanging plant of ivy colored the corner to the left of the window and a Christmas cactus with pink buds was beginning to bloom in a brass pot sitting in the sill. The kitchen was so neat and clean. Ruby could've eaten off of the floor.

The stereo was located under the TV. Ruby rummaged through the albums, picking out Bing Crosby's Christmas Album.

"Good choice, Ruby. I haven't heard this one in a while."

As she walked into the kitchen, Matt put his arms around her and kissed her. Ruby's heart was pounding. She needed him so desperately. *Did he feel the same?*

"I better quit kissing you before I can't stop myself. I'll get the fish out of the refrigerator in the garage," he said turning around and heading to a door towards the back porch. He came back with two medium sized trout that had already been filleted.

Ruby began working on the salad while singing with Bing. She set the table and lit a candle in the center of the table. "I better call Sarah. I'll be right back," she said drying her hands on a tea towel and walking into the living room. As she picked up the receiver, she noticed the photo on the desk was a picture of Sarah and her at the lake. She couldn't believe it. She smiled as she dialed her house. She told Jenny she would be home soon and she said that was fine. Sarah had just finished some frozen pizza and was watching the Disney Channel. She returned to the dinner table. Matt looked so handsome in his red and black plaid shirt and jeans that he had changed into before cooking the fish. They sat down and began chatting about Matt's plans to Maui with his brothers. He thought his dad would be better and that they were all still planning to go.

"I sure wish you could join us," Matt said thoughtfully taking a sip of his wine. "What are your plans for Christmas, Ruby?"

"We'll go to Raleigh to see my family. I've missed my sisters and my brothers. We always have a special Christmas…the traditional popcorn on the tree, hot chocolate, singing carols, and cooking breakfast over the fireplace Christmas morning. I want Sarah to be close to them. I know how important family is.

I'm excited about seeing Lilly, Diane's daughter, for the first time. Diane and her husband have jobs on Broadway. I think it would be great to visit them for New Year's in New York one of these days. I'd better start saving my money. You'd really like them, Matt."

"What's Sarah getting from Santa for Christmas? I know we bought her a few surprises."

"I found a secondhand stove and refrigerator at a yard sale. I repainted them last weekend and bought some stickers to decorate the outside. I also bought her a Barbie, and some fancy hair barrettes. That should keep her busy for a while."

"What do you want for Christmas, Matt?" Ruby asked when their eyes met.

"What I want for Christmas, you couldn't give me, but there's always hope for next Christmas." He reached over and kissed her hand. She could feel herself blushing.

"I did have one small gift that I didn't give you after we went shopping. It's something very small but I thought you might enjoy it." He handed her a small blue box. She used her knife to open it. On top of a layer of cotton, was a white airplane pin with several pastel colored stones set in the wings. She picked it up to examine it closer.

"Matt, I don't know what to say. You really shouldn't have. I don't even have a present for you." she said opening the clasp and pinning it to her sweater. "It's the most beautiful pin I've ever had. I will always think of our trip to the mountains when I wear it." She leaned over and kissed him on the cheek.

"Thank you. You are too good to me. Oh, I didn't realize the time…I need to be going in a few minutes. Let me help you with the dishes," she said getting up and taking his plate and glass into the kitchen.

"I'll do them later. Let's go sit by the fire for a minute. You have to sing a Christmas song before I let you escape."

He tuned the strings and played a few chords…

"Are you ready?" he asked strumming the strings.

"What are we singing?"

"White Christmas, what else? You know I won't see one of those where I'm going." They harmonized to the song.

"Merry Christmas, Ruby," he said walking her to the door and hugging her. He leaned down and kissed her once more. "Happy New Year! I leave tomorrow for Maui and won't be back until next year."

* * *

Christmas was a happy time for Ruby because she spent most of the holiday with her family. Sarah and Lilly helped her decorate cookies. They made a large gingerbread house for the centerpiece on grandma's kitchen table. Ruby loved the smells of Christmas. The spiced bread was a familiar and traditional fragrance that lingered throughout the house. The girls made hot chocolate and the adults visited Auntie Josephine to have some of her special homemade eggnog…The heavy duty one with more liquor than eggs! It was always a treat for them. Ruby's family went to the Midnight Christmas Eve Service. Troy complained about having to wear a suit and how much his knees and back ached sitting on the pew. When they returned home, he had several beers and soon seemed to be in a world all of his own. Ruby was sure he had taken some drugs, but didn't catch him in the act. He started picking on her about her hair and the way Sarah was being taken care of. When they were alone in the bedroom he made love to her. Troy became rough and interested in his own satisfaction. Angrily he told her she was lousy at lovemaking so he dressed and left the house. She cried herself to sleep dreaming of Matt and his family enjoying the warm Christmas Eve Service in Maui. She tried to visualize the Hawaiian dancer and the music that was being played.

Sarah woke up for Santa just as Troy was sneaking back into the house. His eyes were red and glazed. He told her parents that he had gone for a jog. He was wearing his Nike outfit and he looked like he had been running. Their eyes met when Ruby came into the kitchen and he said smiling, "Merry Christmas, honey. I trust you slept well."

"Merry Christmas, Troy. Yeah, out like a light," she answered him looking away rubbing her covered bruised arms.

Instantly the door banged open and Sarah was shouting, "Did he come? Did he eat the cookies we left him?" she asked running into the living room to inspect the empty plate. Then she noticed all the presents. She ran to get Lilly. Paul brought her down the stairs cuddling her blanket with her thumb in her mouth. She didn't quite get the idea of Christmas, but Sarah did. Sarah didn't know which present to open first.

Ruby's family had bought her clothes for work and outfits for Sarah's growing body. Ruby gave Troy a brown leather briefcase and a silk, conservative tie to go with his new expensive suits. He handed her a turquoise sweater and a pair of gold earrings in the shape of daisies. She wondered who was wearing the pearl necklace.

Ruby shopped with her sisters and mom the day after Christmas leaving Sarah with Troy. He watched TV and drank beer, while she played with her toys.

Ruby purchased an airplane silk tie for Matt, a Boy Scout knife and compass. She also bought several dresses on sale with the money her dad had given her for Christmas. Her first item was a long red evening dress with a dressy black shawl. For work she bought a black knit dress and sweater to match and a light green linen dress with a large cream colored collar and buttons sewn on the front. She pulled out the plane pin from the black purse Matt had bought and placed it in front of each work dress to see if she could wear it. Perfect!

CHAPTER 8

Ruby received an invitation to one of President Reagan's Second Inaugural Balls. She was surprised to find out that no one else in the office had one. She was perplexed.

After retrieving a cup of coffee she sat down at her desk when the phone rang. It was Matt.

"Hi, Ruby! Do I get some coffee too?" he asked waiting for a response.

She hung up and fixed another cup. At first when she opened his door she didn't see him. It was dark inside and she felt her heart sink. A hand out of the darkness took the coffee from her hand and placed it on the desk. Matt gave her a big hug. "I missed you, Ruby," he whispered in her ear. "I couldn't wait to fly home to tell you."

"I missed you too."

They hugged each other for several minutes silently. Matt turned on the light.

"Stand back and let me see this pretty green dress on you," said Matt whistling. "Nice pin."

"It's my favorite," Ruby said examining him closely. "Look at that tan, Matt. Don't stand too close to me or I'll be jealous."

"I had an awesome time with the boys. I flew over the island several times and managed to catch a few monstrous fish. I had my brothers take pictures because I knew you wouldn't believe me!" he remarked sarcastically.

"It's easy to pick up a fish to claim as your own."

"I'll ignore that remark," he replied shaking his head.

"How was your dad?"

"Dad was in a little pain but enjoyed the sun and being outdoors. He looked really good with his dark color when we all parted at the airport. He was even flirting with one of the stewardesses on the plane."

"Well, good for him." Ruby squinted with her eyes and wrinkled her nose. "I thought about you often over the holidays. I'm glad it worked out that you could all be together again."

Ruby handed him his coffee. "Here. This will be cold before you drink it and I'm not going to get you another one. I can see out of the corner of my eye all those letters to be typed on your desk. I'll be here for weeks!"

"Thanks for reminding me," he smiled handing her the new batch of correspondents. "We need another lunch date. Twelve work for you?" he asked sipping his coffee

"I'll see you at twelve only because you're paying me!" Ruby joked as she turned around and left his office with her arms full of papers.

The restaurant was busy as they finally were seated and ordered salads not waiting for the menus.

"I brought this invitation from work to show you. It's for one of Reagan's parties on the 18th. Did you get one too?" Ruby inquired taking a bite of her lunch.

"No, I didn't. Whom do you know to get an invitation to the ball?" asked Matt puzzled.

"I have no idea. But the invitation is for two. Troy will be out of town that weekend on business in Chicago. He's having his second interview for the job in California. Would you like to go with me?" she said watching him smile.

"Of course, I'd love to be your date, Ruby. But two conditions," he said wiping his lips with his napkin and placing it in his lap. He reached into his pocket and produced a small box wrapped in blue paper and a gold, curly bow. "Happy Birthday," he whispered handing her the present.

"How did you know it was my birthday?" she said drawing her hand to her chest.

"You know us British Intelligence have our connections…We get paid to know these things

"Matt, you have to stop spoiling me."

"One condition is that you can't open the box until you get back to work. And the other is you have to wear these to the ball, Cinderella"

"I should've known you would make me wait until I finished my letters."

As she slid the box into her purse she noticed Marla being seated with two other friends.

"Matt, over in the corner is Marla, the girl Troy has been spending so much time with."

Matt looked over. "Well, I must say Troy is a fool. Let's get out of here."

They slipped out of the restaurant unnoticed by everyone, except Marla. She revealed her toothy grin. *Well, well, well. Look what the cat drug in.*

Walking back to the office, Ruby stopped and sat down on one of the park benches. She opened the small box. She lifted the lid and found a beautiful pearl necklace and matching earrings.

"Oh my…" she said at a loss for words. "How lovely, Matt. Thank you."

"I bought them in Maui. I hope you like them."

He looked at his watch, "Well, I hate to run but I have a plane to catch with the Senator to New York again," said Matt sadly checking his watch. "I'll be back in time for the dance."

They were too involved to observe the woman in dark glasses eavesdropping. She skirted away to find a phone booth.

Ruby was anxious to put on the necklace and earrings in the bathroom before typing all the letters Matt had left for her. She admired her new jewels in the mirror. She covered the necklace up with her blouse and let her hair down to hide the earrings. She didn't want the girls to notice the new additions to her outfit.

As she entered the office, balloons and flowers from the staff and a big "Happy Birthday" sign adorned it. "Oh my gosh! I can't believe you guys. I don't know what to say. Thank you all so much," she said hugging each of them.

On the way home Sarah had fun hitting the balloons flying around in the car. Ruby could hardly see out of the back window. She played with them in the apartment and would run away, as if the balloons were chasing her.

Ruby cooked fried chicken and mashed potatoes and bought a small box of ice cream cones for the two of them in the convenient store. She put a candle in each and they both sang Happy Birthday to her. Ruby blew out both candles with Sarah's help. Ruby sang and rocked her to sleep. She kissed the top of her head and pulled the blanket up to cover her. Finally, she was alone to enjoy the rest of her special day.

Relaxing in the bathtub, she was having a glass of wine and letting the soap bubbles float all around her when she heard a key enter the lock. Troy came in. It was already ten o'clock.

Ruby continued to sip her wine and soak. Troy opened the bathroom door and used the toilet.

"Honey, do you mind closing the door? You're letting in a cold draft," Ruby asked frowning and sinking further down into the tub.

"Sure," he said opening the door more and then swinging it quickly back and forth to make more cold air circulate in the bathroom.

"Troy," Ruby said again angrily. "Please stop. It's not funny," she said listening to his laughter.

"What are you going to do about it?" he said picking up the hair dryer and turning it on. He pointed it at her.

Ruby quietly unplugged the tub and stepped out trying to reach for her towel. He grabbed it first and threw it down the hall still keeping the hair dryer on her.

He raised his voice and said mockingly, "You're the ugliest wife anyone could ever have. Look how fat you are. Your hair is never combed and you keep our child looking like she's from a homeless shelter. You suck at love making, and as a mother." He yanked so hard on the hair dryer that the plug came out of the wall. He threw it down the hall at her. He continued to yell, "Where's my dinner? I work too damn it, to provide for you and my daughter. You didn't even fix me anything to eat."

"Stop," Ruby hissed through her teeth shaking more from fear than freezing, picking up the towel again. "It's cold and I don't want to wake up Sarah. What's wrong with you? There's leftover chicken and potatoes in the frig. Turn on the oven and heat it up yourself. How do I know when you are coming home? You never call or write me a note. I can't read your mind."

Troy continued to laugh and pulled the towel out of her hands and wouldn't give it back. He started cursing at all the balloons that had begun to fly around wildly with all the added turbulence in the air.

"God damn it Ruby, where in the f…did all these balloons come from? Are you wasting money on Sarah again, spoiling her?" he asked raising his voice again.

He grabbed all the balloons and opened the sliding glass door on the balcony. He was giving them a punch through the cold opening. Ruby missed the show but could hear him counting them as they were launched.

She ran into the bedroom and grabbed her robe using it as a towel to at least wipe off the water that was freezing her to death. She went back into the bathroom afraid to lock the door because Sarah was still out there all alone. She finished dressing and chugged what was left of her wine. Troy was standing there with his suitcase leaning against the wall. She could see his eyes were red and he was out of it.

"I'm leaving tonight to catch a plane for Chicago. I don't know where I'm staying, but if you're lucky I'll call you later to let you know."

Ruby's anger got the best of her. "Hurry and get out. I don't want you around anymore. You're different from the man I married. God, what happened to the Troy Slader I knew in college? And by the way, thanks for the birthday present. Sarah will be disappointed in the morning to know that the balloons are gone," she added while tears streamed down her face.

Suddenly Troy changed and became docile. He sat down on the floor and started sobbing like a baby. He was becoming too hysterical for her to quiet him. "I'm sorry honey, I forgot your birthday. I'll get you something in Chicago."

Sarah woke up and started crying. Ruby went in to pick her up and rock her back to sleep. When Ruby laid her back down, she noticed that Troy was gone. *Happy 27th Birthday!*

* * *

Troy didn't go anywhere that night except to Marla's house. He came back to the apartment several times during the day while Ruby was at work to pick up his clean clothes He left dirty ones for her to wash in the bathroom hamper. Ruby was tired of his inconsideration. She would take his dirty clothes out of the hamper and fold them. She neatly put them back in his drawers and closet. Ruby figured that if he wanted his own space, he could wash his own clothes. It was a known fact that Troy had a very high IQ, but the drugs had confused his common sense and reasoning, not to mention his personality. He truly believed that he fooled everyone. He was like an ostrich with his head in the sand. He was the fool and didn't even know it.

Troy returned home to pack for his trip. He made up some story about his Chicago meeting and how much work he had to do in the office before his trip. She just nodded her head up and down.

As he opened the door to leave with his suitcase in hand, Ruby told him in a nice, but nervous voice, "Troy, please get off the drugs before coming home or else just stay away. Sarah doesn't need to be around a father who's a drug addict."

He walked over and slapped her. "Don't ever tell me what to do," he yelled pushing her down. "And another thing, don't ever tell anyone I hit you or I'll kill you and whoever you tell." Then he slammed the door and left.

Ruby was shocked. Troy had been mean mentally, but this was the first time he had physically hit her. She cried herself to sleep with an ice pack on her cheek.

The next morning she applied heavy foundation to cover the bruise on her face before going to work. With Matt out of town, Ruby felt abandoned and alone. She decided she needed some spiritual support so she phoned the minister of the Methodist church she had attended several times while living in Virginia. She arranged for her transfer of membership from her church in Raleigh. She had always attended church with her family. Ruby missed listening to sermons and the religious uplifting that transpired. She was so confused. She was married to one man but falling in love with another. *Was that not a sin?*

She felt like she was trapped in a bottle and couldn't get out. Ruby wanted to sleep with the man she loved and divorce the man she was growing to hate.

That evening she listened to Elton John's song. 'Someone Saved My Life Tonight' over and over. She wanted to be that butterfly... 'and butterflies are free to fly...fly away...bye bye...'

* * *

Ruby was looking forward to going to the Ball with Matt. It gave her something to look forward to. She had arranged for Jenny to spend the night just in case she came home without her glass slipper after midnight.

On the eighteenth, a dozen red roses were on her desk with a note. Again the girls teased Ruby...Flowers..., invitation to a President's party..., secret calls,'..."Go girl, Work it, Own it!" they laughed. The card said, 'Mockingbird, I'll be around to pick you up in front of your apartment at 6…'

Ruby dressed in her red formal adding the pearls around her neck. She put on black silk stockings and sandals with silver sequins sewn on the straps. She left her hair down and curled it with hot rollers. She placed two simple glittery barrettes in her hair to hold it away from her face. Ruby applied makeup and sprayed perfume gingerly. She did feel like Cinderella going to the Ball, except she was living with a wicked husband.

She wondered if Matt was as excited about the evening as she was. She couldn't wait to see him. She decided not to tell him about the threat Troy had made before leaving on his trip.

The doorbell rang and Sarah was already at the door letting Jenny in as Ruby walked towards it. Sarah gave her a big hug and the girls became involved in playing dolls on the living room floor. Ruby handed Jenny a paper with the name and phone number of the hotel. She told her to eat whatever she wanted and to try to get Sarah in bed around eight.

Ruby put on her coat before she entered the lobby because she didn't want anyone to see her dressed up and not with Troy. She carried a small bag which she held under her arm. Matt drove up in his sports car. He hopped out and opened the door for her. She was glad that darkness was upon them.

"Where to Miss?" he asked bowing and opening the car door.

He was incredibly handsome in his black tuxedo and smelled delicious.

"I have a special invitation to the President's party. He and Nancy are expecting me," Ruby replied with her nose a little tilted in the air.

She placed the present in the back seat as he ran around to the driver's side.

"I feel privileged to know people with such high connections! I'm still trying to figure out who you know on the Hill to get such a special invitation," he said driving to the end of the oval and stopping to kiss her on the cheek.

"Did I mention you look beautiful tonight, Ruby? I especially like the jewels you're wearing. Did you get them abroad?" he asked raising his eyebrows.

"As a matter of fact, I did. My best friend gave them to me in Rome. We vacationed there and traveled on one of the little love boats one night when the moon was full. He sang, "Mockingbird" and I fell in love with him. Do you know where I might find him? Some people call him Matt, but I call him, Bond, James Bond," Ruby smiled with her hand touching the necklace. They both laughed.

The hotel was beautifully decorated with red, white, and blue colors. There were ice sculptures in the center of wine and champagne fountains. The food was elegantly displayed throughout the many rooms that had been reserved for this special occasion. There were separate tables for fruits, cheeses, meats, breads, desserts, vegetable dishes, seafood, entrees, and an open bar. Disco lights were going around in circles to the live music and people were dancing and having a wonderful time. She still didn't know who paid for her tickets that she later found out cost one hundred dollars per person. But she was honored to be a witness during this historical event. She was a huge fan of Ronald Reagan and loved the way he doted on Nancy. They had not arrived yet, probably because they had four Balls to attend.

Matt took their coats to the cloak room and then they searched for vacant seats at one of the tables. Matt recognized several friends but chose a quiet table near the piano bar. It was probably the best decision since she was the married woman.

"Can I get you a drink?"

"Yes, I'd love some champagne."

He made his way over to the fountain and came back with two flutes. "I heard the Reagans will be here in about half an hour. They said there's quite a crowd following them. Our Senator and his wife should be here soon too."

"This is so exciting, Matt. Thanks for the champagne," Ruby remarked when he handed her the glass.

"Cheers! This is our Happy New Year's Toast," he beamed.

They clinked glasses.

"You look so elegant in that red dress, Ruby."

"I bought it in Raleigh the day after Christmas. But it's really the pearls that give it that classy look and my glass slippers add the final touch!"

"I'll try to remember not to step on your toes when we're dancing. There are too many lawyers in this place that would love to take the case!"

"I'd be afraid to find out how many guests here are actually attorneys."

"Don't forget you're with one. Be careful. I've already told you I can't be trusted."

"Well, that makes two of us!" Ruby said before sipping her champagne. "So did you rent your tux or is it yours?"

"It's mine. But as you know, I have numerous black tie affairs to attend during the year. I have to admit though, I'm usually bored with most of these parties unless I can play my saxophone or can find an excuse to leave early. But being here with you tonight only makes me want to make the night last forever."

"I was hoping to hear you play the sax. If the opportunity arises, I hope they let you join them. I'm looking forward to hearing you play if not tonight sometime soon. The girls in the office could talk of nothing else after the Christmas party."

"This is a talented jazz band. I've played with them at the Blue Note Jazz Club in New York. I may have to accommodate your wish but dancing is first. Are you ready? I can't take another minute just looking at you," Matt said wanting to hold her close.

They played many popular pieces. Matt sang the words into her ears and hugged her while moving to the beat of the song.

The lead singer of the jazz group pointed to Matt and spoke in the microphone. "We have a gifted saxophone player amongst us tonight. Maybe if we put our hands together we can coax him to join us for a song or two. Ladies and Gentlemen, put your hands together for Matt Connery."

Matt left Ruby's side and walked up on stage. He whispered in his friend's ear.

"This song is for all the special young ladies," said Matt finding Ruby in the crowd. They performed "I Love You Just the Way You Are."

The rest of the evening seemed magical, as though Ruby was in a dream. The Reagans mingled and danced with the crowds of people, laughing and enjoying the festivities. Flash bulbs flickered everywhere.

Matt had played a set with the band before returning to Ruby.

"I told you to be careful for what you wish for. Sorry I was up there so long. I just get into the music and it takes over."

"I enjoyed every moment, are you kidding? I can't believe how easily you play. It's like you and the instrument are one."

"Time to sweep you off of your feet," he said taking her hand and leading her back to the dance floor. Her dress was soaked with perspiration, as was his suit.

On the way home, Ruby told Matt she wanted to divorce Troy.

"You'll need a good attorney so you can start putting your legal matters in order. I can recommend one of my friends if you'd like. He isn't very expensive and will be fair. That is if you don't want to involve your family."

"That would be great. I've thought about this for a while now. Troy needs help and I'm not the one to give it to him. Sarah doesn't really miss him anymore because he's never home. I may as well be a single parent. Besides I'm in love with my boss."

"I'll phone you in the morning to give you that number. I'll stay away from you for a while to give you some time to sort things out. Make sure this is what you want, Ruby. I know it's what I want. But I've wanted you from the first moment I saw you."

When Matt stopped the car in front of the apartment, Ruby said,

"Oh, by the way, I almost forgot. I have a few small Christmas gifts for you." She reached her hand around to the back seat.

"These are little things," she said handing him several wrapped skinny packages. "You are always giving me gifts and now it's my turn."

Matt opened the presents. The first one was the airplane tie. He wrapped it around his neck. "I'll model this late one night when you come to visit," he grinned.

Next, he opened the Boy Scout knife and compass. He laughed so hard Ruby thought he would fall out of the car. "Now what am I to do with these?"

"You know, in case you get lost in the mountains rescuing people."

"OK. Well, you're first on my list!" he said nodding his head.

Last, he unwrapped the thin, flat present. It was a watercolor picture she had painted of his Cessna with Asheville Mountain Lake in the background. She had used one of her photographs as a guide. She even painted the tail numbers 942 Foxtrot Bravo and a small Bond emblem.

"It's wonderful. You're truly a gifted artist and I have a signed original. I don't know what to say," he said giving Ruby a hug and kiss.

"That's unusual for an attorney to be speechless. I'll have to see what else I can do to make you that way again. Goodnight, Matt. I had a really good time," Ruby said kissing him one more time before her dress turned back into rags. She closed the car door and waved.

Ruby waited until his car lights disappeared. She entered the elevator and leaned against the wall as she was lifted up to her floor. She practically skipped down the hall. She slipped her key quietly into the lock not wanting to wake the girls and closed the door. 'Jenny must be asleep too,' she thought. But as her eyes became accustomed to the darkness, she could see a dark figure in the corner or was she imagining it from all the champagne?

"Did you have a nice time, dear?" asked the all too familiar voice. She heard a loud crack and Ruby didn't remember anything after that.

CHAPTER 9

It was the violent wind and rain beating against the bedroom window that woke her. A few tears unconsciously trickled down her cheek. Suddenly Ruby became aware of the aches she felt from head to toe. She could barely see out of her right eye. Peering through it resembled a bamboo shade that someone had pulled down in front of it. Ruby tried to recall where she was and what had happened to make her feel so terrible. She turned her head and looked around her bedroom. She was aware of the smell of bacon cooking in the kitchen. She could also hear the faint sound of a cartoon on the television. Her first thought was Sarah. Was she alright? Ruby heard her laugh and it eased her mind somewhat. She tried to get up because she needed to use the bathroom but she couldn't move her legs. Shakily she used her arms to pull the sheet down, but she discovered it was too painful to use any of her muscles. It was all she could do to roll over and force one leg in front of the other trying to sit up, letting her legs dangle over the side. When she did this, an excruciating throb began to attack her head. Ruby thought she was going to faint. She stabled herself with her two arms holding her upright and breathed deeply.

"Focus," she kept saying over and over again to herself.

Ruby examined her condition. Her naked body was covered with dark, purple bruises and dried blood. She was scared. She could see swelling on both knees and it was incredibly painful to bend them over the bed. The blood seemed to come from her face and between her legs. She used the sheet to wipe away the tears that kept dripping down. Ruby put one hand up to feel her face. She put her hand over the shade gently but could hardly see out of it at all, much less feel her own touch. She trembled. Her lips felt like she had used them to open a sharp can. She needed to use the toilet to empty her bladder.

She painfully stepped down touching the floor. Ruby slowly grabbed the furniture and the walls to support her weight. She made her way to the bathroom. She felt the cold tiled floor under her feet and placed the palms of her hands on the edge of the sink. She looked into the mirror. "Oh my God," she exclaimed at her reflection through her one good eye. Ruby's face was one distorted mess. She looked like a freak at the circus. More tears fell down to the floor.

Ruby used a dirty washcloth hanging on the towel rack. She tried to recall what had happened after she left Matt. She couldn't. She used the toilet finding it difficult to sit with her swollen knees. When she finished, she turned around and threw up. Every muscle ached with the heaving that continued for several minutes. Her body yelled out in agony as she brought up the dinner and champagne from the night before. *Or was it the night before? How long have I been like this?*

She weakly turned on the shower and carefully helped lift one leg and then the other over the tub wall. Ruby let the water wash away her blood, sweat, and tears. It hurt to feel the rain beating down upon her pulverized body. She shampooed her hair and kept scrubbing, using more and more soap. She felt like this was a nightmare and she would soon wake up.

Suddenly, the door opened and Troy was pulling back part of the curtain to the side. He was staring at Ruby. She started to shake under the water.

"Good morning, Ruby. How are you feeling?" he paused, as she continued to shiver at the sound of his voice. When she didn't answer he continued, "I couldn't believe the way you slipped on the floor in the dark when you came home the other night." He acted like he was concerned rubbing his hand over her wet hair. "I tried to clean you up the best I could, but you went to sleep on me," he added as if she was part of a jury and he was trying to convince her to believe his story. "I hated to get rid of your nice dress, but it had a tear you see, so I put it in the dumpster. Unfortunately, everything had to go."

Ruby kept the water running just to give her courage to face him.

"When did you return from your trip?" she asked barely able to hear her own voice.

"About an hour before you came home. I arrived home early to tell you the great news, but you weren't here. Anyway, I've forgiven you for that," he replied happily. "I guess I'll tell you now. I've accepted the offer in California and you, Sarah, and I will be leaving within the week. You won't be able to work at the Senate. I already called your office yesterday and left a message with the secretary telling her you had the flu and that you wouldn't be back. I guess you could say I officially quit for you. Today is Monday and you see I was right. You've already missed a day of work." He left the room whistling.

Ruby turned off the shower and stepped out, slowly feeling the suffering of her injuries screaming out throughout her body. Drying herself with a towel, she found some pajamas and a robe to cover her horrible figure. She didn't want Sarah to see her like this. She applied makeup but it didn't help hide her red puffy face. She put on sunglasses and decided to tell Sarah that she had a terrible headache and the glasses kept the light from making it hurt more. She used dark lipstick to cover the scab on her swollen lip.

Troy packed boxes while Sarah watched cartoons.

Troy wrote down several messages for Ruby from Mary, her close friend at the Senate. The other girls in the office expressed their concern about her illness and sadness that she was leaving. Ruby was sure they were upset with her for not giving the required two weeks notice, but she never had the chance to talk to them personally. Troy asked them for a letter of reference. Troy said he found it in the mailbox downstairs without a postmark. Ruby stared at his signature. Matt had given her a glowing recommendation. He must have delivered it himself.

"If I didn't know better, I'd think this guy likes you," said Troy with an annoyed look. "I know for a fact that you don't deserve half the credit this Matt guy has given you in the letter," he added tossing it on the floor. "I've heard from a reliable source that you two were seen together at a restaurant and you were given a present. Can you deny this rumor?"

"I have no wish to deny it. I was having lunch with my boss while catching up on work I needed to finish because, like you, he was going out of town. As for the gift, he remembered it was my birthday. She would have mentioned not receiving a gift from Troy but thought better from provoking him. "I'm going back to bed. I have a headache." Ruby cried alone in her room, afraid and caged like a prisoner.

She wondered who had seen her and Matt together. Marla was the only one who came to mind. Troy did not leave the apartment until the end of the week. They packed and left for San Diego.

* * *

They drove for four days through snow, rain, and windy conditions across the states to California. Ruby was still recovering from her bruises and achy body. She was in constant pain taking aspirins to relieve some of the swelling. She continued to apply heavy makeup, wear long sleeved shirts, and sunglasses to conceal her battered body.

On the trip Troy seemed like his old self, but Ruby had been tricked many times before. She hoped and prayed he had given up the drugs if not for her for himself. She didn't trust him. Why should she? He had beaten her and taken away any happiness she could have. She wondered where Marla fit into the picture. She knew it had to be somewhere.

At least she had Sarah, but what about Matt? How could he ever forgive her? Ruby thought of him constantly and wondered how close she was to where he had grown up. There wasn't a day that she didn't picture him flying around in his plane with her and Sarah in the back seat. She knew she had to stop thinking about him because it only made her depressed. But so many things she saw, heard, or did reminded her of him. Ruby wondered what Matt thought of her now. Maybe she could write him a letter, but what would she say? She couldn't change anything, at least not right now.

The weather was beautiful when they arrived in California. The palm trees flapped their beautiful leaves as the gentle West Coast winds tickled them. It was nice to see the sun and feel the warmth it had to offer. Troy phoned Ruby's parents at her request after their arrival in San Diego. Her mom and dad weren't happy about them moving across the country but promised to visit when they saved enough money. Ruby agreed to keep in touch as often as she could.

A realtor helped them purchase a two bedroom townhouse in Riverside. Ruby found the suburbs refreshing. There was a small yard for Sarah and Ruby had a place where she could plant flowers. No more shaking while watering them high up in the air. Ruby bought a small plastic pool for Sarah and a few buckets and shovels to use in the dirt.

Ruby enrolled Sarah in a daycare and began seeking employment by checking ads in the newspaper. She was hired as a teller at a nearby bank.

Troy seemed to love his new job at first. Ruby thought the sun and warm climate also contributed to his cheery disposition. He was home for dinners, and they cooked out often on a small hibachi. He read to Sarah, and they were regular visitors to several parks. Ruby started taking pictures again. She was beginning to feel like she had a real home.

One Saturday they drove to Laguna Beach. They sunned and swam in the freezing Pacific. There were other beautiful places in the state to explore. Little did Ruby know that God had placed the sunny sky for them to enjoy, but it was only a small light that was in the way for what was to come.

April brought the dark clouds, rain, and the beginnings of more problems.

It all started with numerous hang-up phone calls. Troy was the only one who talked to a voice on the other end. When he shut the door for a private conversation, Ruby knew it was a dangerous sign. It seemed like the dark cloud they left behind in Alexandria found them and were sauntering towards them.

Ruby was in a staff meeting when Troy telephoned. He was in a bad mood and cussing. He said he needed to get away from her and was driving to Las Vegas to gamble with some law school friends. He informed Ruby he would be back sometime Sunday night. The call unnerved her. Her mind raced with the thoughts of only one former law student and she had been the one hanging up on Ruby.

Before she left the bank, she attempted to withdraw some money from their checking account. She gasped when she saw the two dollar balance. Troy had depleted their savings as well. Ruby had no money. She wouldn't get paid until the following week. Her car was almost out of gas and was experiencing engine trouble, which Troy knew and ignored. She was angry and upset. She'd finally had enough.

Ruby picked Sarah up from her school. Her bright smile and strong hug around Ruby's neck convinced her it was time to leave California. Her mind was already making the necessary preparations for their escape.

Ruby noticed the crumpled ten dollar bill on the counter and a gas credit card Troy had left for her before abandoning them. Troy left no phone numbers where she could reach him. She didn't care any more, meaning she had a lot of work ahead of her. She didn't sleep at all that night. Ruby decided she was never going to shed another tear for Troy. For the first time in ages, she stood up and laughed. It felt good.

The next morning, it was pouring buckets. Ruby fed Sarah breakfast and dropped her off at school. She headed towards the bank trying to see the road in front of her high speed wipers. The wall of water was so thick she felt like she was inside a car wash. She was afraid to drive fast. Suddenly her car began to smoke under the hood. She was frantic. She pulled off the road while the car kept steaming. She noticed a white pickup truck stop behind her in the rear view mirror. A man with a baseball cap and tank top tapped on her window. She was a little nervous about trusting him, but who else was there? She rolled down her window as the rain splashed her face.

"Howdy. Can I help you?" he asked getting drenched in the rain. He had a thick southern accent.

"My car started smoking and now I can't start it," Ruby replied helplessly.

"Can you unlatch the hood? I'll take a look," he yelled over the traffic whizzing by.

She unlatched it and watched through the windshield while he checked it out. She guessed he was about her age. The wet shirt revealed his muscular physique.

"I think you need to take it to a garage. Seems like your radiator burst," said the rescuer. "I can take you to where ever you need to go," he offered.

"Thank you. If you could just take me home, I only live about two miles from here. I can call a tow service and have them pick up the car. I'll leave the key under the seat. Do you have the time to do that?" Ruby said because she was still worried about getting into his car. *What if something happens? No one will ever know my story. What choice do I have? I have to take a chance.* She reached for the car door latch and climbed into the white Ford.

He introduced himself as Carl Lawson. Carl said he was on his way to his realty office. He was a co-owner and informed her he had only been working there for a year. He was originally from North Carolina. Carl handed her one of his cards with a red and white emblem with Lawson Realty surrounded by a semi-circle. He drove slowly through the rain and inquired about her family. Ruby lied and said Troy was home sick. Carl told her about his wife and twin girls. Before she knew it he dropped her off at home.

Ruby offered to pay him but he tipped his hat and winked, "My pleasure, Ruby. Good luck with your car." He drove off in the downpour.

She called work and explained her situation. She didn't want to give notice until she had everything in order.

Next, she thumbed through the phone book and located a service station that honored her gas card Troy had left. She told them to fix whatever was wrong. Money was no object. *Troy is going to pick up this tab.*

Ruby placed a collect call to her parents in Raleigh and explained partially what had happened. They wanted her home. Her mom said she would purchase an airline ticket and would be there by the next day. She would drive back with Sarah and her to North Carolina.

Ruby was going to 'Fly Away'. She began to call moving companies. If she couldn't find one to move her on Friday, her other thought was to have them move her things to a storage place in Riverside and then pick them up the next week. Her calls turned out to be unsuccessful. They could only give her estimates for the following week.

Ruby called, Mr. and Mrs. Walton, a nice couple she and Sarah had met while walking through the neighborhood. When Ruby explained her predicament, they offered to pick up her mom from the airport.

"You know, Ruby, our daughter is married to a fireman. Sometimes they move people as a side business. Do you want me to call and ask?" said Mr. Walton.

"Yes, thanks. That would be great."

Ruby packed boxes until the phone rang.

"Good News," Mr. Walton said. "If you can rent a U-Haul on Saturday, they can come, load you up and drive the truck to your home."

"Excellent," she said smiling, "I will call right now. Thanks so much for your help"

Ruby phoned the men and they agreed to her price and promised to be at her townhouse at 7a.m. on Saturday morning.

She continued packing all afternoon. She had some folded boxes stored in the shed that she hadn't thrown away. She placed her Maui cap on her head and walked to the store fighting the rain and wind that twisted her umbrella into interesting shapes. Ruby bought duck tape and a black marker with her ten dollars.

Mr. Walton drove Ruby over to pick up Sarah and waited while she withdrew her from the school.

The next morning, he drove them to the airport to meet her mom.

Ruby's mom came towards them with a mass of people. She looked tired and worn from her worried face. She was still the beautiful blond haired, blue-eyed woman that had grown old gracefully. She was dabbing her eyes as she approached them. Ruby was sure her mom knew she was at her wits end if she was finally leaving Troy. She hugged Ruby.

After introductions were made, Mr. Walton suggested they go to a Mexican Restaurant for dinner. The food was great and the margarita helped the pain go away, at least for a little while.

The packing was finished Friday morning and Ruby's car had been fixed. Sarah stayed with her grandmother while Mr. Walton drove Ruby to the gas station to pay the bill and collect her car. She visited the U-Haul rental office and used money her mom brought to help pay for the move.

Ruby made the call to the bank and apologized for her necessary departure. They were wonderful.

She told her mom she didn't want to move back to Raleigh because she wasn't ready to deal with all the gossip and with Troy's family not far away. Her mom phoned home to let John know they were fine.

"You're in luck, Ruby. Your dad has a friend, Charlie Jacobs, who owns a vacant small fishing cottage in Wrightsville Beach, North Carolina. Charlie said if you repaint the inside and outside of the dwelling he won't charge you rent for three months. He also said the rugs needed cleaning. I think it only has one bedroom. I understand it's snuggled in a sand dune facing the Atlantic Ocean. I don't know if that interests you or not," said mom smiling. "But the community is friendly and it's a place to get yourself back on your feet. Knowing you, it won't take long. You're a fighter. At least you used to be. But as the saying goes, 'once a fighter, always a fighter'…that damn Troy!" she said angrily. Her mom never cussed, so for her to 'damn' anyone was a shock.

Saturday arrived and still no calls or word from Troy. It was easier that way, Ruby thought. The firemen began loading the truck with Ruby's instructions. Unfortunately, the rain did not let up. However, they were able to fit most of the antiques she had inherited from her family in the small truck. She gave the firemen the leftover items. She hated to leave some of the heirlooms, but she had to. The king mattress was too large to fit in the truck and after becoming drenched in the rain, Ruby decided to take it back to the bedroom as a small gift to Troy, who truly deserved it.

Ruby had given the firemen the address to her new cottage and they took off. They were to call her dad when they reached North Carolina so he could drive down from Raleigh to meet the truck with her brothers to help unload it.

Farewells were given to the Waltons and a promise to keep in touch.

The girls climbed into the car and headed for Nevada. They passed an exit leading to the Las Vegas strip. Neon lights could be seen lighting the skyline. They pulled into the Flamingo Hotel and registered. The lobby was full of casino nightlife. *Too bad I don't have amy money to gamble with. I've never been to Las Vegas!*

It took them eight days of hard driving and frequent stops to stretch their legs before reaching North Carolina. The firemen had already emptied the truck and taken off. Ruby's dad was glad to see them. He gave them a big hug and handed Ruby the keys to her new house.

CHAPTER 10

The cottage was white with gray shutters. It had a small porch surrounding the front of the house. Once inside, Ruby examined the work that lay ahead. There were several throw rugs that appeared to have been a bright mustard color at one time, but now resembled an African spotted tiger. She opened the windows to air the place out. Luckily, it was an easy remedy that a little elbow grease and a strong sea breeze could take care of.

The walls were covered with dark, cheap veneer. The kitchen was white with an open wall facing the living room revealing the ocean view. There was a window above the sink that overlooked old beach apartments. Opening the back door, Ruby saw the remains of a small garden and was excited about growing her own herbs and vegetables. Sarah would be able to help with the planting. She was going to love it here.

Ruby dreaded the thought of facing Troy when he finally showed up. *Will he fight me for custody of Sarah? Will he try to hurt me again?* Even though California was a long drive, Troy could show up at any time and she knew he would soon. His ego was too big not to have the last word in their marriage.

The first thing on her agenda was to phone the Senate to talk to Matt. But she was informed that he no longer worked there and they had no forwarding address. She was devastated by the news. The pain was almost too much to endure after all she'd been through. There was so much she wanted to tell him. She knew she would never see him again.

With the news about Matt, Ruby concentrated intensely on repairing the cottage to make it livable. She seemed to focus on the work so she wouldn't be distracted about the unexplained closure of their relationship. She ripped up the old carpet and stripped the grime showing off the natural wood beneath. Once the floors were sanded and polished with a protective sealer, they were beautiful.

Two months of hard work paid off with their adorable home. Sarah and Ruby shared a king size bed, two chests and a small closet. Ruby hung several pictures of the sea to give it that beach look and framed a fishing picture Sarah had painted. She envisioned a few scenes to paint for their bedroom and for the dining room, but they would have to wait for a while. She hung yellow flowered wallpaper in the kitchen and replaced the old green stripes in the bathroom with pastel seashells. She placed a welcome mat at the front door.

***

Mark Snyder was dressed in a dark suit and definitely had a preppie look about him. Ruby had to meet with her lawyer about the divorce. They shook hands and he escorted her into his plush office. He had blond hair and a well trimmed beard. His blue eyes sparkled through the wire rimmed glasses. He sat behind a large oak desk covered with files and pictures of his family. He handed her a copy of the agreement so she could follow along while he explained the terminology.

"Troy has finally signed the papers for separation, Ruby, but he's being difficult about the terms for your divorce. He doesn't want to pay you alimony even though you're entitled to it, especially since you helped to put him through undergraduate and law schools.

"He has only agreed to pay child support, of course, because he is required by law, but he is offering an amount much lower than he can afford according to his salary at the law firm." He paused looking up at Ruby before continuing.

"He has agreed to pay for Sarah's health insurance until she is eighteen. Additionally, he accepts the responsibility of payment for her college but only under the condition he approves of the college choice. What are your thoughts on these terms I've just read to you?"

"I'm not going to ask for alimony, Mr. Snyder, but I do want a fair settlement each month to raise Sarah. What amount do you suggest?"

"I recommend at least six hundred a month, plus the insurance. That should make paying for her day care and other expenses affordable to you. I do advise you to have the payments go directly through the courts. That way you won't have to deal with any delinquent payments or having any extra contact that you don't want."

Ruby thanked him for his counsel and was told the papers would be sent out that afternoon.

She had given a lot of thought to having her name changed back to Fraser and to make out a will. She decided to have her cousin, Martin, draw up papers. Even though she didn't have a lot to leave anyone in a will, she felt it necessary to have some legal papers to provide Sarah with whatever she had and to designate a Power of Attorney. Martin was more than happy to help out.

Ruby was employed by Wilmington University as the Dean of Student's secretary. Working at the university allowed her to take free part time classes. She was thrilled about going back to school and finishing her degree. Unfortunately Wilmington didn't offer the film courses she needed to complete her previous major so she was naturally disappointed. But she decided to take education classes and become a teacher allowing her to have summers off with Sarah. She entered the Adult Studies Program.

Night school would have been a problem for Ruby if it hadn't of been for Karen and Robert Marshall. Karen was an attractive blond with beautiful blue eyes. She owned a gift boutique and had a keen eye for intriguing art pieces to sell in her shop. Her husband, Robert, was a chemical engineer originally from Kentucky. He had dark features and a muscular physique that he kept in shape from lifting weights on a daily basis. Robert was a former football player in college and loved a good Redskin's game with a few cold beers in his comfortable chair on Sunday afternoons.

Their daughter, Amanda, was Sarah's best friend. When Ruby needed someone to watch Sarah on the evenings of her classes, the Marshalls agreed to help her out. In exchange for their generous offer, Ruby would baby sit Amanda on weekends, so the couple could go out or leave town for a weekend excursion if they wanted. Money was never exchanged between them. It worked perfectly.

Karen and Robert were both gourmet cooks and every once in a while invited Ruby over to try a new recipe. Of course, she didn't mind being a guinea pig.

Dean London was a kind boss. He was married with three teenage daughters and one son. He was tall and handsome, always wearing a matching tie and suit to work. He was a real perfectionist, reminding Ruby often of Matt. Dean London had dark features and wore glasses. He drove an old Porsche that was kept in mint condition.

Freshman orientations often became quite hectic with students running around trying to get settled into their housing, meeting their roommates for the first time, adjusting to where things were located on our campus, and making sure they had the classes they needed for their major. Ruby's job was to make sure the students had packets with name tags, schedules, housing rules, planned activities, picnic lunch tickets and details, and a group games activity schedule for the afternoon to help students break the ice meeting their new classmates.

The Dean annually organized a rally for students to kick off their first day and a small speech to welcome the new recruits. Of course, there were inevitably the last minute enrolled students who didn't have a name tag, much less a schedule. Word processors were just beginning to be purchased at the college, but their small office didn't have one yet. A new invention called *Whiteout* was very popular for secretaries.

A mocktail and air band event was a tradition put on by the student council. They asked faculty and staff to volunteer to be waitresses, so Ruby did. Karen had offered to let Sarah spend the night, giving Ruby an evening off.

Ruby was issued a black tuxedo tails jacket and red cummerbund to wear over a white button down blouse. Black shorts and tennis shoes were suggested because of the hot and humid climate. It was going to be an oven inside the building without air conditioning in the student lounge.

Ruby brought her blender so that the cafeteria director, Josie, and her assistant, Lena, could use it to make the non-alcoholic drinks for the students. The director of student activities, Rose Martin, also volunteered to help waitress. The girls were originally from Pennsylvania. They were all single and instantly hit it off with Ruby.

The air band performances were great—Bryan Adams, the Supremes, the Beetles, Elvis, and Tina Turner. During intermission, a DJ put on disco music. The Pennsylvania girls and Ruby couldn't stand it any longer. They insisted Ruby go in front of the line they formed behind her. They started weaving through the tables, holding on to each other's waist. Ruby saw an opening to the stage and headed for it. The DJ started playing 'New York, New York' with Frank Sinatra. The girls started jumping and kicking their legs in sequence high up in the air. The students went wild and the cameras were flashing... Then Ruby looked down and saw her boss. His mouth was agape, but he also had a smile on his face. He watched the dance until it was over, then he turned around and left. The Dean never mentioned that night until the yearbook came out in the spring, and there was his secretary with the other girls dancing on stage kicking their legs high up in the air...

It was only ten when Ruby drove up to her cottage after the show. There were a group of people cooking on a grill and playing loud oldies music from the apartments next door. Ruby dimmed her lights just before stopping and put her gear into park. She opened her car door and reached in the back seat to retrieve her blender.

One of the guys ran over and said, "Hi, my name's Doc. You must be the new kid on the block," he smiled noticing Ruby's outfit. "Are you a bartender?"

"No, just for tonight." Ruby explained looking down at her costume. "Actually, I work at Wilmington University as a secretary. We had an air band night and the staff had to be waitresses. I must look a mess. We danced at the end of the show and I got a little hot," Ruby said taking a free hand, trying to smooth her hair. She had dumped so much hair spray in it to make it have a wild look. After all the sweating, she knew it must look a sight. "I'm glad it's finally starting to cool off."

"Yeah, I know what you mean. I live over there," said Doc pointing. "We're cooking oysters on the grill. Why don't you come over, have some food, and meet everyone?" he said reaching for the blender and tucking it under his arm.

Ruby agreed and followed him through the narrow path to the grill. Whistles started as Doc walked her over in her tux.

"Everyone this is…I'm sorry, I don't think you told me your name," he said with his palm raised upward.

"Hi. I'm Ruby. I just moved in a few months ago from California."

"You have a little girl don't you?" said one of the guys.

"Yes, Sarah. She's spending the night with a friend tonight."

"Nice outfit. Where've you been?" asked another guy.

"I don't always dress like this, but I had a job to do tonight and this was the outfit I was given."

"Well, we'll still talk to you," someone answered sarcastically. He continued, "I'm Chris and this is my place on the corner where the music's coming from, and this is my grill, and that is my old orange car over there." He laughed and pointed to an old Cadillac. Ruby knew it was covered with rust because she had seen him working on it. "We have beer and our most popular requested drink, Captain Morgans served in ice tea jars." He held his up to show her and toasted her before taking a swig.

"I'll try some of your Captain Morgans, thanks," Ruby replied.

"You got it," he said turning to go inside to make her a drink.

"Hi, Ruby. We haven't had much time to talk since you moved in except to wave. I live upstairs in the building next to you. I'm Josh." he smiled.

"Yes, Josh. I've seen you at your window with a typewriter quite often. Are you a writer?" she asked taking a sip of her drink when Chris handed it to her. "Thanks," Ruby said.

"Yes, I do a little free lance when I can. I'm also a naval reserve officer. I'm working on a few short stories about my travels overseas."

"I'd love to read some of your work sometime."

"I'll bring a book over tomorrow if you're home."

"Josh, you're not going to make her read those boring navy books are you?" teased Chris. "We're trying to make friends with Ruby, not scare her away," he laughed. Chris fixed her a plate of oysters and a salad. "Sit here. Enjoy," he said bringing out an extra chair. He handed her a fork.

"Just because *you* lead a dull life, Chris, doesn't mean the rest of us do. It's obvious you're jealous of my talents," he added taking a swig of his drink. "Seriously, Ruby, don't listen to these losers," he joked. "Every once in a while, I have to do some work for the Navy Seals. I was very active at one time," he answered watching her eat her dinner.

"Do you enjoy that part of your job?" Ruby inquired putting an oyster in her mouth.

"Yeah, it's interesting. But I'm ready to give it up and just write," he added sipping his drink.

"How do you like your dinner?" asked Chris changing the subject.

"These oysters are wonderful. Did you get them here?" Ruby asked Chris changing the subject.

"Yeah, one of the guys picked up a bushel at the market. I love to eat them right off the grill," he said dipping one in sauce and popping it into his mouth.

113

"Let me introduce you to the rest of the gang out here," said Doc interrupting. He walked Ruby around the corner of the building and led her to a circle of guys standing around drinking out of their ice tea jars. "This is Kyle, Dugray, Mason, and John. They smiled and said their "hellos".

Suddenly a girl with long black hair came down the steps from a middle unit and said, "Does anyone have a light?" She was barefoot wearing cut off jeans and a t-shirt.

"Theresa, this is Ruby. She lives next door. You've seen her daughter playing outside," said Doc.

"Hi. Glad to have some more girls around here. There are way too many guys. Enough to drive a woman crazy," she added lighting her cigarette and blowing a puff of smoke in the air.

"You're always whining about something, Theresa," said Kyle winking at Ruby.

"Are we still going over to the Island Hotel to dance? I'm ready to move around a little bit," she replied in her husky voice, beginning to dance to an old Beetles tune. "Turn that up!"

"Yep, we're going as soon as the oysters are gone. Do you want to come with us?" asked Chris watching Theresa go into his apartment and turn up the stereo. "You still haven't met Elizabeth," said added raising an eyebrow, grabbing a beer bottle and dancing in his cheap flip flops.

"She Loves You, yeah yeah yeah," Doc sang along with Theresa. She held a bottle and linked her arm with his so they faced each other and continued singing into the bottles.

"Let's walk down to the beach hotel. The oysters are gone and I'm ready to clean up," suggested Chris turning off his stereo and throwing away the empty plates and beer bottles. He emptied the trash in the dumpster.

"I better go home first and change," Ruby said.

"No way. You look great. Let's go," said John ushering Ruby towards the hotel. "Besides I want you to meet Elizabeth. She's working there tonight."

They could hear a man singing and playing an electric piano

through an open door. The singer smiled when they walked in and waved to the gang. He wore a yellow and blue Hawaiian shirt and a straw hat. Ruby could see he was heavyset and he had a dark mustache. 'They must come in here a lot,' she thought.

It was crowded but they managed to find a table in the back. A pretty dark, headed waitress came over to John and kissed him.

"Hi baby," he said. "This is Ruby. She's the new neighbor with the little girl."

"Hi, I've seen you two from a distance. How do you like living here?" she asked politely.

"It's great. I've been working tonight and that's why I have this outfit on. I don't usually dress like this," she found herself feeling self-conscious about her clothes again, especially when the customers stared at her when she walked in.

"Don't worry. This place, anything goes. Would you like something to drink or eat?" she asked while collecting some dirty glasses.

"Sure, I'll have a Coke."

"You're not really going to have coke are you?" asked Chris listening to her order.

"I better sober up a little. Otherwise I'll have a serious headache tomorrow and I have to pick Sarah up at nine in the morning. You're lucky. You guys get to sleep in,"

"Well, I don't think one more could hurt. But you know best," he said ordering a beer.

The entertainer welcomed his friends on the mike and said, "Here's one that the gang always request."

"Oh when the sun beats down...Under the Boardwalk."

Someone grabbed Ruby's hand and led her on to the dance floor. They closed down the place and hugged each other goodnight.

Ruby could tell these vivacious friends were full of life and fun to be around. She didn't know much about them, at least not yet. But what she did know was that they were bonded by a simple night of oysters, singing, dancing, and Captain Morgans.

CHAPTER 11

It was Labor Day and the girls were ready for the beach. A day off from school and work was just what the doctor had ordered. They followed the narrow, public path and found their next door neighbors sitting in a circle surrounded with coolers, chairs, a loud radio, and a volley ball. A net was already up waiting for players. Ruby waved and joined them.

Chris was wearing blue swim trunks and a beige baseball hat that had 'Bubba's' written across it. His hair was as red as hers, but he had sky blue eyes. He was greased up with suntan lotion and looked tan from the previous summer days and the numerous freckles that covered his body. He smiled at her and jumped up to help with the chairs and umbrella revealing his skinny legs.

"Hi, Ruby. This must be Sarah Sue," said Chris patting Sarah on the head, reading her bathing suit. "Or is it Barbie?" he said teasingly.

She frowned at him behind her pink flowered sunglasses. "I'm not Sarah Sue. I'm just Sarah," she corrected him.

"Nice bucket and shovel you have there, Sarah. Can I use it today too? I want to build a sandcastle," he implied trying to make up with her.

"OK, but I get it first," Sarah told him pointing to herself. Ruby blew up her water wings and then Sarah sprinted down to the ocean to fill up her bucket. She started playing with another little girl forgetting about Chris. Ruby was pleased Sarah had found a playmate.

"Hey, we missed you Saturday night. Everybody went back over to the Island Restaurant and noticed your lights weren't on. Were you still sleeping from Friday?" Chris teased, tapping her on the shoulder.

"As a matter of fact, I'm sure I was up long before you. Sarah and I had to drive to Raleigh to pick up some personal items and to see my family. We decided to spend the night," Ruby said with a smirk on her face.

"I'm sure she's telling the truth," said Doc reaching for a beer in his cooler, coming to her defense. "I knocked on her door around nine to return her blender, but she didn't answer," he informed them shrugging his shoulders.

"Ruby, would you like a beer?" he offered. His jet-black ponytail swung to the side of his muscular body as he leaned over to open the cooler again.

"No, thanks," she replied. "I'm still trying to recover from Captain Morgans. That's some strong stuff. I've been fighting a slight headache for two days. "But," she said with her finger in the air, "I wouldn't trade it for all the fun we had." She grinned and took several sips of water enjoying the ice cold wetness. "Of course, I can safely say I won't be drinking for quite a long time."

"Yeah, that's what they all say," Chris said jokingly.

"By the way, did any of you guys have a hard time parking on the street or in your parking lot today? I'm about a block away," Ruby said shaking her head.

"No, but there's a sign posted in the street in front of our units saying cars will be towed at the owner's expense if they're not residents. We had a condo meeting last month and that issue was discussed. I volunteered to paint some numbers and lines on Saturday," informed Chris. "It's a big problem in the summer."

"That's probably a good idea. Sometimes I come home and have to park in the street late at night. It makes me a little nervous being so far away from my door in the dark. I guess I'm just a little scaredy cat,"

"No, it's good to be careful, especially when you have a little one to look after. Say, you're an artist, right? How'd you like to help paint a few lines in the lot next Saturday?" he asked raising his eyebrows.

"Not really, but if you promise not to laugh, I'll try to find an hour or two in my busy schedule. I know it can't take too long to paint a few straight lines. Of course, it's probably harder than it sounds," she said sarcastically.

As she finished her water, Ruby pulled up a chair beside Theresa under the umbrella. It was too hot to sit for long in the sun and the humidity was stifling. The boys ran down to the water to cool off and flirt with two busty girls in bikinis.

"Looks like the guys will be entertaining those beach bunnies for a while," said Theresa lighting up a cigarette. "I can't even tell what color their suits are, they're so small."

"I don't think the guys are looking at their suits."

"You're right. Their heads are drooping, along with their mouths. I think they better stay in the water a lot longer to cool off." Both girls giggled.

"Well, I personally am glad we have some time alone together. It gives us a chance to get to know each other a little better. How did you end up in Wilmington?"

"Well, there's not much to tell about me. I'm from Las Vegas originally. Although my family moved around a lot," Theresa revealed taking another drag from her cigarette and blew smoke rings in the air. "I found my way to the east coast with a previous lover. But he's history," she puffed once more before burying her butt in the sand. "I go to the community college at night. Some day I want to be a CPA, and start my own company. I like being in control, in case you haven't already noticed," she laughed.

"I can see that about you," Ruby smiled nodding her head. "Are you dating anyone now?"

"Sort of. There's this guy at the law firm where I work. We have a date tonight."

"That's great," said Ruby sincerely.

"OK, Theresa, now tell me about the guys. It's obvious they're close friends, almost like family," Ruby said pointing to the ocean.

"Yeah, I've never seen neighbors get along as well as these guys and I've already told you I moved around. She looked up and waved to them talking to the girls, "OK. Do you want the quick or the short version?"

"Short works for me."

Theresa swallowed several swigs of her beer. "I'll start with the twin brothers, Dugrey and Mason. They're from Laramie, Wyoming and fly jets for the Air Force. I think they're hot, don't you?"

"Yeah," Ruby replied thinking about their muscular physiques, dark hair, and blue eyes. "Personally, I have a hard time telling them apart. I bet they get away with mistaken identity often, especially with many girls I would venture to say."

"I know. I always call them by the wrong name," she admitted. "They can be a little too serious for me though. I think they like those high-maintenance chicks if you know what I mean."

"I get your drift," Ruby replied wiping her sweaty forehead. "Tell me about the others."

"Kyle's from California and decided to move to the East Coast after serving in the Navy in Norfolk. He's defiantly a tall blue-eyed, blond knockout, don't you think?" she asked while allowing her opinion to be known. "He's going to school to be an engineer."

John's from New York. He's a Navy Seal and gone most of the time training for 'secret missions'. He and Josh go way back. They're pretty tight.

Keith attends medical school and he's in his second year residency. He's from Asheville. We all call him 'Doc'. Appropriate don't you think?" she added finishing her beer. "After today, we probably won't see him very much until Christmas."

Chris is the only native from Wilmington and we named him our social event commander-in-chief. The Coast Guard owns him one weekend out of every month and the rest of the time he's is a loan officer. Chris attends community college at night with me. We usually carpool together. Well, speak of the devils. We can't talk about you guys now that you're here," Theresa said loudly.

"Ruby, don't you believe a word Theresa says about us handsome duds," Chris retorted defensively. "I have you know our intentions are one hundred percent dishonorable."

"I've heard already," she answered shaking her head.

"Hey ladies, how about a game of volleyball, or are you going to keep nursing those beers?" said Dugrey picking up the ball and tapping it lightly in the air. He reached over and turned up an Eagles song on the radio.

"Doc, come on and show us how you mountain boys play," teased Mason going to the opposite side of the net from his brother.

Theresa put down her drink and wandered over to choose a side.

"Do you play, Ruby? We need another player on our side," said Chris reaching his hand out to help her get up.

"I'm sorry, Chris, but I can't play because I have to watch Sarah. I can fill in if someone gets tired or wants a drink, and they don't mind keeping an eye on her," she answered pointing to Sarah playing with her new friend.

The group started out small, but the busty girls came over and joined the teams. Elizabeth arrived and participated with an amazing serve.

Ruby adjusted her camera and snapped pictures while they played. She also photographed Sarah building her sandcastle and captured several sailboats passing by.

She substituted for a couple of the players. She knew she wasn't very good but she tried her best.

"OK, Everyone line up! Last one in is a rotten egg," yelled Kyle making a line with his foot in the hot sand.

"On your mark, get set, GO," Kyle shouted.

Ruby raced against them down to the water, jumping, splashing, and swimming into the cool, refreshing Atlantic Ocean. Soon the boys started dunking the girls. They fought back losing more than winning.

Chris came out of the water and started playing with Sarah's sandcastle. He decorated it with shells and made a flag from a stick and a piece of trash that had blown his way. Doc assisted with the moat that went around the castle. Sarah spied them working and went over to help. They were having as much fun as she was.

Kyle came up and asked, "How about a canoe ride? Mine is up there in the dunes."

"Sure," Ruby answered. "Let me check with Chris to see if he can watch Sarah." She walked over to get an "OK" from the babysitter. She was informed she had fifteen minutes of enjoyment but it would cost her.

Ruby and Mason followed Kyle to the dune. Mason helped carry the boat down to the water. Ruby was glad for the extra muscles.

Mason asked Kyle, "Can I come too? Ruby can sit in the middle and then she won't have to row."

"Sounds like a plan to me," Ruby happily replied, thinking about being a queen for fifteen minutes.

The waves were quite mild making it easy to pass the steady swells that broke on shore. Ruby devoured the scenery and soaked in the rays.

"I think you like this service, Ruby," said Mason glancing back watching her as she relaxed and became lazy.

Ruby looked up at the clear blue sky. Sea gulls were searching for food. "It doesn't get much better than this," Ruby whispered closing her eyes and relishing the moment.

"It's hard to believe the summer's almost at an end. I guess we have a couple of warm months of fall before the cold sets in though," said Kyle taking a rest with his paddling. He tipped one oar in the water and made a small splash, getting Ruby wet.

"You are a troublemaker," she said pointing her finger at him. Ruby put her hand in the water to return the splash.

"And you are a fighter. I like that in a woman," he retorted splashing her again.

When they approached the beach, Kyle and Mason gave each other a signal. Suddenly they stood up and made the boat tip over.

"You guys can't be trusted!" screamed Ruby wiping the water from her eyes when she bobbed up for air. Her lips tasted salty. She rode the waves back into shore.

"Oops! I forgot. I'm not supposed to stand up in a canoe," Kyle exclaimed sarcastically becoming an actor in the water pretending to drown.

Mason swam to collect his paddles that had started making their way to the beach. "We should do that again!"

Ruby dunked under the water again to make her hair look presentable before coming out of the water. Then she said in her best Scarlett O'Hara accent, "Thank you both for that spectacular finale."

They grabbed opposite ends of the canoe and returned it to its natural position.

"You're a good sport, Ruby," said Kyle winking.

"You can paddle me around anytime."

Elizabeth had been watching them. When Ruby sat down, she picked up her chair and came to sit closer to Ruby.

"Looks like you got thrown overboard by two pranksters," she said laughing.

"Yeah, they're definitely twisted," Ruby replied wiping her face with a beach towel. She combed her hair and put her hat and glasses on. "But I have to admit, I did enjoy living like a queen while it lasted." Ruby spread out her blanket and relaxed in the sun.

Elizabeth reached into her bag and pulled out her nursing book. "I hate to even look at this today but I have a huge exam on Wednesday. I have to waitress tonight, so it was either study in the sun or at home. Tough decision!" she said laughing.

"I've always had the philosophy that you have to keep a balance in your life. You have work on one side of a scale and play on the other. When one becomes too much, you need to do more of the other. Otherwise, for myself, I come completely unglued and I have too much on my plate right now to do that."

"I definitely agree with that balance thing. My only playtime lately has been working. But I have fun joking with the customers and raising a little 'hell' when the gang comes over. It's probably a good thing that John is gone most of the time so I am able to concentrate on my studies. What about you? Didn't I hear you say you were going to Wilmington University too?

Ruby nodded her head 'yes'.

What classes are you taking?" she asked reaching for a cracker.

"Algebra and Speech. I wish I could take more classes, but with Sarah, it's all I can do with working a fulltime job. I don't think I'll be able to count on much money from my soon to be ex-husband. So far, I haven't received a dime from him since I left in June. I should have taken my lawyer's advice and gone through the courts. I guess I'll do that this week. I have to admit, I'm a little nervous about seeing him again." Ruby revealed.

"Are you dating anyone now?" Elizabeth asked.

"No, I'm in the midst of a divorce and need to get out of that situation before thinking about dating."

Ruby explained a watered down version of her escape from California.

Sarah ran towards her castle to help Chris and Doc. "That looks awesome," Ruby replied walking around to check out all the details. Instead of one flag, they now had three, different sizes and colors. "I'm impressed with all the details, you guys. Such hidden talents!"

"Mom, I'm hungry," said Sarah looking up at her with one hand on her hip.

"Mom, I'm hungry too." parroted Doc and Chris with their hands on their hips.

"Go wash your hands in the water and come up to dry off. I'll give you some crackers and juice," Ruby said pointing to all three, rolling her eyes when she looked at Doc and Chris, before walking back up to her chair. Ruby pulled out Sarah's beach towel and opened it in the shade under the umbrella. Sarah walked up and sat down and ate her snack hungrily.

Doc and Chris sat in their chairs while the rest of the gang had laid out their towels and were soaking in the rays. Chris picked up his towel and walked over to sit next to Sarah. "Can I sit with you?" he asked her.

"Sure, want some crackers?" she asked handing him one with a semi-sandy hand.

"That's OK. I'll wait for your mom to give me my own," he answered looking at the sandy one with a frown.

He shoveled several into his mouth. "Thanks."

"I also have some homemade chocolate chip cookies," Ruby smiled looking at Chris with a grin on his face.

"I knew Betty Crocker would bring the cookies," he said looking over at Doc.

"Betty Crocker, huh? I guess I'll take that as a compliment." Ruby passed around the Tupperware container. "Good thing I brought enough."

"Thanks guys for today. I loved playing in the sand and the volleyball game was awesome! I've had such a hard time sitting still on the beach, especially after being cooped up inside the medical labs. I can't get enough sun and fresh air," said Doc looking around at the scenery. He took a bite of his cookie. "And these cookies are out of this world. You can bake for me anytime, Mrs. Crocker," he added munching on his second one.

"You tell me when your next exam is and I'll bake a huge cookie just for you, Doc," Ruby pointed in his direction.

"Gee, Betty, you're the best!"

"I have a paper due on Friday. You don't by any chance like to type, do you?" Chris asked with raised eyebrows. "I told you the babysitting would cost you."

"I had a feeling it wouldn't be long before your payment would be rendered."

"Seriously, I'd be glad to pay you. It isn't too long, maybe a couple of pages."

"Give it to me tonight and I'll type it tomorrow during my break."

"I might owe you another fifteen minute ride," he replied smiling.

"So tell me Ruby," said Chris changing the subject, "What do you like to do in your spare time, when you have any that is?"

"Oh, I like to play tennis and read. I also like to paint when I can. But I've been so busy that I'll have to put those luxuries on hold for a while I'm afraid."

"What medium do you prefer?"

"I like to mess around with watercolors and acrylics. What paints do you use, besides sidewalk lines in parking lots," Ruby teased.

"I like oils and using florescent colors. I minored in art in college. I've always loved to draw and stroke a brush, probably ever since I could hold them in my hand," he added making his hand paint something in the air.

"Chris is a good artist. Have you ever seen his pictures on his walls in his condo?" asked Kyle. "He painted me a sailboat last year for my birthday. It's hanging over my bar."

"No, I haven't seen his work. I'll have to check it out sometime." Ruby suddenly realized how long she'd been out in the hot sun. "We have to go, Sarah."

As they were leaving, Chris offered, "Dinner at my place around 7, if you're interested. Bring Sarah and whoever."

"I'll bring a fruit salad and chocolate cookies," Ruby smiled.

"I knew we could count on Mrs. Crocker to bring some dessert," Doc replied elbowing Chris.

The following Saturday, Chris was outside painting white lines on his side of the condo building. He smiled at Ruby when she came over.

"Hey, thanks for typing that paper for me. You're a lifesaver," said Chris finishing the end of the line he had started. "Want some coffee? I just made it," he said putting his brush down and walking her into his apartment.

Ruby nodded, "That'd be great. I can't believe that I haven't seen the inside of your place before. It's really charming for a bachelor," she laughed teasing him.

"Cream or sugar?" he asked avoiding her comment.

"I'll take both, thanks."

Ruby glanced around the room and noticed the walls were painted a shrimp color. A cream colored couch and chair circled a TV and stereo, which was playing the oldie station. His unit was small. She could see an unmade bed and clothes thrown around on the floor in his bedroom.

"Rough night?" she asked pointing to the bed.

"They're always rough," he retorted handing her the coffee mug.

There was a bright oil painting of a bunch of wildflowers in a field with a shining sun off to the side.

"Wow, Chris. I love your bright colors! Where did you say you studied art?" Ruby inquired.

"I went to UNC Asheville for my undergraduate but it was hard being so far away from the beach. You know it sort of gets in your blood. It was a great school though and I had some awesome teachers," he commented.

Chris gave her a paintbrush while she sipped her coffee. She found a spot on the pavement where she thought a line should go and started painting. Suddenly Ruby heard a scream from next door. It was Theresa yelling at Chris, "How dare you paint a white stripe down my black cat's back! Chris, you are such a pervert! Poor kitty, come to mama."

"She needed a little color," said Chris laughing uncontrollably.

"I'll get you back, Mr. Murphy," yelled Theresa from her upstairs window. Furiously she started throwing kitty litter from one of the window to make it stick on Chris's newly painted lines. The wind was doing a super job swirling it around the parking lot.

The war began.

"Stop messing up my work, Theresa. I've been out here all morning trying to give you your own space to park. Your cat walked up to my leg and asked for the hair color!" he yelled up at her.

She disappeared from the window and came back throwing a dirty bucket of water on him. He threw down his brush and ran around the side of the building and turned on the hose. He faced it towards her window and let the geyser enter her living room. More screams and windows started slamming. Chris was on the ground laughing hysterically. Ruby didn't want to miss the fun so she grabbed the hose and sprayed him. He was stronger than her and had it back in his hands in no time. Ruby lost!

Elizabeth didn't come out of her apartment the rest of the day. In fact, she stayed mad at Chris for the entire week.

Ruby had been looking for legal papers her lawyer had asked her to send him. As she unpacked one of her boxes she found the Senate directory. She stared at Matt's number and picked up the phone. Ruby was anxious to get in touch with him. She needed to explain so many things. She was nervous and didn't know exactly what she was going to say. The operator came on the line after three rings and said the phone had been disconnected. Her heart sank but she was determined to find out where he went.

Undeterred she tried to reach Mary, but her answering machine came on. Ruby left her name and number on the tape. Since it was Saturday she knew Mary could have gone away for the weekend.

Ruby was angry with herself. Why hadn't she tried to call him before now? Almost eight months had passed since she last kissed those sweet lips and told him of her plan to get a divorce. What must he think of her now?

She decided to write a letter to the Senate addressed to Matt. Maybe if the office knew his forwarding address, he would at least have the choice of contacting her or not. She told him she thought of him constantly and how much she would love to see him again. She asked him if he could ever forgive her. She told him she loved him.

She had made him the happiest man alive—he had told her so himself. Ruby had to find him, no matter how long it took.

* * *

The next month, Ruby received the letter she had sent Matt stamped with Return to Sender; Address Unknown. Ruby immediately called Mary from a pay phone at school. Mary apologized for not getting back to her earlier but her mother had been ill and she had gone to Maine to take care of her. She told Ruby, Matt had quit working for the Senator the month after she left. In fact, the week she did not return, he gave his one-month notice. He left no forwarding address or phone number except with the Senator. No one else knew where he went.

Ruby shared a short version of what had happened since leaving D.C. Mary wished her well and they both promised to keep in touch.

Matt had left his work for the Senator. Ruby was stunned. *Where could he have gone? Jackson Hole? Back to California? Maui?* Oddly she thought of the cabin in Asheville. Ruby would have to call her cousin and tell her she was coming to visit.

Brigette was thrilled that Ruby was coming to visit. She and her daughter, Michelle planned to meet them at The Pine Tree Restaurant for lunch and then take a hike around the lake. Michelle was Sarah's age and they had only seen each other once during a family gathering since her wedding. Brigette lived about an hour's drive from the lake.

Ruby called Doc to let him know she was going to his home town and to see if he wanted her to take or pick up anything from his folks. He told her that he did.

Doc placed several items in the trunk. He drew Ruby a map of how to get to their house. She hugged him goodbye noticing he looked exhausted. He informed her that he had been up all night and was on his way back to the hospital. This was his weekend on call.

It was the perfect clear day. When the girls arrived at the lake, Ruby found the airport sign. She followed it so she could retrace her steps to Matt's cabin. Two airplanes were chained at the tiny airstrip but neither was his. Ruby didn't see Matt's car parked in the lot so she turned her car around, and began the drive twisting around several roads and up the hill to his cottage. It looked deserted. There was a "For Sale" sign on the door and a phone number to call. The curtains, porch furniture, and potted plants were all gone. Ruby was devastated.

Sarah had been sleeping, unaware of her surroundings. She didn't seem to remember being there. Ruby parked and both girls stretched.

"Are we there, mommy?" asked Sarah looking around.

"No, honey. This was my friend's house and I wanted to stop by to see if he was home. But I don't think he is."

She gave Sarah some water and an apple on the porch. Ruby walked up the steps and peeked inside the window cupping her hands, to block out the reflection. The furniture was there but covered with white sheets. Ruby noticed there was wood stacked in the fireplace. She wondered if it was the same stack of wood she saw him place there.

Ruby walked to the car to get her purse, fumbling for paper and a pen. She used the mailbox to press against her writing. She looked at his name "Connery" on top of the mailbox carved in wooden letters. She took her hand and followed the spelling of each letter with her fingers. Tears formed, spilling over her cheeks. She took out a tissue to wipe her eyes. She wrote down the number under the "For Sale" sign. Maybe these people would know how to contact Matt.

Ruby didn't know why she wanted to look in the mailbox but she pulled down the lid. She peeked inside and saw something crammed in the back of it. It was a small plastic bag. Inside the bag, there was an envelope with 'Ruby' written on the outside. Her heart skipped a beat. Her hands were shaking as she opened the letter. Small dried rose petals fell to the ground. It was dated the day Troy and she left DC.

It read:

Dear Ruby,

By now you are living a different life than the one you and I tried to start under strained circumstances. I don't know exactly why I am writing you this letter because some mischievous kids will probably read and destroy it. But I guess I'm writing it to you because if things didn't work out for you in California, I was hoping you would come here looking for me. I'm sure it is just an ego thing because I believe that you still love me, as I do you. If you are here reading this, it proves my case.

As you can see, I'm selling my cabin and have decided to invest in another one further out west, closer to my family. I have a new job beginning at the end of this month. I will be traveling quite a bit and living in different parts of the world for extended periods of time. So I am sure our paths will never cross again. I wish you and your little one well. I will always cherish my pictures, (the ones you photographed and the one you painted for me.)

I love you, JB

P.S. Keep painting!

How did he know I would come here to look for him? Looking at the cabin, she pictured Matt carrying the fishing gear and loading the car. She closed her eyes and prayed that he was safe. Whatever it was that he was doing, she was determined to search for however long it took. She placed the note and the realtor's information in her bag. She took a deep breath and smiled. She was loved.

* * *

Ruby parked her car in front of a small, white country house with a wrap around porch and two swings. The backyard bordered the lake, with a short dock holding on to a row boat. A beige and white collie greeted her with his barking. A stocky man and slightly plump woman came out to see what all the noise was about. Ruby introduced herself to Doc's parents. They were a sweet elderly couple dressed in jeans and plaid shirts. His dad wore a baseball cap and Ruby noticed Doc favored him. They invited the girls in for cake and cookies, but Ruby told them she was already late meeting her cousin. She told them what a great person Doc was and that he was going to become a wonderful physician.

They seemed pleased and proud of him. His mom gave Ruby several tin cans of baked goods and some new shirts she had bought. She packed them away in the car. She and Sarah waved goodbye as they drove towards the restaurant.

***

"I'm so glad to see you" Ruby replied putting her arm around Brigette.

"I can't believe you're actually here," smiled Brigette. "But Ruby, you look tired. Is something wrong?" asked Brigette concerned with her cousin's puffy eyes.

"I'm OK," Ruby reassured her. "We can talk later, but let's eat and wait until we're hiking. How's John?" asked Ruby changing the subject.

"He's fine. He's playing golf today with some of his buddies," said Brigette.

"And how's your job?" Ruby asked referring to her nursing in the hospital.

"I love working in the ER. There's always so much going on and medicine changes almost every day. There're new techniques, equipment, and medicines to learn about constantly. Sometimes it's hard to keep up. There's never a dull moment. Trust me."

Inside the restaurant, the waitress came over and took their orders of grilled steaks, salads, and fries. They splurged and had ice cream sundaes for dessert. After lunch, they left for a hike around the lake. They walked until they found a small group of ducks swimming near a wooden bridge. The girls fed the ducks bread that Brigette had brought. When the bread gave out, the girls played on a miniature jungle gym nearby.

Brigette and Ruby sat on a huge rock sunning. It was there that Ruby told her life story. It felt good to finally tell someone the truth.

"I can't believe that Troy Slader treated you so horribly. I hope I never have to see him again."

"I have to admit I'm still afraid of him, Brigette. I know it's just a matter of time before he shows up on my doorstep."

"What ever happened to Matt?"

When Ruby finished talking, she showed her the letter that was left in Matt's mailbox. Brigette was flabbergasted.

"Ruby, you must try and find him," she encouraged. "How romantic! He must really love you and it sounds like you do him. Why else would he leave that note?"

"Brigette, I don't know how to find him. I called the Senate last week and Mary said he left no forwarding address. Then the letter I mailed to him was sent back to me. The only lead I have right now is the phone number on the for sale sign outside his cabin. I will call tonight when I get to Greenville.

When Sarah was asleep, Ruby called about the cabin. A man with a low voice answered her call. She left her Wilmington information. He said it would be several days before he would be in touch with the owner. Ruby wanted to reveal her connection with him, but decided against it. She would have to be patient.

The next day a letter arrived from her attorney informing her that she and Troy would be divorced in March.

CHAPTER 12

It was a Friday night in October and Sarah was spending the night with her best friend, Amanda. Ruby had received a white, grape-shaped invitation that had been placed under her windshield wiper that morning. The gang decided to have a toga party before the cold weather set in. Ruby had never been to a toga party, but smiled at the thought. At the bottom of the invitation it said:

The costume requirements: You should be dressed up in a sheet or tunic, sandals, and wearing some sort of crown (Be Creative). It also said to bring a Greek dish to share with the Greek Court.
It was signed: Caesar

She jumped into the shower and put on her robe. She prepared a Greek salad and started looking around the apartment for something she could drape over her for a costume. She had two choices: a queen sized yellow sheet or a faded blue sheet with gigantic daisies. She chose the yellow and wrapped it over her shorts and tank top. She pulled one end over her shoulder and used her airplane pin to secure it. She made a crown of leaves out of Sarah's construction paper and taped the leaves to a bendable vine she found outside. She left her hair down which had grown about two inches during the summer. Ruby put on gold hoop earrings and a necklace. She added dangle bracelets and placed one around her ankle. She quickly painted her toenails peach and put on her blue flip-flops. She didn't think anyone would see her feet. She wore extra layers of green eye shadow, dark rouge, and lipstick. She turned off the lights and closed the door.

It turned out to be a beautiful night. Doc was home for the weekend and had mixed a huge tub of grape juice and grain for the drinks, using a soup tureen decorated with plastic flowers. He even added grapes and orange slices as a garnish. There were plastic cups on a small white table nearby with a lit tapered candle stuck in a wine bottle. The wax dripped down the sides claiming its holder. There were extra tables with lit candles and fruit for the guest to display their Greek dishes.

Ruby was already an hour late. The dean had several important letters that had to get mailed before the weekend. Everyone was sampling the grape and grain beverages and looking festive in their costumes. Chairs covered in sheets had been placed around the parking lot and several of the guys were sitting with their legs crossed, listening to the music and deep in conversations.

"Hi everyone," Ruby said placing her Greek salad and pita bread slices beside a cheese platter. She inspected the dinner. Chris had prepared a large pot of lamb stew. Ruby put a fork in it and decided to try it before it was all gone. It was wonderful. Theresa had made a huge bowl of humus. She served it in a huge hole dug out of a round fresh loaf of bread. The extra bread was put in a basket next to the dips. There were also dishes of cut up veggies and fruits. Elizabeth had put together some skewers with meat and veggies marinated in a special sauce on the grill. The brothers had picked up some baklava and sweet round bread with raisins and custard from a bakery.

Ruby sampled another bite of stew before she left the table. She was starving. "Wow, yummy stew! You should keep your parking lot decorated like this. It looks so festive."

"You're late. Where have you been you gorgeous Greek woman? I saw your car and knew you were home," quizzed Doc taking a puff of a cigar. He was quite handsome in his white sheet, dark sandals and crown of real leaves. His ponytail was tied back behind his head.

"Nice toga, Ruby. A real goddess," said Chris handing her a drink, eyeing her sheet.

"Thanks," Ruby replied. She emptied the cup enjoying the grape taste. She couldn't taste any alcohol, but she knew these guys liked their parties and there was a large portion of the grain in there somewhere.

Chris had on a white sheet with an obvious Burger King kid's hat that had been covered with real leaves and stapled to the paper. "How do you like my crown?" he asked touching it with the palm of his hand.

"It's very original, Chris. It's so you!"

He sat back down in his chair and crossed his legs. He took a sip of his grape beverage, tapping his foot to the Greek music he had checked out from the library. He too had a cigar that he played with, shaping smoke rings into the air. He and Doc were trying to see who could blow the largest ones. Of course, they looked the same to Ruby, but they argued and laughed about it as they drank. It was just a guy thing, she guessed.

"This is a Kodak Moment! Everyone looks fantastic. I'll take some pictures before the sun goes down," Ruby remarked walking over to use the ladle.

Elizabeth followed her to refill her own glass. "I have off tonight for the first time in I don't know how long. I'm glad to be here to keep that balance!" she laughed serving another spoonful.

"I'm glad you're here too. Do you have to work tomorrow night?"

"No, thank goodness," she answered sipping her drink.

"I know John's glad. I haven't seen him in about a month. Where did they send him this time?"

"I think he said he was in the Sea of Japan at the beginning of the month practicing some underwater drills and then they sent him to Maui the last two weeks," she smiled. "Did you see that tan he has? I'm as white as a lily."

"Well, your skin will be more beautiful a lot longer than all of us who worship the sun. Some day you'll be glad you stayed out of it," Ruby assured her. Ruby took several pictures of the punch and buffet tables before assembling the toga party members.

"Ruby, I'll take pictures of the goddesses first," Chris said slipping the camera out of Ruby's hands. "Now ladies, show some legs," said Chris insisted while snapping several shots. The boys whistled. Theresa asked the guys to give up their cigars for the next pose. The girls held the cigars in their fingers while taking a puff of smoke and trying to create smoke rings.

Finally the guys were ready for their turn. They stood with serious looks and then several athletic ones for the Greek theme while Ruby captured the party on film.

All of a sudden, Theresa's cat came prancing by her leg. She let out a scream and then yelled, "Chris, you are such a pervert." But she couldn't keep a straight face. The cat had been decorated with a small crown and it was tied around his neck so he couldn't get it off. A small white cloth was also tied around the belly and looped around the neck. Ruby caught the image in her camera. Everyone was in hysterics. She let the cat wander around the party. If the cat didn't seem bothered, why should she stress over it?

A red convertible with four girls dressed in togas drove up and parked on the side street. They were the girls from Labor Day weekend. Dugray was in conversation with a pretty blond. Soon more people showed up and it turned into a large crowd.

It was almost midnight and Ruby decided she was tired. She grabbed her dishes suddenly feeling the effects of the alcohol. Ruby quietly left the party, entered her cottage, and locked the door. Ruby turned on the living room light with her elbow trying not to drop her plates. She opened the bathroom door and used the toilet in the dark. When she walked into the bedroom, she was grabbed forcefully from behind. Ruby was pushed down on her bed as the yellow sheet was ripped off of her back. She was terrified. Ruby started to yell, but she felt a hard slap against her face. She could feel the sting and began fighting back. Again he hit her this time over her right eye, knocking her head against the wall. Ruby cried out in pain. She was dizzy from the alcohol.

Finally a voice said, "So you thought you could leave me without saying 'goodbye'?"

Troy's voice echoed in her confused state of mind. She started shaking. What was she going to do? The party next door was too loud for anyone to hear her scream or yell.

"You're hurting me, Troy. You need to leave or I'll call the police," Ruby tried to say as he pinned her under his heavy body. She realized her sheet was gone, but her shorts and top were still covering her.

"You're still my wife. We're not divorced yet, Ruby! Though I have to admit it'll be a pleasure to get rid of you but not until I've had the last word," he remarked angrily, slurring his words.

"Are you drunk, Troy?" Ruby asked trying to adjust her eyes to the darkness.

"No baby, just high as a kite. I love life when I'm on Cloud 9. Now give me what I came a thousand miles to get!" he demanded rubbing her all over with his hands roughly.

He started to kiss her and she yelled out in pain. She could dimly see his shadowed profile looking down at her, rubbing her face with a smile saying, "I'm sorry, Baby. Did I hurt you?" He still had her trapped on the bed. Soon he started tearing off her clothes. She could feel blood trickling down from her nose and mouth. Her eye was beginning to swell. She reached for the corner of the sheet and wiped her face with it. She was glad it was dark when he raped her because she didn't want to see his eyes. The alcohol she had consumed helped ease her pain. She felt nauseated. When he finally reached his climax, he became quiet and distant.

Out of nowhere, she could hear two voices outside. Ruby knew it was Chris and Doc. They were drunk. They were yelling, "Ruby" at the top of their lungs.

Troy became furious. "Tell them you're tired and that you were asleep," he said angrily pulling her hair, pushing Ruby in front of the dark window.

Ruby slowly opened the window, couching low and whispered, "Goodnight you guys. I need to get my beauty rest."

She could hardly talk. Her voice was unsteady as Troy pulled her hair again from behind with a yank.

Doc yelled, "Your presence is required at the Island Restaurant. Everyone's going. You have to come. We'll wait for you."

"I can't really. I've already dressed for bed."

"Come on, Ruby. Will you come if we sing you a song?" asked Chris swaying and grabbing Doc for support.

Then the two of them started to sing "Oh Ruby...Don't take your love to town..." They were singing as if they were rock stars and the whole neighborhood had to hear. Soon they couldn't remember any more words. They continued to have their arms around each other. Chris said, "Common, Ruby."

"Sorry guys. I've had too much to drink. I'm not feeling so good. I'll try to go next time."

They finally gave up and staggered away. Ruby could hear them whispering and laughing as they left.

Troy let go of her hair and pushed her again on the bed. "So you're screwing someone else! Didn't take you such a long time to get over me now, did it?" he hissed through his clinched teeth.

"Why are you here anyway? You stopped loving me a long time ago," Ruby whispered holding her hand over her forehead. It was pounding so loudly in her ears.

"I always have the last word, you know that," he said smiling. "Goodnight, bitch! You're a terrible lay." He turned and let himself out. Ruby followed behind him locking the doors and shaking.

She put ointment on her cut lip and nose. Her eye was swollen and was developing a dark circle over it. She folded some ice in a cloth and held it in place. She found her pin on the floor. It was bent from the rough force of Troy's hands when he ripped her toga. She tried to straighten the small dent. She placed it in her jewelry box.

Ruby balled up the wet sheets and put them in a garbage bag. She cried herself to sleep after taking two aspirins.

The next day her body reminded her of the previous night's intruder. She ached all over. She experienced dajevu while she applied heavy makeup and dressed. She grabbed her keys and purse. She placed her dark shaded sunglasses on and opened the door. She walked over to the trash can and tossed in her bag of wet sheets. When Ruby moved towards her car, Chris was outside cleaning up some of the Greek night cigar butts and moving the chairs back on the deck.

"Good morning. I trust you slept well," he said waving. He also wore dark shades and moved a little slower than usual.

Ruby unlocked her car door to get in quickly trying to avoid a confrontation, but Chris dashed through the bushes and tapped on the window for her to roll it down.

"How are you feeling? My God, Ruby. What happened to you?" he asked lifting up her shades with his hand.

A tear trickled down Ruby's face. He opened the car door. He took her hand and wrapped his arm around her. More tears appeared as Ruby tried to hide them.

"Here's a tissue. I'm going to fix you a cup of coffee," he said pouring a cup and fixing it with cream and sugar. "Now, when did all this happen? Where was I? Maybe we should go get Doc," he questioned upset about her appearance.

"No, Chris. Please don't bother him. It will go away soon."

It was then that Chris and Ruby become devoted friends. Not the kind that are lovers, but a serious closeness that develops between siblings. It happened that day when Ruby explained her marriage from the beginning to end. He became a protective brother, friend, and father figure for her daughter. God must have known she needed him, and the rest of their friends. Ruby felt like her life was a soap opera. She wondered if she was always going to have to fear Troy showing up at inconvenient times. Would she never find peace like she did with Matt?

"I have to pick up Sarah. I'm already late. I need to be going," Ruby said placing the coffee cup on the counter.

"I'll get her. Tell me where to go. You're in no condition for her to see you like this. And Amanda's parents will be asking questions too. You stay right here. I'll be right back," he replied getting his keys.

Ruby revealed the information he needed to find Sarah, and she gave him an extra key to her cottage. He left immediately. Ruby had fallen asleep on Chris's couch. When she finally woke up, it was late afternoon. She saw his car parked outside. Ruby wandered over to her place and found them both asleep on the carpet. Ruby woke Chris and thanked him.

"If that ass comes back here again, let me know. Maybe he can fight with someone more his own size," he whispered lightly tapping her chin.

Ruby hugged him for a long time. She was afraid to let go. "I love you, Chris."

"I know. I love you too." He turned around and quietly walked down the front steps.

CHAPTER 13

Ruby enjoyed her evening classes and working at the university. But the full time job, night school, domestic shopping, and the other single parent responsibilities exhausted her. She found herself setting her alarm for four in the morning to study for tests and to complete whatever papers she needed to type. She often wondered how women with more children managed their busy schedules and financial burdens.

Sarah's fourth birthday was celebrated at a local pizza parlor with Amanda and a few other girls from her school. Ruby bought Sarah books and drawing supplies. She also purchased several outfits for school. She selected a pair of purple tennis shoes to replace the old ones that were hurting Sarah's feet. She was growing up so fast.

An ice cream birthday cake was included in the party package and small favors were placed on the decorated table with a helium balloon tied to each chair. Everyone sang 'Happy Birthday' when the candles were lit. Sarah loved opening her presents and getting the special attention she needed. It had to be one of the hardest birthdays Ruby would ever have to attend for her daughter. So much had transpired since Sarah's little life had begun. Ruby was sorry Sarah didn't have two happy parents to celebrate with her, but at least she had one. Maybe one day, Troy would change into the man Ruby used to know, and Sarah and her dad would have a close relationship. But for now, Ruby had to keep her life focused on the assumption that would never happen.

When the party was over, Ruby drove the girls to their homes and collapsed on her bed. She had taken a math test the day before and had crammed long hours memorizing the algebraic equations. Math was not her best subject.

Mrs. Fraser phoned and wanted her daughter to drive to Raleigh to celebrate Sarah's birthday, but it was a little too demanding for Ruby. She convinced them to wait until Thanksgiving when the Fraser clan would be together. That seemed to appease them.

Troy's mom also phoned to wish Sarah a 'Happy Birthday'. It was the first time Ruby had talked to her since leaving her son. It was a difficult conversation for the two of them but before hanging up, Ruby promised to visit them during the Thanksgiving holidays.

Ruby's parents came running out to the car to carry in some food Ruby had prepared for the Thanksgiving feast. Her dad reached in the trunk to lift out their suitcases and sat them on the ground. He wore an old pair of jeans and a red plaid shirt that was his familiar attire. He was sweating from stacking wood.

Her mom looked pretty but tired in her peach dress that was covered with a stained pink apron. She had her hair up in a French twist. Even with all the company and cooking, Ruby knew she was pleased to have all of her children home for the holidays.

"How's my little girl?" asked Sarah's granddad handing her a green candy out of his pocket and giving her a big hug.

"Yummy, grandpa. Thanks," she replied opening the treat and putting it into her mouth. She handed Ruby the paper, of course.

Sarah ran into her grandma's arms. "Grandma, I'm four years old. Do you want to see my crown?" she said putting her hand on top of her head to show off her royalty.

"Oh, that is such a beautiful crown. You are a little princess!" said Sally Fraser hugging her again. "And I love your purple outfit. Did you get that for your birthday?"

Sarah smiled and nodded.

"Don't I get a candy too? I've been a good girl," Ruby sulked sticking out her lower lip.

"Are you sure you've been good?" he said squinting, with a twinkle in his eye. "I've known you to have a little mischief up your sleeve, behind those pretty green eyes."

"Dad, you know I'm your angel," Ruby smiled, hugging him and then holding out her hand. He gave her a red candy and he ate a yellow. He gave Ruby his wrapper too.

"How do you like your cottage? Are you able to make ends meet?" he asked seriously.

"Yes sir. In fact, I've written you a check to pay for the moving truck you advanced me during my crisis," she replied handing him a prewritten check. "My job's going great, and I even have a little money left over if I'm extremely careful," She lied not wanting to tell him how tight things really were.

"I'll put this in a savings account for you. You may need it some day," he said in his business tone, folding the check and putting it in his shirt pocket. Then he put a hand on her shoulder and said, "I'm sorry Troy turned out the way he did. But," he added, "I'm proud of your hard work and especially for continuing your education."

"Thanks, Dad. I couldn't have made it financially or mentally without yours and mom's help. You've given me extra support that so many other stranded and trapped women don't have. I really appreciate it," Ruby said hugging him again and wiping a tear from her eye.

He smiled and said, "I love you and so does your mother. You'll be all right. You have an incredible amount of strength and talent inside you. Let it shine."

John Fraser picked up the bags and carried them upstairs before returning to sweep off the outside walks. He spent as much time as he could out working in the yard. John couldn't handle too much commotion around the house, now that he was getting older. He was gearing up for retirement in a few years from the bank. John was looking forward to traveling cross-country and overseas with his wife. They had already bought a camper to prepare for their adventures together, after the twins went away to college.

"Wow, mom, the house looks beautiful," Ruby said walking into the living room and putting her arm around her. She held Sarah's hand with her free arm.

Her mom had placed fall flowers on the coffee and hall tables. She had mixed yellow mums and red roses in two different shaped gold vases adding greenery and baby's breath. The rug had recently been re-carpeted to a light green, making the room look larger and brighter. It was amazing how a color could change everything.

She also had a cornucopia full of bright fall leaves and fruit spilling out over the lace runner, decorating the dining room table. A white tapered candle was added in the center of the fruit.

"I've been cooking all morning. Come in and see your sisters. They've been waiting for you," she said walking into the kitchen where everyone was nibbling on appetizers and having a glass of champagne.

"Hi everyone. I'm glad to see you guys and the champagne too. Did you save any for me?" Ruby asked holding up the empty bottle. "Guess not."

"Don't worry, we have another bottle chilling just for you," said Lizzy retrieving one from the refrigerator. She opened it and poured Ruby a glass.

"Thanks, Lizzy. I knew you wouldn't let me down." They clinked glasses and gave each other a huge hug.

How is New York treating you?" Ruby asked Diane turning around to hug her.

"It's wonderful. I love living in 'The Big Apple'. I've been exhausted lately, but happy," she replied making a click with her glass to Paul. "Paul and I are performing almost every night until Christmas. I can't believe we were able to get away today."

Diane had met Paul Mierra at her college in Boston. After a year of living in New York, he was now a rising, talented new star on Broadway and she worked as his agent, helping manage his career. Diane's musical background had originally brought them together, and she appeared in a variety of choruses on the stage with him. Paul was a tall, blond with blue eyes. He had a boyish way about him that appealed to the Broadway crowd, and his tenor voice could make your heart melt. Ruby appreciated his easy, laid-back style and his down-to-earth personality. He was originally from a small town in Ohio.

"How's it going you gorgeous red head?" asked Paul giving Ruby a kiss on the lips.

"I'm fine, Paul. It's great seeing you again. Congratulations on all of your successes. I'd love to come to New York one of these days and see your show. I only hear raves about it," Ruby commented smiling up at him.

"You just need to say when and it can all be arranged, Ruby," Paul replied pleased with her comments.

"And where is Miss Lilly? Sarah's anxious to see her, aren't you, sweetheart?" Ruby asked.

"Yes, where is she?" questioned Sarah looking around.

"Lilly's been waiting for you too, Sarah," Paul said hugging her. "Say, are you a princess?" he teased pointing to her crown.

"Yes, I became one on my birthday. Did you know I'm four years old?" she asked holding up four fingers.

"I heard it from a little bird that you had a birthday last month, and I think Miss Lilly has a present for you. Come with me and let's go find her," said Diane taking her hand and leading her into the den. Ruby walked into the room with her to give Lilly a hug and kiss too. She couldn't believe she would soon be two in January. She had beautiful blond curls and blue eyes that she inherited from both sides of the family. Lilly could easily have been Sarah's sister.

"How long can you stay?" Ruby asked Diane after the girls had started playing together.

"Unfortunately, we can only stay for the day. We have to head back to New York tonight. You know how the show must go on. Ruby, you really should think about coming up to see us. How about Christmas or New Years?"

"I'd like that. I'll put it down on my calendar."

Leaving the girls alone, they wandered back into the kitchen.

"Lizzy, how's law school going? I bet you don't let any of those law school boys get by with anything," Ruby said laughing and hugging her. Lizzy was living in Durham and pursuing a law degree from Wake Forrest. She was in her second year.

"I guess it's OK, but the work's hard and the studying is unbelievable. At least Alan helps to keep me out of too many arguments with the guys in my class," she winked pouring Ruby another glass of champagne and handing it to her. "Cheers."

"Cheers."

"I think those guys enjoy her confrontations. She keeps them on their toes," laughed Alan, Lizzy's boyfriend.

"I think she's going to be a wicked attorney," yelled Liam from the other room walking in to get a glass of water.

Lizzy chased him into the other room and attacked him on the couch. It didn't take long for Brad to join in the wrestling match. Their height over the years was to their advantage. Lizzy yelled for assistance from Alan. He helped to free her and she rejoined the party in the kitchen. She did look a little ruffled in the hair department.

Alan Thomas also studied law at Wake Forrest, but was originally from Florida. He was a few inches taller that Lizzy and had a muscular build. Alan had dark hair with a nice trimmed beard and wore black framed glasses that circled his brown eyes. He worked out at the gym at the university every day, especially swimming laps. He was a super tennis player, as was Lizzy. 'He is a good match for her,' Ruby thought, remembering no one messed with Elizabeth!

"All I can say is that when you finish law school, I want you for my lawyer!" Ruby added tapping her shoulder. "Too bad you couldn't have gone up against Troy."

"I would have loved that," retorted Lizzy. "I'd probably be arrested first for using karate on him in front of the judge. On second thought, maybe it's best I'm not the one. But you can be assured, I'll catch up with him somewhere else."

They all laughed but really wished deep down inside, that she was Ruby's attorney.

"Where are the twins going?" Ruby asked changing the subject.

"To shoot hoops. They have a big game in a couple of weeks and they wanted to get a little practice in before dinner," said Mrs. Fraser opening the oven door and basting the turkey.

"Can I help with anything?" Ruby asked her mom, spying the rolls on the counter that waited to be buttered. She began slicing the rolls and putting a thin slab of butter inside.

"I'll make the salad," said Lizzy putting her champagne flute down and opening the refrigerator to find the vegetables she needed.

Diane came back into the room and offered to fix the tea. "The girls are so happy to have each other to play with. They're making a house for their Barbies. Do you remember when we used to do that?" she laughed shaking her head.

"Oh, yes. I couldn't get enough time in the day to play with mine. I spent hours changing her outfits and putting straight pins in her head to give her a new hairdo," Ruby added smiling thinking about the scalp damage she had put Barbie through.

"I don't think Lizzy ever owned a doll, did you?" Diane asked teasing her.

"You know I never cared for dolls. A bow and arrow suited me just fine," snubbed Lizzy wrinkling her brows. "Someday, if I ever have a girl, God will probably punish me and give me the prissiest one of us all," she added laughing.

Paul and Alan were huddled in a corner involved in a heavy discussion about politics. They continued to talk and joke with each other, as they carried their drinks into the den to watch the football game that was beginning on TV. The Redskins were playing the Eagles. Soon the men in their household would be lost for the afternoon rooting for their favorite teams. Ruby knew the twins and her dad would be joining them soon. It was a good thing they had a couple of hours before dinner. At least Ruby had a little selfish time alone with her sisters.

"Ruby, how are you managing life on your own?" asked Diane, curious about her single parenting.

"I guess fine. I've met some nice neighbors, and I love my job at the university. Sarah seems to be well adjusted at her school, and she's beginning to make friends in the neighborhood. Wrightsville Beach is awesome."

"Have you heard anything from Troy?" asked Lizzy while she continued to chop up the carrots.

"Yeah" Ruby nodded. "He came to visit one night several weeks ago, but he never saw Sarah. We had an argument and then he left. I was nervous about seeing him again. I could tell he was still using drugs and I don't want Sarah or myself around that situation ever again. I know I don't love him anymore, nor does he love me. I guess he went back to California. I haven't heard anything from him since the fight." Ruby didn't go into the details of his abuse because she was embarrassed, and knew she would be free from him in a few months.

"I'm sorry about your marriage. I always liked Troy. It's too bad he changed—he had a bright future facing him," said Diane sadly.

"Yeah, well. I'm glad to find out now instead of later. I think I would have had a miserable life if I had stayed married to him. I'm happy for any other girl to take him away. They can have him."

"What classes are you taking?" asked Lizzy changing the subject from Troy.

"Education courses. I dread having to give my speech though. It's in December, about three weeks from now. You know how nervous I get when I have to get up in front of people," Ruby replied pouring more champagne into everyone's glasses. The champagne tasted good and the bubbles were going to her head. She started nibbling on a cheese cracker to get some food in her stomach.

"You'll do fine. Just practice and pretend the people in the class don't have any clothes on," said Lizzy. "That's what I do."

"You're right. I'll learn to overcome this fear," Ruby said, making a tight fist and lifting it up in the air. She continued to hold her fist up as she walked into the den. Ruby wanted to give her tall brothers a hug. Luckily, her timing was good. Thank God for commercials.

"Hey, sis," said Liam towering above her and wrestling her to ground to give her a hug and kiss.

"Help, someone. This big ape is messing up my hair!" Ruby wiggled away from his hold.

"Hey, I was wondering when you were going to come in to say hello," said Brad, squeezing Ruby with his hot sweaty body. "Sorry about getting you all wet," he teased. "I guess I need to take a shower before we eat. Mom will have a fit if I don't smell better than this," he replied sniffing under his armpits and smiling.

"I can vouch for that," retorted Ruby.

Brad and Liam had grown to be six feet and were extremely handsome. They were sophomores in high school. *Where had the time gone?*

"Thanks a lot for the smelly hug. I bet you don't do that to the girlfriends," she said holding her nose and using her hand to fan the smell away. She backed away from the body odor.

"They don't care about it. The sweatier, the better," said Brad bragging.

Elizabeth picked up the phone as it rang. "Hello, Yes, he's here."

"Liam, it's for you," she said rolling her eyes.

"Ruby, you won't believe how this phone rings off the hook. Of course, it's all female callers," her mom said irritated.

Ruby could believe it!

Liam hung up after a few minutes of saying 'yes' and 'no" several times. He walked back over and sat on the couch.

"I never did thank you two for helping me move all my furniture into the cottage. I hope it didn't put you out too much," Ruby said looking from one to the other.

"We're just sorry about Troy," said Liam shaking his head sadly. "How's Sarah taking everything?"

"Well, so far so good. I'm staying busy and she's making new friends. It was a wise decision on my part to leave him."

"We want you and Sarah to drive up one weekend to see one of our basketball games. It'll probably be fun visiting the old high school again," Brad said with a grin. "You might see some of your old flames now that you're single again," he needled.

"I don't think I need to see any old flames right now, but watching your basketball games would be fun. Let me have a copy of your schedule before I go back to the beach. Maybe I can work out a weekend to come up."

"Did you see the old truck dad got for us?" questioned Liam. "It's really neat. I can't wait until I get my license in a few weeks,"

"Yeah, that's a really cool truck alright. You can put all your ski equipment and surfboards in it. But where do you fit the girls?" Ruby said giving them a hard time.

"We'll fit them in the front seat somehow," said Liam. "Those are just minor details, right, Brad?"

"Yeah, we can carry a whole truck load of girls if we want," bragged Brad.

The commercials were over and the game took over their attention again. Ruby returned to the kitchen. She knew when she was being dismissed.

The football game was in the fourth quarter and only a two-point difference. It kept the guys yelling and howling all through the last few minutes. Soon bets were being placed and winner's scores were being predicted.

"John Fraser, your mom's waiting to be picked up. You're late."

"Honey, the game's almost over. The boys and I are watching the end. Then the twins can take their showers and I'll pick up mother from her house," he replied glued to the TV, annoyed that she wanted him to miss the last few plays.

The Redskins won the game by two points causing a lot of shouting and yelling from the living room. Dad grabbed a few carrots, munching them on the way out the door whistling. Obviously, his team won.

Ruby's grandmother lived alone not far from her parents. She entered the house looking beautiful. She was a tall, gray haired woman, dressed in her Sunday yellow flowered dress. She wore a string of white pearls and earrings to match. A small yellow hat covered her head

"I've been praying for my girl. How are you, sweetheart?" she asked holding Ruby's hand.

"I'm fine, grandma. You're looking elegant in your yellow dress," Ruby replied returning the squeeze.

Ruby's grandmother walked into the kitchen to visit with the rest of the family. She was so amazing for her age and had such an incredible memory. She was the youngest of ten children, raised on a farm in South Carolina. She had attended Converse College and majored in music. She played the piano, but arthritis had invaded her hands and it was too painful for her to play anymore. She also was losing her sight and couldn't read books or music. Ruby couldn't imagine why God would take away one of her favorite and most precious gifts.

"Something smells wonderful, Sally," Grandmother said to her daughter-in-law. "You're an excellent southern cook."

"Thanks, Grandmother. Most of these recipes are from your cookbook, you know," Mrs. Fraser replied welcoming her with a smile and handing her a glass of iced tea.

Grandmother blessed the food as they gathered in a circle to hold hands. She had been raised in the Methodist Church and her faith in God was incredibly strong. She always had such beautiful prayers. Ruby needed to learn from her.

Grandmother had lived during the Great Depression and knew what it was like to go hungry. She explained that many nights they would have strangers on their doorsteps begging for food. Ruby's great-grandmother always shared what her family had from the farm with the poor. She talked about the old days as they questioned her, wanting to know what her life had been like. It was amazing to see how many changes had taken place during her lifetime.

It had been a tradition in the Fraser family to play a game or some sort of sport outside, if it wasn't too cold or raining. It was still light and the temperature was perfect. Everyone was keen on a game of basketball. They chose sides and played until they couldn't see the ball anymore. Ruby's mom and grandmother watched through the glass door.

When the game was over, they all clustered around the piano to sing, 'We Gather Together, To Ask the Lord's Blessing'. Diane played the piano and her dad pulled out his hammered dulcimer. He followed along with the piano keys and their harmonizing voices. They sang many other hymns that evening before Diane's family had to take showers and drive back to New York.

Ruby felt lucky to have such a close relationship with her family. Little did they know that their grandmother would not be at their next Thanksgiving gathering.

CHAPTER 14

Ruby had planned to visit Diane in New York for Christmas, but she couldn't afford it. 'Maybe next year,' she thought to herself. To celebrate the season, Chris offered to help select and carry home a Scottish pine for the girls to decorate. Chris placed the tree in front of the bedroom window. Soon the fresh scent filled the air. They listened to Christmas music while Sarah threw tinsel on the branches, humming along with the familiar carols. She helped Ruby string popcorn and make paper ornaments. The girls baked sugar cookies adding icing and sprinkles. They danced around the room with ribbons in their hands. Chris had brought Sarah a present for under the tree.

Ruby was running errands, when the mailman brought a package to her door. Chris noticed her absence and signed the acceptance register. Sarah's name was written on the front of the brown paper with a no return address stamped on the front. Sarah opened it and was thrilled to find two Dr. Seuss books. There was no note. Ruby thought perhaps a relative sent them and forgot to include one. She didn't know whom she should thank.

Troy stayed in California over the holidays. He promised to send Ruby money to buy Sarah gifts but he never did. Ruby worried constantly about her finances. Without Troy's checks arriving on time, she didn't know how she could manage the bills that seemed to pile up. For some reason, she never overdrew.

Oddly, Ruby began to realize her checkbook didn't match her monthly bank statements. She retraced previous ones and found an extra deposit dating back to September, when she had started school. Her monthly statement consistently showed two hundred dollars being deposited into her account. Ruby suspected her dad was contributing to the 'Ruby Fraser, Single Mom's Club Fund' anonymously. It would be easy for him to do. When she questioned him, he denied it sincerely. Ruby couldn't find out any information from the bank. She was clueless.

July was the month Ruby and Sarah stayed in the Frisco cottage. The first two days were beautiful. The girls went to the beach and set up their chairs. They took long walks, collecting shells in Sarah's bucket and had picnic lunches under the old, rustic umbrella that belonged to the cottage.

They showered together outside and dressed in shorts and t-shirts. They painted in the hot sun, sitting on the top deck. Ruby was thrilled to sketch some beach scenes, before applying the acrylic paints. She happily expressed her artistic abilities on canvas and felt rewarded when she completed six large pictures and four small ones.

Suddenly an airplane flew over and Ruby waved to the pilot. It was a white and blue Cessna that she knew belonged to Mr. and Mrs. Carlson. They were an elderly couple from Washington D.C. who owned the cottage next to her dad's. It was a split-level building on top of stilts surrounded by several acres giving them total privacy. They had been vacationing on the island as long as Ruby could remember.

A storm was brewing from the south that was quickly approaching Frisco. The girls collected their things and carried them inside while the sky darkened and the wind howled. It wasn't uncommon to lose power, so Ruby located candles, matches, and flashlights and placed them on the kitchen counter.

The thunder cracked loudly displaying streaks of lightning that zigzagged across the sky. The rain sounded like bullets hitting the deck and roof. The lights went out almost immediately. They were sitting in the den when a loud clap of thunder made Sarah put her hands over her ears closing her eyes. She started to cry. Ruby rocked her and started to sing a lullaby.

"Is anyone here?"

"Mr. Carlson, please come in out of the storm," Ruby insisted unlocking the door as a strong gust of wind forced the door open. He stepped inside and shook the rain from his coat and hat. He was carrying a small suitcase.

"Hi Ruby," he said shaking her hand. "I just landed and barely tied down my plane before the storm opened up. Then the electricity went out all over the island. I'm alone on this trip because my wife passed away several months ago, maybe your dad told you," he said sadly. "Anyway, I didn't want to go to the cottage in the dark tonight, just in case there are snakes nesting inside like they've done in the past. Do you mind if I stay here for the night?" he inquired still shaking water from his hat.

"Of course, you can spend the night," Ruby replied reaching for his wet things and hanging them on the coat rack. "We have plenty of extra sheets and towels. Come in and dry off, Mr. Carlson. I'm sorry about your wife. No, I had not heard the news," Ruby added sympathetically.

Sarah was holding her hand and still squirming when the claps of the thunder barreled down on the island again.

"Honey, you remember Mr. Carlson, don't you?"

"Hi," she said shyly hugging her mom.

"Hi Sarah. My how pretty and grown up you are," he said bending over to shake her hand.

A loud crack of thunder boomed over their heads and lightning followed revealing fireworks.

"I hate that noise. I wish it would go away, Mommy," squealed Sarah holding her blanket and sticking her thumb in her mouth. She put her face into Ruby's legs.

"This is a bad one, Sarah. But we're safe in the house so you'll be OK." Ruby tried to reassure her. "Let's put Mr. Carlson's things in the bedroom and then I can fix both of you something to eat and drink," she offered leading him inside, down the hallway with the flashlight. He placed his bags in the dark room and asked about using the bathroom.

"Do you need my flashlight?" Ruby inquired.

"No, thanks. I brought one here somewhere." He pulled out a small flashlight from his pocket to use.

"Would you like a sandwich and some iced tea?" Ruby asked.

"That would be great. I was planning on eating BBQ at Bubba's when I got here, but I didn't count on running into Mother Nature. I'm really hungry, thanks," he replied entering the bathroom.

Ruby made a ham and cheese sandwich on homemade bread she had picked up at the Gingerbread Bakery, with a home grown tomato. She added chips on the side and fixed his iced tea. She lit a few more candles for the table.

"Are you girls here alone?" asked Mr. Carlson using his hands to slick back his wet salt and pepper hair.

"Yes, as a matter of fact we are. Troy and I recently divorced," Ruby explained. "Mom and dad offered the cottage to us and I was able to take off from work. I can't think of any other place in the world I'd rather be, except during a bad thunderstorm," Ruby said taking a sip of her tea.

"I'm sorry about your marriage," he said sincerely. "Troy seemed like such a nice young man the few times I spoke with him."

"Yes, he had a lot going for him. He's living in California now, so Sarah doesn't see him often," "How long will you be vacationing here?" Ruby inquired looking into his blue-gray eyes.

"I'll be here for two weeks, if I can stand myself that long," he laughed. "I have to also travel to New York sometime this month and maybe even Jackson Hole, Wyoming."

"What exactly do you do, Mr. Carlson?" Ruby asked curiously. She had known his family for a long time but never really inquired about his life outside of visiting Frisco. She knew it involved traveling.

"I fly around the world to different museums buying and selling art. I'm a curator for international art exhibits. My wife used to enjoy traveling with me because she was an artist. Did you know she studied in Paris when she was in college?"

"No, I knew she painted but I didn't know she lived and went to school there."

That's where we met," he responded before taking a bite of his sandwich.

"What medium did your wife prefer?"

"She enjoyed oils mostly. I loved her beach scenes," he said losing himself in fond memories. A loud crack of thunder seemed to snap him back to reality. "I can't paint at all but I admire people that have talent. For myself, my hobbies are photography and flying. I guess you could say those are my two passions," he added with a grin. "There's nothing in this world like flying and looking down on the beauty of our world." Another flash and big boom made Sarah cover her head with her arms knocking over her juice.

"Mommy, I'm scared," said Sarah getting out of her seat and jumping into Ruby's lap.

Mr. Carlson immediately found a wet cloth to wipe up the spill.

"Thank you," Ruby said embarrassed.

"Sarah, you know what is going on up there, don't you?" he asked her while he squeezed out the cloth and put it back in the sink.

"What do you mean?"

"Well, the lightning is a ballet dancer in a fancy white dress. She tip toes across the sky so quietly that you hardly know she's there. The thunder is the tap dancer, and he likes to step quick and hard so he can have fun keeping up with the ballerina. After a while, they become exhausted because they have used up all their energy. Eventually the wind blows them away until they find another place to dance."

"I like to dance too. But why do they dance so loud?"

"You see, they are so high up in the sky, they don't realize the noise they make is bothering anyone."

"I want to see what they look like."

"It's really hard to catch them because they are so fast. But I have something very special for you," he said handing her a silver dollar from his pocket. "Will you keep this lucky coin for me? It's magic and it will always keep you safe."

"Wow, mom, look at this. Can I really keep it?" she asked eyeing the coin and turning it over in her small hand.

"Yes, honey. What do you say to Mr. Carlson?"

"Thank you, Mr. Carlson," she said getting out of my lap and kissing him on the cheek.

"Do you ladies like to fly?" questioned Mr. Carlson smiling.

"As a matter of fact, we do."

"If the weather's nice tomorrow and I get the cottage opened up, would you like to fly over the island?"

"I would love it. What do you think, Sarah?"

"Oh yes mommy!" she exclaimed excitedly jumping up and down. "Is it like Matt's plane?"

"Yes, honey it is. I didn't know if you would remember Matt?" Ruby answered happily and surprised.

"Mom, you know I remember Matt. He was nice."

Ruby smiled.

"Great, then it's settled. We'll head out to Ocracoke and have lunch somewhere."

"Do you have children, Mr. Carlson? You seem to have a nice way with them," Ruby said looking around for some dessert to share. She opened the freezer and pulled out some ice cream.

"Ruth and I always wanted to have children, but for whatever reason we couldn't. I'm close to my nieces and nephews in Willow Springs, though. They belong to my younger brother, Abe. They're all farmers in the North Carolina Mountains. Charlie, my oldest nephew runs things now that Abe's arthritis has given him a fit. They visit me in D.C. every once in a while," he replied taking another bite of his sandwich. "By the way, Ruby, please call me John."

"OK, John, would you like another sandwich and if not, would you like some chocolate ice cream?

"The sandwich hit the spot, but now I'd love some ice cream, thanks."

The rain continued during the night and finally went out to sea. The electricity was still out so they went to bed. Ruby awoke the next morning smelling the aroma of coffee. It took her a minute to remember that John had spent the night. She put on her robe and looked around the kitchen. He had set two places for Sarah and her with a note thanking them for their hospitality. He said he would pick them up at eleven for the plane ride. It was signed John.

They were waiting for him when he drove up Seaside Drive. He sat in a new Safari Jeep, just like the one Ruby had always dreamed of owning. He had the top down and waved for them to hop in. He came around and opened the door.

John was dressed in khaki shorts and a nice short sleeved white shirt with a collar. His hair was cut a little above the ears. He was extremely handsome, Ruby thought.

"Good morning, beautiful ladies," he said smiling. "I love those sun dresses you both have on. Wow, I must be the luckiest guy on the island to have two pretty girls to escort to lunch," he beamed.

"What time did you get up?" Ruby inquired loving the jeep she was sitting in and appreciating the compliment. Ruby was glad she remembered to bring along her straw hat she had picked up at the souvenir shop. She had bought one for Sarah too.

"I don't remember, but I ate a doughnut at the bakery and then went to open up the house. I didn't see any snakes this time, thank goodness. Maybe the poison I'd put around the cracks last year before I closed it up, helped to keep them away. There were a few dead mice laying around that I dumped in the trash. I vacuumed and dusted pretty well. I also wiped the counters and windows. Other than that, it's a little musty inside, but after the ocean breeze and sun get to it, it'll be like new. I'm sure it will be a hot and humid day, so I'll run the air conditioner tonight after it airs out."

"Was it hard for you to go in with so many wonderful years of memories?" Ruby asked.

"Yeah, that's why I had to go in there alone. I'm sure time will help with the healing process, but it sure is hard on me," he said looking away and out of his window. Ruby could tell he had some tears behind those sunglasses.

"The day is perfect and not much wind yet. I'm looking forward to our trip," Ruby said smiling placing her hand on his shoulder.

They drove to the Frisco airport where John's plane was chained down on the yellow T. He checked all of his gas lines and equipment, as Ruby had seen Matt do before. It brought back a lot of deja vu for her too. She found herself wishing he were here instead of John. Wasn't that selfish of her? And he probably wished she was his Ruth.

Ruby could've sat beside him in the plane, but Sarah wanted to hold her hand. They taxied down the small runway and lifted up, ever so gently, over the sand dunes and ocean. Small fishing boats looked like play toys in a bathtub. They flew in the direction of the Cape Hatteras Lighthouse circling the island heading south towards Ocracoke. Ruby couldn't get Matt's face out of her mind. She was enjoying the view and thinking about the time he told her about his trip to Ocracoke. John made small talk over the headphones but was relatively quiet on the trip. Ruby thought he was probably having love loss pains too.

"We're almost at the airport. Would you like to go a little further south and then come back? I know a great place for a seafood lunch. You do like seafood, don't you?" he questioned turning around to see Ruby's face.

"Yes," she nodded. "The scenery's beautiful, John. Thanks for this," she said taking in the nature from a bird's point of view. Wasn't that her fortune once at the DC Chinese restaurant when she dined with Matt? Ruby was pretty sure that's what the paper had read. She thought to herself remembering Matt making his fingers work like chopsticks. *I wonder what Matt is doing at this moment?*

They landed, and John made a phone call to someone he knew on the island. "I phoned this kid earlier this morning. He said he left his truck for us to use, and I wanted to tell him we were here."

He chained the plane and located the truck parked behind the fence. They drove to the Back Porch Restaurant to have tuna, cooked in special island seasonings, along with a baked potato and salad. Sarah had chicken finger and fries, her favorite food. The restaurant was homey and not too crowded. "How's my little friend doing?" John asked Sarah in his southern accent.

"Good," she said nodding her head up and down. "I like it," she said, dipping a fry into the ketchup and putting it into her mouth.

"What type of work do you do, Ruby?" John asked taking off his sunglasses and putting them into his pocket.

"I'm a secretary for the dean of my college. I'm taking night classes to pursue a teaching and art degree."

"Oh, are you an artist too?" John inquired surprised.

"Well, I don't know if you call it that. I'd like to teach art someday, maybe even overseas."

"What type of paints do you work with the most?"

"I'm an acrylic fan. I like to use bright colors."

"Do you have any of your work here in Frisco?"

"I've done a few pictures, but they're just for fun. I like to paint beach scenes and pictures that I take with my camera. I look for the unusual shot, if you know what I mean."

"I'd like to see your work. Will you show it to me?"

"Of course, but I'm afraid that since art is your business, my little paintings will be very simple for your taste," Ruby replied a little hesitant to share that part of her soul with him. She had never had an art critic look at her pictures before. She knew the ones she painted the day before were done quickly.

"Please don't feel that way. I'm interested in you as a person and what you enjoy doing. There are many artists that never are discovered because of their insecurities about their work. You should always be proud of what you accomplish, even if you're the only one that appreciates its beauty. I used to tell my wife that all the time. She never would have tried to show her pictures at an art gallery if I hadn't pushed her. I'm a business man, that's what I do best."

"I appreciate your words of encouragement, John," Ruby said feeling relieved.

"Speaking of pictures, I'll get the waitress to take a picture of us here at the restaurant. Would that be OK with you ladies?"

"Sure, and I'll also ask for one with my camera," Ruby added smiling at him. He really was an attractive man, Ruby thought guessing he was around sixty five years old. She knew John was wealthy. She imagined he had many women after him. Ruby liked him and was grateful for his friendship.

After lunch they traveled to the village of Ocracoke and watched the ferries and tourist while eating ice cream. John insisted on taking Sarah to the Pirate's Chest to buy her something pretty. She picked out jewelry and ended up with three rings, two bracelets, and one necklace. *If John had children, especially a girl, he would have a hard time telling her 'No'.*

The return flight to Frisco was as beautiful as the morning, but a little bumpier because the winds had shifted and picked up speed. It didn't bother Ruby, but Sarah kept squeezing her hand.

When they returned to the cottage, Ruby thanked him again for the lunch and flight. "Would you like to come over for a cookout tomorrow night?"

"Sure, what time should I come over?"

"How about six?" Ruby suggested.

"Can I bring anything?" John asked.

"No, just yourself," Ruby answered waving goodbye.

CHAPTER 15

The next morning the girls walked along the shore and climbed the airport dune to see John's plane. Ruby captured several images of it and of Sarah exploring the beach. On the way back to the cottage they collected shells with small holes to make jewelry. Ruby had brought yarn and embroidery thread from home. Sarah rinsed them off in the ocean and placed them on a towel to dry in the sun.

Sarah jumped waves with a new friend while Ruby relaxed with a book, *The Agony and The Ecstasy* by Irving Stone. She read it slowly absorbing the life of Michelangelo and learning about his passion of sculpting marble. Ruby was fascinated by his life story. She couldn't imagine the time he spent on his back, high in the scaffolds painting the Sistine Chapel with oil dripping in his eyes. His muscles must have ached constantly while holding his brush up in the air and completing the detailed artwork. She closed her eyes as she dreamed of visiting Rome and Florence one day to see his acclaimed masterpieces.

After absorbing enough rays and exhausted from the heat, the girls showered and went to buy groceries. They weren't home long before they heard a tap on the door. Sarah ran to let John in.

"Hi, Mr. Carlson," she said giving him a hug and taking his free hand.

He had on a red plaid shirt and a pair of jeans. "Can we go flying again?" she asked excitedly.

"Hi, sweetheart. Maybe we can go for a short one tomorrow if the weather's nice. The airport closes at night so I don't think we'd have time this evening," he said handing Ruby a bouquet of fresh flowers.

"Thanks, John. They're beautiful. I'll put them in a vase," Ruby said looking under the cabinet and finding a green one. She filled it with water and placed the flowers on the kitchen table.

"And this is for you," he said to Sarah handing her a small white bag.

She opened it and took out a decorated chocolate cupcake from the bakery. "Mom, look what I got. Can I eat it now?" she asked wide-eyed begging for a 'yes' answer.

"Not now, Sarah. But after dinner," Ruby said looking at her and placing the cupcake on a small plate. She had a disappointed look.

"Thank you," she said giving him another hug

"Something sure smells good. I've been looking forward to this all day."

"It's the apple pie Sarah and I made for you."

"That's one of my favorites. I can't tell you the last time I had a home cooked meal. How can I be so lucky?"

"It seems luck is on our side too, John."

"Can I do anything to help?" John asked.

"As a matter of fact, how are you at grilling steaks?" Ruby inquired handing him the tray and spatula. She set two potholders on top. "I just checked the coals, and they're red hot."

"I'm not too bad on a grill but I don't think you'd want me in the kitchen," he laughed. "If the coals are ready these will only take a few minutes to cook," he informed Ruby taking a swallow of the beer she offered. He disappeared outside.

They made small talk during the meal discussing the changes that had taken place in Hatteras. John mentioned the decision he faced about selling his home in D.C., now that his wife was gone. He shared his feelings of love for her and the emptiness he felt after she died. Ruby listened with sympathy while they cleared the table and washed the dishes.

"Now, I want to see those paintings you were telling me about yesterday," he said drying his hands on the tea towel.

"OK, but I hope you aren't expecting Monet," she said feeling a little self conscious about her talent. She left to retrieve them from the bedroom.

John studied each one without saying a word, lifting them up and examining the strokes. Finally he said, "Your paintings are innocent and childlike. I like that. They're bright and fresh. You have your own unique style, Ruby. How long did you say that you've been painting?" he inquired looking at her while holding one of the lighthouse pictures.

"I've never really had lessons, but I was hoping to take some next year, if I can fit them into my busy schedule. A good friend of mine told me to keep painting, but I thought he was just being polite," Ruby replied thinking about Matt's note in the mailbox.

"Ruby, you definitely have a gift. I personally don't think you should take lessons because it might ruin your individual style that I admire. That's what makes your work unique. If I can, I'd like to take these up to my meeting in New York and see if I can talk to a few people I know. Do you have other pictures at your house in Wrightsville Beach?"

"Yes, I have a few."

"Well, if my colleagues see the genius in your work like I do, maybe eventually I can help to organize a show for you. There are many cities throughout the world that are open to us. I don't want to get your hopes up, Ruby, but I think it might be a realistic possibility. What are your thoughts about that idea?" he asked grinning.

She looked at him in disbelief. "John, I don't know what to say. I know my paintings are simple, but do you honestly think I'm ready for a show?" Ruby asked still trying to grasp the conversation that had transpired. "What's involved?" She inquired curiously.

"Well, you need a sponsor. I'm right here," John offered. "And you'll need to have approximately thirty or forty pictures of different sizes.

We'll select the best and frame them. You may have to make a trip up to New York. What do you say?" he questioned.

"I'm just shocked, I guess," Ruby said placing her hand over her heart. "It'll take me at least a year or so to have that many pictures ready with working fulltime and night school, not to mention taking care of Sarah," she said suddenly becoming overwhelmed. "I guess I could paint on weekends," she said still unable to grasp the seriousness of his proposal. "Of course, I'd love to try a show. It sounds challenging and exciting. I've never been to New York. I could visit Diane and finally see her Broadway show. I better start right away," she continued, thinking about the labor that lay ahead.

"I suggest you try different scenes and objects to see which ones compliment your style. I'll need your address and both phone numbers for work and home."

"Thanks again, John. This is so unbelievable to me," Ruby said writing down the information he requested.

"I have to admit, when I first asked to look at your art, I wasn't expecting such a talented painter. I hope you realize how exciting it is for me to find an artist such as yourself. It's funny to think how much time and money I've spent looking for new talent and here you are right next door making me apple pie. I can't wait to introduce you to the public," he said sincerely. "I wouldn't just say this if I didn't think you had a chance to become known. I know the art world is competitive, that's why it's important to be different. This is my line of work. After all, I know many artists and judges globally," he added raising his eyebrows and smiling.

"I don't know what to say. But I'll take your advice and look forward to working with you."

Ruby covered her art with plastic garbage bags. John went over to sit down next to Sarah.

"How was your cupcake?"

She smiled, still showing the chocolate on her lips. "It was yummy. Can you bring me another one tomorrow?" she questioned leaning over to give him a chocolate kiss on the cheek.

"I'll see what the bakery has tomorrow. You know lots of little girls are staying on this island and they sell them really quickly. Maybe we could try a different one. Would that be alright?"

"OK."

"Now, I need to return home and get some of my business matters taken care of. We can fly again tomorrow morning if you'd like."

He didn't need a reply from Sarah or Ruby. He knew what they would say.

They flew the following day with a perfect, clear sky. Ruby snapped a few more pictures and got one of John beside his plane when they landed.

John invited them to his house. There were pictures of his wife and traces of a woman's touch in the decor. It was the first time Ruby had ever been inside his cottage. It was a split level house but the two circular structures were totally separate and had to be entered from an outside door.

He had a desk full of papers and a tape recorder for dictation notes. His phone rang while they enjoyed cokes on the deck. He explained he had a business call and apologized. "I told my good friend, Bob, about your work. He's anxious to see it. I hope you ladies have a wonderful last few days here on your vacation. I'll be in touch, Ruby."

They said their 'goodbyes' and thanked him for everything.

Before Ruby knew it she was packing the car. The hardest part about being in Hatteras for her was leaving. She stared out into the ocean saying her silent farewell.

Chris called Saturday morning singing, "Time to get up you sleepy head."

"Thanks for the song," Ruby smiled thinking about his deep voice singing in the phone.

"I know I woke you didn't I? I can tell from that raspy sound in your voice."

"I'll have you know, I've been up since the crack of dawn painting. So you see you haven't come close to waking me up." She had heard from John and he wanted her to visit New York after Christmas. She had several pictures to complete before then.

"What are you painting?"

"I'm actually painting a picture of a plane or at least attempting it. It's sort of a Marc Chagall style watercolor picture. Do you like Marc Chagall?"

"Yeah, he's good. I like that type of painting myself. When can I see your work?"

"Maybe sometime this weekend. But I still need to finish the final touches. And, of course, I have to sign it."

"OK. Oh by the way, the main reason I called is to tell you that we're all getting together Labor Day at the beach and later for a chili cook-off. Do you know how to make chili, and if so, do you want to enter the competition?"

"Sure, I can make a pretty mean chili. You can count on me to compete in your contest. Are you my competition too?"

"I'm planning to use a secret recipe that has been in my family for centuries. I'm sure I'll win, but you can give it your best shot," he bragged. "The winner gets to wear a crown and, of course, they have an Alpo Award for the worst chili. You'll get to wear a dog tag," he laughed.

"You better start your chili now because I'm going to give you a good run for your money. The winner isn't announced until the fat lady sings," Ruby said teasing him.

"I look forward to it, Ruby. I'm sure the crown will look good on me."

John and Doc were absent for the volleyball game on the beach. Sarah had been invited to spend the day with her friend Amanda. Kyle brought his jet ski, and they all took turns zipping across the water. The water was cold but refreshing.

Doc had been on call most of the weekend but managed to escape for the party. He was able to whip up a chili and enter the contest too. Dugray, Elizabeth, and Theresa also entered. The pots were set up on a card table with numbers taped to each. Paper and pencils were provided and a mason jar was used for votes.

Chris was slyly offering one dollar bills to everyone to persuade them to vote for his gray concoction. Supposedly he had cooked it for two days to get that incredible color. Many voters obliged him and took his dollar.

An older friend of Chris's, David, showed up to join in the fun. He had brought some French bread and butter placing it on one of the tables. David had been in the Navy for twenty years and now lived off of his retirement fund each month. This allowed him to take monthly hikes down the Appalachian Trail or climb Mt. Everest, or whatever challenge he was willing to take. David was about fifteen years older than Ruby and very attractive. He had short salt and pepper hair with bright blue eyes. David's tan showed a slight sign of crows feet when he smiled. He wore khaki shorts and a tank top.

Mason was chosen to tally up the ballots and announced the winners. Theresa decorated the crown with sequins made of rope and a plastic card covered with aluminum foil. She wrote

'Alpo Award" in black marker on the side of the dog tag.

"Ruby, did you make chili?" asked Dugray smiling at her taking a dip into one of the crock pots that happened to be hers.

"Yes, I did. All of them are very different, don't you think?" she questioned him finishing her last sample, which happened to be Chris's gray masterpiece. She made a face after putting the spoon back in the bowl and taking a sip of beer to chase down the terrible taste left in her mouth. She continued to make a frown and Dugray shook his head up and down to mean he agreed with her.

"This is the best," said Doc taking a taste out of Ruby's pot. "Didn't you make this one?" said Doc winking at her.

"You know I can't divulge that information, Dr. Sunderland. But if you vote for that one, it won't hurt my feelings," she replied reaching into her own pot and enjoying the savor of beans and meat she had thrown together.

"This gray one is scary!" he remarked pointing to it and shuttering.

"That seems to be the consensus. I think Chris is going to be disappointed and broke from all the dollars he's handed out for votes. Crime just doesn't pay!" They both laughed.

John drove up in his jeep honking. Elizabeth ran over to greet him. They kissed and everyone clapped.

"John Boy, good to have you home," yelled Kyle walking over to shake his hand.

Sarah ran up to him and tugged at his shorts.

"Hi, Sarah. Gosh, you've grown so much and you have such a dark tan! Have you been hanging out at that beach again?" he teased. "Your hair's almost white."

"Yep, I played with my friend Amanda," she said.

"John, where've you been? I haven't seen you in the last two months?" Ruby asked him munching on a corn chip.

"Well, you know the Seals. We can be anywhere," he grinned not wanting to tell.

"Well, wherever you've been, you have a great tan. How long are you home for?" Ruby inquired still pumping him for more information.

"Elizabeth and I are planning to go away next week to Nags Head. I've arranged to have some time off. I can really use it. We've had some unreal drills lately," he said sipping his beer.

"John, come over and vote for the best chili. Here's a dollar for you to write the number three on your ballot," Chris said slipping a rolled up dollar into John's hand.

John walked over to the table. "Three looks a little sick. Why does it have that color?" he said checking out the other pots. He handed Chris the dollar back. "I'm not that desperate for a buck. Besides I'd like to live a little longer. Being a Seal is risky enough," he retorted.

"Why hasn't anyone turned up the music?" asked Theresa walking into Chris's apartment and turning up the volume.

"Now shake it ah baby now...shake it ah baby, Twist and Shout, Twist and Shout..." They danced in the parking lot. Even Sarah was dancing with Doc. He showed her how to twist. She was laughing and swinging her arms wildly.

"Mom, look at me. I can dance."

"She's a pretty good dancer. Does she get that from her mom?" asked Doc pointing to Ruby.

"I think she's better than me. Look at her go."

When the dance was over, Mason called everyone around to find out the name of the winners of the contest. Ruby's name was called for the first place award. Everyone clapped and the crown was placed on her head. She had to sit in a decorated beach chair with a red towel in front. She could see flashes of light blinding her as she posed for her title.

"I have the results of the worst chili here tonight. Ladies and Gentlemen: The vote was unanimous. The Alpo Award goes to none other than that Irishman, Chris Murphy.

Chris's mouth almost dropped to the deck railing. Everyone started clapping and whistling for him to accept his award. He bowed as Elizabeth put the dog tag around his neck accepting it with disappointment and slight embarrassment. He raised one eyebrow and scoured a frown, "I paid for these votes, didn't I? I think I need my money back. I demand a recount!" He held out his hand to collect his money.

"Chris, that had to be the worst chili I've ever tasted. Where did you say you got that recipe?" questioned Kyle shaking his head sadly. "I was afraid to have more than one spoonful because I didn't want to die. I have to work tomorrow!"

"I'll have you know, that recipe has been in the Murphy family for generations. It was passed down from my relatives in Ireland. The secret is to cook it for two days soaking in all the spices and flavors into the meat," he proudly replied. "Obviously, none of you have the gourmet pallet for such fine cooking," he said shaking his head and smiling.

"Well, I think you cooked it too long. I can't eat anything that has that color and not feel nauseous," said Kyle holding his stomach. "It's a good thing we have Doc here to save us if we start dropping off," teased Kyle.

CHAPTER 16

John phoned in October and wanted to know if Ruby and Sarah were available on Friday for dinner. They set a time and Ruby gave John directions to her cottage.

They exchanged greetings and were glad to see each other.

"Look at my lovely dates in pink dresses."

"You always say the right things to a girl!" Ruby teased locking the door behind her. After she was seated in the car, Ruby spied Chris peering out of his window. When she waved, he sheepishly put a hand up and backed away, out of sight.

"Where's your plane, Mr. Carlson?" Sarah asked leaning forward from the back seat.

John started the car and backed out of the parking space. "I have her chained at the airport. It's not too far from here. I rented this car so I could visit you and your mom."

"We're glad you came," Sarah said talking to the teddy bear she had in her arms. Mr. Carlson seemed pleased.

"Doll, how's everything been going?" he asked Ruby turning his head to check for moving vehicles before pulling out on the main highway.

"Good. I'm taking art history and choir this semester. My history professor is also an archeologist. She brings the class to life with her fascinating stories. She uses her personal slides to share art and the expeditions she's seen around the world."

"That makes a great teacher. I, myself, am a visual learner. I guess that's why I'm in the art business. Does she also paint?"

"She's more of a sculptress. She has some of her work in her office. I especially like her cast iron molding of a ballerina."

"And what are you singing in choir?"

"Handel's Messiah. We started practicing it this week. It's one of my favorite pieces."

"You'll have to let me know when your performance is so I can come to hear you sing. I also enjoy Handel's masterpiece too," he said stopping at the red light.

"I'd be happy for you to come. I think the concert is the first week in December, probably on that Saturday. Put it on your calendar."

John drove another mile and pulled into the restaurant parking lot. When they entered the building he told the hostess, "Reservations for Carlson." She grabbed menus and led them to their table. John pulled out a chair for Sarah to sit and then he did the same for Ruby.

Sarah busied herself with a coloring book the waitress had provided. John removed his glasses from his suit pocket and studied the menu. He ordered a bottle of Merlot.

"So what are you doing here at the beach?" She was anxious to ask him about what his colleagues thought of her art. She decided to let him bring it up.

"I actually made a special trip to see you," he smiled. "I've thought a lot about you two ladies and how much fun we had in Hatteras. You see, sometimes my family can be a little too intrusive and often I think they just want my money. I don't get that feeling from you, Ruby," he said sincerely. "And right now I need to be around someone like you."

"John, I'm flattered that you came down here just to see us. I know you're a busy man flying all over the world and married to an incredible, busy itinerary. But I'm sure your family does care for you a great deal.

Have you thought that maybe they feel uneasy about their relationship with you since your wife's death, not knowing what to say or how to act."

"Perhaps you're right. I'm still emotional and having a rough time of it. I thought if I worked all the time, it would fill the emptiness I feel inside. Since her passing, I've had insomnia and grieve her absence. I returned to Hatteras last month to spend some time alone and try to make peace with God. Did you know we were married for twenty five years? You see, I was a confirmed bachelor until I met my Ruthie. I was forty five when we married."

"How did you meet her?"

"I was drafted into the service during WWII. It was my junior year of college. I was put in command of a unit of twenty men. They were all like brothers to me. We were from all parts of the United States but we were bonded because of our military situation. I'll never forget the terrible sounds of my men being shot and wounded, dying with so much pain and agony. I went back into the line of fire to carry two of them back to the camp, but they died shortly after receiving medical attention by the Red Cross. I was the only survivor in my unit and to this day, I think I should have died with them. The good Lord must have had a special reason why I remained on this Earth."

He took a sip of his wine and continued, "And later after the war, I returned to college pursuing a business and art history degree. After graduation, I worked my way up the corporate ladder and made a lot of money. I was living in Washington D.C and soon became president of The World Bank. I was on many committees throughout the city and on the Board of the Smithsonian. I began attending art shows locally and then started branching out to New York, Chicago, Columbus, and Jackson Hole, of all places. Eventually I made contacts with museums in Europe and other parts of the world. I became so busy that I resigned from the bank and started my own business in the arts.

I remember I almost didn't make it home one Thanksgiving weekend with my family because my flight had been delayed in Frankfort. But I managed to switch to another airline and when I landed, I jumped in my plane and flew home. My brother had invited Ruth over for the annual turkey and dressing feast. I'll never forget the first time I saw her. She was dressed in a green and white gingham cotton dress. It matched her eyes. Her chestnut hair was curled around her shoulders. I thought Ruth was the most beautiful creature I'd ever laid my eyes on. She had grown up in another small town close to Willow Springs, but I'd never met her before. Isn't it strange, that I searched for the perfect woman, traveling around the world, and all along she was just a few miles away," he said wiping a small tear that had formed in his eye.

"John, I'm sure you miss her deeply. You know you're always welcome to come to Wrightsville Beach anytime you'd like."

John realized he had dominated the conversation with his personal sorrow. Changing the subject he said, "Ruby, I need to talk to you about your art. My friends in New York were ecstatic about your paintings. They wanted me to ask you about doing a show, maybe during New Year's. It's a small museum but a nice place to introduce you to the art community. Most of these people have money and don't mind spending it. I don't know how much time you've had to add to your collection. Am I rushing you, Doll?"

"Are you kidding? I still can't believe this is happening. I have to keep pinching myself to make sure I'm awake," she said enthusiastically. "I think you'll be amazed how dedicated I've been with my art. I've built up quite a diverse assortment of subjects and interpreted them on my canvas with bright acrylics. But I must warn you, a few of them are really out there."

"I can't wait to see your newest additions."

"How long does the show last? Do I have to be there every day?"

"Only for the reception that will be in your honor, of course. I'm trying to arrange the date on January 2nd. I thought it would be easy for you to take one or two days off from your job if you had to."

"I'll call my sister to let her know we're coming to visit. She won't believe it. But I won't tell her about the show until we're there. I'd like that to be a surprise."

"Doll, when you girls visit me in New York, I promise you won't have to lift a finger to do a thing. I'll pamper you so much, you won't want to leave," he joked, but was truly serious.

Before Ruby could comment, the waitress placed salads on the table and she poured more wine into their glasses. She refilled Sarah's coke. "Everything alright?" she asked.

John nodded and replied, "It's wonderful, thank you."

A pianist began playing popular tunes in the center of the dining room. The tables were adorned with white lit candles and a red rose was in a vase on each table. There were several ship pictures and hurricane lamps with white electric lights that were hung on the dark, wooden walls. This was such a romantic place to dine. Ruby hadn't been treated with so much attention and class since her days with Matt. As if reading her mind, the piano player began playing and singing "Your Song." Ruby listened while memories danced in her head.

When the last bite had been placed in her mouth, John smiled. "Are you enjoying your meal?"

"I don't think I've had steak since dining with you at Hatteras. I'm trying to savor the moment," Ruby replied closing her eyes. She wiped her lips with her napkin.

"Dessert anyone?" questioned John looking at Sarah and moving his eyebrows up and down.

"Oh, Mr. Carlson. I want chocolate ice cream. Can I?" begged Sarah looking up at him with a twinkle in her blue eyes.

"Of course, Doll. You can have anything you want." And he meant it. *She had him wrapped around her little finger.*

They decided to take a quick spin over the night lights of Wrightsville Beach and Wilmington. They climbed into a six passenger white Cessna, with a thin green and blue stripe down the side. John's initials JJC were on the pilot door painted in black.

"What does the middle "J" stand for?" Ruby inquired touching the initials.

"It was my dad's name. It's Joshua," he said smiling.

Ruby mailed John a hand written invitation to the Messiah. He showed up early for the concert and sat in the front row. He wore a grey suit with a conservative maroon and blue tie. Ruby saw him reading the program and waved from behind the curtain. He grinned.

Ruby was dressed in a white, long sleeved blouse and black skirt required by her choir master, Mr. Martin. The women soloists sang in red evening gowns while the tenor and bass each wore a black suit. Mr. Martin had hired several symphony members to accompany the pianist. They performed in the small theatre at the university. The room was packed. The dean brought his family and most of the faculty showed up for the music, as well.

Kevin and Doc came in late to listen to the music. They had to stand in the back of the room. They were wearing dark suits and ties with white shirts. Two handsome young men, she thought as they waved when their eyes met. Ruby couldn't help but feel like the luckiest person in the world, to be surrounded by all these loving and caring friends. Her recent past was beginning to fade, and she was able to hold her head up and feel proud of herself again.

Ruby met John and the guys in the foyer. The tables displayed red and white poinsettias, cake, and punch.

"The choir was fantastic, Ruby," said John handing her a glass of red punch.

Ruby wiped perspiration from her forehead. "Thanks, John. My throat is so dry. This punch tastes great," she added emptying the glass. "Oh here come my neighbors I've told you about."

She introduced them and they shook hands.

"We've heard a lot about you Mr. Carlson. Did you fly your plane here from New York?" asked Chris interested in his means of transportation.

"Yes, as a matter of fact. It sure beats sitting on Interstate 95 for hours waiting for the bottleneck to clear. Have you ever been stuck in traffic there at rush hour?" he asked raising his eyebrows and smiling.

"Yeah, I know what you mean. It's a total nightmare. If I knew how to fly and had a plane, I'd do the same thing," said Chris shaking his head and reaching for a piece of cake.

"So Ruby, where's Sarah?" asked Doc patting her on the shoulder changing the subject.

"She wanted to spend the night with Amanda. She's having a better time there."

"I agree with her decision. It's a long piece of music to sit through for a young lady," Doc commented looking serious.

"Doc almost made us miss the first part though," complained Chris. "I don't like being late."

"I was detained at work because I couldn't get anyone to cover my rounds at the hospital and then we had an emergency," Doc said apologetically.

"I know that was frustrating. I'm glad things worked out so you could enjoy most of it," said Ruby.

"Your choir was excellent. I'll have to come back again next year. Who were the two gorgeous soloists?" asked Doc looking in their direction.

"Which one are you interested in, Doc," Ruby wanted to know.

"Whichever one is available," he said. "Actually, I'll take the brunette and Chris can have the blond soprano."

Doc glanced at his watch. "Well, I hate to rush off but I have to be back in the O.R. in the wee hours of the morning. John, it was a pleasure meeting you. Come by and see us sometime," said Doc sincerely, shaking his hand.

"Yes, take care with your trip back to New York tonight," said Chris. "You are going back tonight, aren't you?" he pressed John further, trying to find out how serious the relationship was.

"Yes, as a matter of fact, I do have to leave. Nice to meet you gentlemen," he said waving goodbye. When they left he smiled and looked into Ruby's eyes. "If I didn't know better, I'd say that young fella has a crush on you!"

CHAPTER 17

Ruby escorted Chris to his Christmas party at the bank. She enjoyed the celebration that included dinner and dancing. Ruby met a few of his close colleagues and their wives. She adored Chris. Six years stood between their ages and she loved him as a younger brother. He was fun to tease. But she knew the gang thought maybe it was more than friendship.

Ruby wore the black dress John Carlson mailed to her after the concert. In his note, he wrote that it was a small present and that she could wear it on the night of her show in New York. Ruby was grateful for John's gifts, especially since living paycheck to paycheck didn't allow her to be extravagant. She was only able to make ends meet because of the extra money that consistently appeared each month in her account. It continued to be a mystery where the cash originated.

Ruby was pleased having a party to attend but she longed to see Matt again. No matter where she went or who she was with, something always triggered a memory, whether it was the sounds of an airplane, an Elton John song, Chinese food, typing at her desk at work, James Bond movies, or whatever. Ruby tried to divert her thoughts on her art show.

She knew he would be proud of her. She needed to forget him. But deep inside, she couldn't.

Diane invited Ruby to see the Rockettes and their play, which was showing two days before Christmas. She had hired a babysitter to watch the girls. Ruby was thrilled. She decided to keep the art show a secret until she heard from John. He had flown to Wrightsville Beach to collect her work and returned to New York.

The highway became a little congested when they reached the New Jersey Turnpike, but other than that they made good time. Ruby phoned Diane when she reached a convenience store near the apartment. Diane met the girls and Ruby followed her to their high rise. Diane obtained a guest pass from the attendant that greeted them at the front gate. They parked the cars and filled their arms with luggage to the elevator. Paul returned several times to retrieve the remaining items.

The couple lived in a small two bedroom apartment on the fifth floor. It was tastefully decorated with modern furniture and mostly black and white decor. There was a small baby grand piano in the corner and a life-size black and white poster of Paul and Diane on their wedding day enclosed in a plain, gold frame.

A black dining room table and chairs fit nicely next to the open kitchen space. Pots and pans hung from ceiling hooks and colorful ceramic tiles graced the kitchen walls.

The master bedroom had a king-size water bed covered with apricot and sea foam green. The stained green furniture matched the wallpaper and bedspread. The floor length curtains were a solid peach.

Lilly's room was pink and purple. She had her name painted in wooden letters on the door as you entered her room. The walls were light lavender and pink ballet slippers had been stenciled around the top of the walls. Pink lace curtains hung from a tiny window. She had her own child-sized vanity with perfume bottles, play makeup, a jewelry box, and a brush adorning the glass top. Her Barbie House occupied one corner of the room and her stuffed animals were sleeping on shelves in the other. Ruby was to sleep in Lilly's bed and the girls were to sleep in sleeping bags on the floor.

The apartment was located on East 52nd Street near most of the Broadway Theatres. The show, "My Fair Lady" had been a hit for many years. Paul continued with his successful Professor Higgins role, as critiqued by all the New York critics, and Diane appeared in the horse race and street scenes part-time because of her new role as mother.

The sisters caught up on family gossip before retiring to bed.

Diane had invited a friend of theirs to sit with Ruby during the performances. Robert Williams was from Chicago and visiting New York for the holidays. He was tall with dark hair and eyes. He looked extremely handsome in his black suit. He worked at a night club in Chicago and was hoping to start a new club of his own. He wanted to see as many clubs as he could while in New York and to analyze what people wanted in an establishment. He informed Ruby he was staying until New Year's Day and asked if they could go somewhere to celebrate the New Year with Paul and Diane. Ruby agreed.

Ruby wore a green evening gown her mother had purchased for her as an early Christmas present. It revealed her slender figure. She borrowed a pair of pearls from Diane, similar to the ones Matt had given her.

'My Fair Lady' was spectacular and Ruby felt honored, knowing the stars personally. The cast received a standing ovation, which Ruby was sure was a common occurrence judging from their performance.

"You were fabulous, Paul," Ruby said congratulating him backstage after the show.

"Did you enjoy my English accent?" he said smiling wiping the sweat off of his brow with a handkerchief.

"It was amazing how you imitate the Brits so well. Where's Diane? Is she changing?" Ruby inquired looking around for her.

"Yes, you can go back there, if you dare," he laughed pointing to a door. "Beware of naked bodies!"

She opened the door and went inside. It was full of fast talking ladies from the cast undressing and redressing back into their street clothes. It was a chaotic scene. She'd never seen anyone change as fast as they did. They didn't even acknowledge her presence, as she walked past them. Finally, she spotted Diane.

"Wow, you were great and your husband is so perfect for Henry Higgins. I love his voice," Ruby exclaimed expressing her enthusiasm. "Do you need any help?"

"Can you hang these clothes up and put them on that rack?" she asked unzipping her dress and stepping out of it. Ruby grabbed a hanger and hung up her dress. Diane put on the sequenced red dress she had worn from home. She slipped on her red heels to match. She looked in the mirror and brushed her blond hair before adding a dab of red lipstick. "Let's find the boys and go. I'm starving."

Their dates were waiting by the lobby door. "Are we listening to jazz tonight, Paul?" questioned Diane.

"Yeah, let's go to the Blue Note. Robert wants to check out the club anyway," said Paul.

"Do you know who's playing tonight?" asked Robert.

"No, but whoever it is, I'm sure they're good," answered Paul confidently.

Inside the Blue Note Jazz Club they could hear a woman singing 'Summertime'. It was smoky and dark making it difficult to see empty tables. Finally, Paul discovered one in the back of the crowded room. They ordered champagne to celebrate. Another waitress came over and took their food orders.

It was hard to see the band members, but the female singer wore a blue sequenced dress that sparkled with the lights. The third waitress returned quickly with four flutes and a champagne bottle. New Yorkers definitely did things faster than the old south Ruby thought.

The lights on stage turned to blue and the singer started to sing, 'I Will Always Love You'.

"Want to dance, Ruby?" asked Robert standing up and offering his hand.

"Sure," she answered taking another sip of her champagne. She set the glass down and followed him to the dance floor. It was quite crowded, but they managed to find an opening in front of the stage. The black singer's voice was powerful and convincing as she sang the words. Suddenly, the saxophone player stepped into the spotlight and played his solo. Ruby couldn't believe her eyes. It was Matt. She was so shocked she almost fell over Robert's feet. *Why is he here? Doe he see me?* Robert circled her around again and Matt's eyes met Ruby's. He finished playing his part and stepped back out of the lights. Ruby tried to find his eyes again in the shadows, but she couldn't. She was convinced he could see her. What would he think, about her dancing with another man?

When the song was over, the jazz group announced they were taking a break. Ruby thanked Robert for the dance and excused herself to use the ladies' room. She detoured towards the stage, but Matt was no where to be seen. Ruby asked a member of the jazz group if they knew where Matt went. They said she must be mistaken. There was no one in their band by that name.

Ruby knew it was him. Maybe he went out to get some fresh air. She stepped outside holding her arms because it was below freezing and she was cold. She looked around the street and didn't see him. She sauntered back into the club and found the bathroom. When Ruby came out she felt a hand grab hers. He pulled her behind an artificial tree where it was dark and kissed her. It was as if time stood still while they held each other for those brief minutes.

"Ruby, I can't believe you're in New York! I can't talk to you or explain why I'm here, but you have to pretend like you don't know who I am," he said softly with a worried sound in his voice. "Your life could be in danger if you don't ignore me," he added looking through the branches.

"Matt, why are you acting so strange?" Ruby whispered looking up, trying to see his eyes. It was too dark to see what she longed for. But she could feel his breath close, as he brushed his lips to hers. "Do you really want me to forget you? I tried to find you after Troy took me to

California but you disappeared," she admitted as a tear fell down her cheek. "I don't want to lose you ever again, Matt. I'm still in love with you."

"And I love you, Ruby," he answered kissing her again. "Did you know, Ruby, I think about you every day? I know a lot about you, more than you're aware, but I have to say you surprised me tonight," he added holding her close. "I've been keeping up with where you live, what classes you're taking, what perfume you wear, and what men are interested in you, your art show in January. I know almost everything!" he said convincingly squeezing her hand. "But that's my job. It's the kind of work I'm involved in now. I don't have a life of my own, at least not for a while." He wiped the tears from Ruby's cheek with his fingers.

"What are you talking about, Matt? You're making me scared for you. What exactly is your job?" Ruby inquired.

"I'm here with another woman, Ruby, and I can't risk running into you right now. The gig is part of my cover. Please try to understand. If I complete this mission tonight, I leave tomorrow to be with dad and my brothers for Christmas. I wish you could come with me," he whispered in her ear. "I stay away from you because I don't want anything to happen to you or Sarah. I can't talk to you anymore, right now. They'll start to notice that I've been gone too long." He kissed her for the last time and said, "You'll have to trust me. Remember, 'I Will always Love You'." He lifted the tree branch for her to leave. He squeezed her hand before letting go. He dropped a circular object in it. "I've been carrying this for a long time hoping to see you soon. I'll find you again, I promise. Merry Christmas, Ruby." He left the club a few minutes later with a tall blond with way too much makeup on.

Ruby retraced her steps back to the bathroom and opened her hand. She held a beautiful gold and silver ring with a ruby. It crossed like a bow and displayed a string of small diamonds. She placed the ring on her left finger. She would never replace it. She splashed her eyes with cold water to disguise their puffiness. She was thankful for the smoky, dark room.

Ruby returned to the table as dinner was being served.

"And where have you been, big sis?" asked Diane pouring more champagne into her glass.

"You wouldn't believe it if I told you, but I just ran into an old friend. I was catching up on the gossip. Did you miss me?" she said reaching for her champagne and taking several big swallows.

"Well, it's a small world, isn't it?" said Robert. "I hope you will honor me with another dance after dinner," he remarked smiling.

"But, of course," Ruby said lifting her napkin into her lap. "Bon Appetite, everyone."

She had lost her appetite. She couldn't concentrate on anything but Matt. He said he still loved her. *But what was he talking about? Working undercover? Was he just saying that to 'cover up' his real date and his James Bond image? What did he mean that he knew all about me? The art show? Was he spying on me?* Was he ever close enough to her but disguised so Ruby wouldn't recognize him? She knew she would see him again. Ruby had the ruby ring to prove it.

For Matt's safety, Ruby had to act like nothing was bothering her. She was among actors so why not join the crowd? Robert, Diane, Paul, and Ruby danced until two in the morning and had a good time. The singer continued to belt out the blues, but Matt was no longer playing the saxophone. He had been replaced by a tall, bearded man.

The 1990 New Year's celebration in New York was spectacular with the excitement of the crowd at Times Square. Dick Clark hosted the live show. Robert was her date for the event. He asked to see her again and told her flying to Wrightsville Beach wasn't a problem. Ruby politely told him she wanted to remain friends. He reluctantly agreed. For the remainder of the evening, Ruby's mind was on Matt again. She hoped he was in Maui with only his dad and family. She prayed there wasn't a blond lying next to him on the beach wearing 'way too much makeup.'

The art show was a grand affair. John had personally overseen every minute detail including the champagne, flowers, and pianist. Ruby was amazed how the special lighting brought her pictures to life on the gallery walls. Seeing her photograph and biography printed on brochures forced her to realize the reality of it all.

Ruby humbly welcomed the visitors in her black gown. She wasn't used to the attention she received, especially by photographers and news reporters. John remained by her side supporting the confidence she lacked with the social elite's cliques from New York. He had explained to her that first impressions were crucial in the art world. If they accepted the artist, the art would follow.

Diane and Paul were proud of her accomplishments even though they had given her a hard time about her secrecy. They also received publicity because of their family connections with Ruby.

Ruby listened to comments about her pictures while walking around the gallery. As an artist, she had to be open to criticism and not take it personally. But because the art was an expression of her creativity, she had difficulty with the negative responses.

"Your work is lovely, dear."

"She has a primitive style, similar to my six year old."

"Ruby expresses her subjects with personalities. The colors schemes make her work unique."

"I don't care for folk art, I never have. But the champagne's good."

Ruby admired the ring Matt had given her. She focused on the red stone as it glimmered in the light. She graciously thanked the guests continuing to mingle in the crowded room. The champagne helped to ease her nervousness. Little did she know she was innocently becoming a celebrity.

CHAPTER 18

Chris was washing his car when Ruby drove up from New York. She parked it and helped Sarah unbuckle her seat belt. He motioned for them to come over. "How are my girls?" asked Chris showing his affection.

"We're tired but great. We had a wonderful trip."

"I signed for this last week and threw it in the back seat of my car. I almost forgot it was there until I saw Sarah waving to me," he explained. "It seems to me that you have to leave town at Christmas, Ruby, to get a package," he teased. "Luckily for you, I happen to be around."

"Yes, that's true."

"Oh boy, a present," Sarah exclaimed.

"Open it and let's see what you got!" he grinned raising an eyebrow. "There's no return address. Don't you find that odd?" whispered Chris in her ear. "Another secret admirer?"

"A dress, mom!" she shouted with excitement. "It's blue, my favorite color. Who's it from?" she asked looking at Chris, but he shrugged his shoulders.

"I think Santa must've mailed it here while we were in New York, Sarah!" Ruby replied looking up into the sky and thinking about the obvious sender. She looked at the label and noticed the dress size was perfect. *How did he know?*

"Sarah, I have a present for you too. It's from all the guys. Come into the house and, I'll get it for you," said Chris leading her to his front door by the hand.

She had learned the art of tearing the paper as fast as she could and leaving it on the floor. Ruby collected the trash and threw it into the can under the sink.

She gave him a big hug. "Thanks, Chris."

"They're by a lady named Beatrix Potter. I always liked her stories when I was growing up. Did you know she painted her own pictures, Sarah?" said Chris browsing through the book. "See Peter Rabbit?" he said pointing to a page.

Sarah was interested in learning the tale about Peter. Now that she was seven she could read some of the words with help. "Chris, can I read to you?" she asked. He reached for a small, white plastic bag hanging on the closet doorknob and handed it to Ruby. "Here's the rest of your mail. Do you want to stay here and open it, while I read with your daughter?" he asked when she sat down next to him on his couch. He began with the first story.

"Is it safe to use your bathroom?" Ruby teased looking through the doorway observing his clothes thrown all over the bedroom. "You really should fire your housekeeper. She does a lousy job," Rudy said as she shook her head trying to step on the carpet to the toilet.

"I know. The help you get now a days!" he retorted, before continuing with his reading.

Ruby sat in the rocking chair and began sorting her mail. A few Christmas cards were mixed in with the monthly bills. She needed to check her bank statement. She was shocked to see her balance. Five hundred dollars had been deposited the day after she saw Matt in New York. *He has to be tampering with my account. The presents at Christmas! What else is he doing?*

Ruby opened a card from Troy's mother. She wrote to inform Ruby about her son's marriage on Christmas Day. Ruby opened her mouth in disbelief. Mrs. Slader explained that he was hired by a corporate law firm and was living in Carmel. His new wife, Barbara, was expecting a baby in March. Troy's mom revealed the fact that Barbara had been Troy's secretary at his previous law job. She said they were planning to visit sometime over the Easter holidays, after the baby was born.

Ruby waited patiently for Chris to finish reading before quietly telling him the good news about Troy. "Glad to hear it. Maybe he'll leave you alone for good. You don't need any more hassles like that!" he expressed sincerely putting an arm around her.

"So what did Santa bring you?" Ruby asked Chris while looking around for any recent purchases.

"I got some cheap flip flops for the beach, a brief case, and a coffee mug from a local artist," he said showing her his gifts.

"Oh, I almost forgot. I have a present for you too. Can you wait for one minute? I'll run next door to get it." Ruby turned up the heat once she entered the upstairs entrance. It was extremely cold as she shivered, seeing her breath.

"Here," she said slightly winded. "Gosh, my apartment is freezing. I just turned up the thermostat. I should have done that before coming over here," she remarked rubbing her hands together.

He handed Sarah the gift and asked for her assistance. She started tearing the paper. He turned the book over and read the title: *One hundred Ways to Make Successful Chili.*

He raised his eyebrow and scoured like he had done at the contest. "I'll have you know, you wasted your money on this book. My recipe will win next time. Mark my words." He froze with his finger still pointing upward towards the sky.

"The tin man in *The Wizard of Oz* posed like that once and look where it got him!" Ruby remarked pretending to use an oil can to lubricate his frozen arm.

"Just because yours came in first place, doesn't mean it will happen again!"

Ruby didn't want to burst his bubble, but since she had already won first place, she didn't think she'd push her luck. Besides, he was set on winning. She only hoped he would try one of the new recipes from the cookbook. Anything had to be an improvement from the gray mystery meat!

John phoned Ruby to share his enthusiasm about her sold out show. With her permission, he wanted to coordinate another one during the summer months. He announced that he would be sending her a check. He mentioned the fact that she was beginning to earn world recognition for her art and that her photograph had been selected to be on the cover of 'New Artist'. He encouraged her to think about quitting her job. It would allow her more time to devote to her painting. Ruby couldn't believe what was happening to her.

It was a few days later that Ruby developed a fever. She didn't have the energy she needed. Dr. Johnson ran some tests and felt her swollen glands. Ruby felt awful. Sarah was a sweet nurse. She would quietly tiptoe into the room and stand over her mom's head to check on her. Ruby could feel her breath on her cheeks. Sarah would remove Ruby's damp washcloth and wet it with cold water. She carefully folded it and put it across her forehead saying, "How's that mommy?"

Ruby's pillow had accumulated several big wet spots from the excess water.

Chris made her chicken soup and offered to buy groceries. Ruby gave him a list, and he took Sarah along for the ride. The doctor called while they were gone and announced she had mononucleosis. She was ordered to stay in bed for at least two weeks and maybe even longer. With the substantial check she had received for her art, Ruby requested and was granted a leave of absence.

It wasn't until the middle of March that Ruby's illness finally came to an end. Her parents drove south from Raleigh to retrieve Sarah for the week, allowing Ruby time to get caught up on her school assignments. She had a history test the next night, and she needed to memorize dates and facts.

When the exam was over, she left the classroom thinking that she probably had a B.

It was late when she parked her car in front of her house. She showered and prepared for bed. She was pulling the covers down when she heard a light tap on the door. Ruby thought it must be Chris or Doc. She raised the blinds and cupped her hands to see outside. There was a figure, but she couldn't see him clearly. He stepped back so that the porch light revealed his identity. He was wearing a red plaid shirt, jeans, and a baseball cap. Her heart almost stopped. She froze with disbelief. He whispered her name.

He smiled when she opened the door and handed her a red rose. "This is for your belated birthday. I should have wired it, but I wanted to deliver it to you in person," he said touching her cheek with the back of his hand. "I know it's late, but I just got into town. I've been worried about you. I had to make sure you were all right. I heard you were sick. Are you better?" he inquired.

Ruby pulled him inside, "Shut up and kiss me," she whispered. When they finally let go of one another she said, "Seems like I'll do anything to get your attention! We need to have a serious talk."

Matt removed his hat and put it over her Maui hat, hanging in the hallway. "Nice hat, Ruby," he said pleased to see it there.

"How did you know I was ill? Is that why you're here?" she inquired still shocked.

Ruby directed him to the couch and they sat down facing each other. "I heard from one of my colleagues that you were sick. I'm sure you've figured out who I've been working for. You know our main training base is in Virginia," Ruby nodded as he continued.

"The CIA has kept me in Europe for the past six weeks and I couldn't see you until now. As I explained before, I can't reveal anymore information about what I do. I'm just trying to be the good Boy Scout and catch the bad guys." Ruby listened attentively. "Ruby, sometimes I miss working on the Hill for the Senator with the busy workload and meetings. But this life is totally demanding and challenging in a different way. I've had extensive training, both mentally and physically, learning new languages along the way. When I took this position, I thought you were out of my life, but since our meeting at the Blue Note in New York, I've had a hard time focusing on my job. I think about you constantly. But, Ruby, I can't afford not to stay focused. Not only am I putting myself in danger, but my colleagues, as well," he confessed.

"Matt, I guessed about the CIA, but now you've confirmed it. I know you risk your life for others and I admire that quality in you. But what does it all mean for us? Why are you here?" Ruby asked.

"Ruby, I need to hear the truth about the move to California. I felt helpless when Troy had you quit work and moved you and Sarah within the week of our wonderful evening at the inaugural ball," he hesitated and then said, "I think I already know, but I need to hear it from you."

"Yes, he was waiting for me when I went upstairs that night. I didn't want to wake the girls, so I entered the room in the dark," she spoke softly remembering the terrible night. Matt squeezed her hand. "I must have blacked out because I barely remember hearing that smack on my face and then waking up the next day." Several tears began to trickle down her face. Matt reached for a tissue and dotted her eyes.

"Troy beat me up pretty badly. He couldn't risk having everyone at work see what a battered wife I was," she continued softly. She explained the rest of the night, week, and traveling to California. "I wanted to call you, to tell you about everything, but I was too fearful. I wasn't only afraid for myself, but for Sarah and you. I will always be nervous and afraid of him." She proceeded to tell him about the incident in the apartment and Chris helping her with Sarah.

"It sounds like you have a real friend. I'm glad you have someone looking out for the two of you," he remarked pulling her towards his shoulder. Ruby rested her head against his muscular body.

"When I returned from New York, I received a letter from Troy's mom telling me that he had married again. He and his wife are expecting a child sometime this month. I'm relieved that I won't have to worry about his unpredictable hard hits anymore," Ruby said with tears swelling up in her eyes. "I fear for the new wife. She doesn't know what she's in for."

"Ruby, I'm sorry he's such a bastard. I wish I'd known the truth, but it can't be changed now. If he ever puts a hand on you again," Matt stopped there. He didn't finish his sentence. But she could imagine what he was thinking.

"It's OK, Matt. I needed to get it out. I've wanted to tell you about it for such a long time. I feel like such a great weight has been lifted off of my shoulders."

He bent down and kissed her. "What are your plans for the weekend?"

"It depends on where we're going," she smiled and put her arms around him.

"That's a surprise. You'll have to wait," he said laughing.

"I don't know if I can wait that long, Mr. Bond."

Matt suddenly became serious. "You know what I want, Ruby," he whispered kissing her again on the lips. "What do you want?"

Ruby didn't say a word. She slowly reached for the buttons on his shirt. He lifted her up in his arms and carried her to the bedroom. The room was dark except for moonlight peeking through the white sheers. She could feel his hardness against her body. Their hearts became intertwined, as the passions of their minds and bodies became one. Ruby was his and Matt was hers.

CHAPTER 19

Ruby was sipping a glass of wine and listening to John Denver sing 'This Old Guitar' when the phone rang.

"This is your date for the weekend. I'm one block from your house. Are you ready?"

"Yes, but I didn't know what to pack. It's hard to decide since you won't tell me where we're going."

"Why don't you leave your bag? Maybe we can stop back by here later," he replied. "I'll be there in about thirty seconds."

She barely hung up the phone when she heard a tap on the door. Matt was waiting in a black suit holding a red rose in his hand. She smiled and noticed he had on the airplane tie she had given him. Without saying a word he touched her nose with the delicate flower as she breathed in the sweet aroma. Gently he moved the pedals over her lips before kissing them.

"You look beautiful. I've waited such a long time to hold you in my arms again. Maybe we should stay here and forget about going anywhere," he whispered pointing to the bedroom.

"Say, I thought we were going out. Did you just want me to dress up for you so you could undo what took me days to prepare?" she joked.

He reached for her hand and said, "Actually I want to take you somewhere special. I want to cherish the small amount of time we have together. We have many sights to see before Sunday." He hooked his arm in hers and said, "Charles is waiting to take us anywhere we want to go."

"Who's Charles?" Ruby asked noticing the black limo parked across the street. "Oh! Is this really ours?" she asked anxious to ride in it.

"How else can I make-out with my girlfriend in the back seat?"

"How many have you had in the back seat lately?" she questioned him with a frown.

"I can't remember."

"It's a good thing I like you a little," she remarked to his loss of memory. "Nice tie," she added giving it a tug before the chauffeur opened the back door for them. She'd never been inside a limo. The couple snuggled close together as Matt instructed the driver to head towards the beach.

"Would you like some champagne?" asked Matt reaching for two chilled glasses in the ice box.

"Yes, please." Ruby felt the soft leather seats with her fingers. "Matt, I can't believe how much room is in a limo. And I can't believe it has a refrigerator with chilled champagne and glasses."

"I knew you'd be impressed," he replied pleased with his choice of transportation.

"I can see, you haven't changed a bit, Mr. Bond," she replied accepting the cold flute. "Always trying to get a girl drunk before taking advantage of her."

"To my girl," said Matt raising his glass to toast her. "The Love of my Life!" He lifted her hand to admire the ruby on her finger.

Ruby linked her arm with his. "Where are we going anyway?"

"I knew we wouldn't have time to drive or fly to Hatteras or Maui, for that matter," he grinned, "so I opted for the closest place. I've made reservations for dinner and a room facing the oceanfront at the Cavalier, knowing how much we both like the ocean. I don't get to see it much with the smoke-filled dingy joints I usually have to hang out in," he added looking into her eyes. "You're the most important person in my life, and I don't want to mess things up more than I already have," he explained.

"What do you mean, mess things up, Matt?"

"I'm talking about my current employment. When you left for California, I didn't think I'd see you again. Now I'm locked into this secretive government position for the next eight to ten years. I've been trained to speak other languages, understand different cultures, locate and destroy terrorists, and blend into any society. I can't go into any other details. I've already told you too much," he said taking a sip of champagne. "But I wanted you to know why I can't contact you often and be with you. I can only tell you that I've become the nickname on my plane," he said. "Martini, shaken, not stirred."

"What made you decide to take it, Matt?" Ruby wanted to know. "I thought you were going to work in Jackson Hole as a forest ranger or with the rescue unit. What happened to that Boy Scout?"

"When I was considering Wyoming, I was thinking about my future with you. But when you left, my interest changed. I only had me to think of," he explained. "Since then I have to admit, I like my work and I guess you could say I'm responsible for rescue missions of a different kind, internationally. You don't know how hard it was for me the night I saw you at the Blue Note to let go of your hand. I was afraid for your safety. Those people are killers. It's The Real McCoy," he said lifting her hand and kissing the ring he had given her. "Do you like the ring?" he asked changing the subject.

"Yes, of course. I can't believe you had it with you that night in New York."

"I bought it in Germany last fall."

"You were in Germany? Where else have you been in the last year?"

"I've traveled to many countries in Europe, Africa, and Russia. I'll be going to the Middle East and/or South America sometime this year and possibly living there for a while," he replied staring out of the window lost in thought.

"I have different alibis and disguises, Ruby," he continued seriously. "If we meet, you have to act like you don't know me unless I tell you otherwise." He took a sip of champagne and added, "I know this is awkward for you. I never would've put you in this position, had I known we'd find each other again, but it must be fate. I understand if this situation is too difficult for you to deal with right now. You have your own life with your art and finishing school. You also have Sarah to think of. I thought perhaps it would be wise for me not to see her, but you know I would love to."

"She remembered you for a long time but I'm not sure anymore. You're a sweetheart for sending her books and the blue dress at Christmas." Ruby squeezed his hand. "I don't think you'd recognize her now. She has grown quite tall, and her hair is all the way down to her waist."

"I've seen her from a distance," he admitted refilling our glasses. "I also know you've been out with several guys? Do you like any of them?" he asked curious about her feelings with his long absence.

"If I did, would I be here now?" she leaned over and kissed him. "And now I have a question for you. Who was that blond you were with?"

"She was involved in a drug smuggling operation. I can't tell you anymore, but we were able to catch many criminals that night and lock them away. The sad part is for how long? Money talks and eventually, if they have the right connections, they get out sooner or later."

Just then their limo pulled up in front of the Cavalier. The chauffeur walked around and opened the door for them. "Thanks, Charles. Goodnight. We'll see you in the morning. Around ten?" said Matt confirming their ride in the morning.

"Yes sir. Goodnight, Mr. Connery, Miss. Enjoy your evening," said Charles closing the doors and then driving away.

They entered the main lobby and Matt asked her to meet him on the top floor at the Shogun Restaurant while he took their coats up to their room. She knew he probably had to check in with 'Q' or 'M', so Ruby didn't ask any questions. She used the ladies' room to apply lipstick and brushed her hair. Matt was waiting for her in the foyer.

"Right this way, Mr. Connery," said the attractive hostess. She was dressed in a white kimono with her hair twisted into a knot.

The room was decorated with flowers and white candles. A jazz band played in the corner. The members were dressed in white tuxes with red and white bowties. The female singer had a short, red sequined dress and red high heels.

Matt had reserved a window seat where they could see the ocean below. The waves were beating the shoreline creating white foam as it churned the sand and shells. Ruby longed for summer and the feeling of salt water splashing against her legs.

Matt ordered an Italian white wine when the waitress came over to take their beverage orders.

"It's been a long time since we had a meal together. Do you remember those great fish dinners?" he reminded her making his eyebrows go up and down.

"I'll never forget your cabin in Asheville. How did you know I'd go back there looking for you?"

"I didn't. I guess it was just an act of desperation and hope I suppose. It was a last minute thing before I drove away. I truly thought some younger boys would find the note and tear it up. I'm glad you called the realtor. It was great to hear your voice," he grinned remembering his disguised voice. "That's how I learned your address and, of course, I had your unlisted phone number. But I would've had it in a matter of time, anyway. You've known me long enough to know I'm good at what I do." Ruby smiled at his arrogance.

"The realtor's phone number was really yours? Did you ever sell your place?" Ruby asked sadly.

"Yes, a single mother bought it the week after you left your message. She has a young daughter too, I believe," he added thinking about the sale.

"Do you miss it?"

"Yeah, but I'll invest in something else later."

"OK, truthfully Matt, tell me, why have you been putting money into my bank account? Don't deny it."

The waitress uncorked the wine and poured a small amount for Matt to taste. He nodded, and she poured each of them a glass.

"I love you," he added toasting Ruby for the second time that night. He reached for her hand and kissed it.

"I love you, too. But you still haven't answered my question," she continued. "How did you know that I needed money? It always seems to show up at the right time."

"I'm glad you were able to use it. I can't think of anyone else I'd rather give it to. I make more than I'll ever spend in a lifetime," he said smiling.

"I see, Matt. You never were a good liar. I'm sure you have your sources."

"I plan on continuing to be of assistance in the future, if that's OK with you. I lost you once. I'm not taking any more chances. I can't do anything about my work assignments, but I can control how I spend my dough."

The waitress came over and took their dinner orders. When she left, Matt asked Ruby to dance.

Matt held her tightly and guided her all over the dance floor. He smelled wonderful. His fingers sifted through her hair. She could feel the muscles of his body respond to her movements.

"You mentioned earlier that you took dance lessons and learned about other cultures and languages. Exactly how many languages can you speak?"

"Currently I speak five and am working on a sixth. Luckily I have an ear for them and am told that I sound like a native when I talk," he said mumbling French words in her ear. He circled Ruby around the dance floor.

"What dances are you learning?" Ruby giggled enjoying the romantic foreign languages he kept switching, as they glided over the tiles.

"Presently, I'm learning Latino dances, which actually I signed up, just for fun. You know how much I love music. The Tango is such a romantic dance, don't you think? You'll have to take lessons so we can show off together," he replied in Spanish and then translated it for her.

He suddenly dipped Ruby and she came up laughing. "You better not be wasting those words on that blond," Ruby said with a touch of jealousy in her voice.

Back at the table, Ruby asked, "Where do you live, Matt? Can I at least know a phone number or some place where I can reach you?"

"I live all over the world, Ruby. I don't really have a life of my own any more, as I've explained. The only normal thing in my life right now is Maui with my family. The rest of the year is not mine to give," he added sadly. "There's a whole big world out there. You'll see it one day, with or without me."

They ate their dinner in silence listening to the band play a few Duke Ellington tunes.

He whispered, "I still have a surprise for you but you have to wait until later."

Matt excused himself to play with the band. The piano player knew Matt when he worked on the Hill. They had performed together at one of the local jazz clubs. He motioned Matt to join them. Ruby twirled the red stoned ring around her finger, while he made love to her through the music in his saxophone.

"Time to get up. We have things to do, places to see. Would you like to take a shower with me first?" he asked kissing her forehead.

"What time is it?" she said snuggling into his arms. Before he could answer she kept her eyes shut and whispered, "I loved sleeping in your arms last night. I don't want to let go of you, for fear I'll wake up and you'll be gone," She squinted trying to focus on the room. The sun's rays were welcoming the morning as it rose over the Atlantic Ocean.

"It's only 8:00, but I told Charles to meet us at 10. We need to shower and eat breakfast," he said squeezing her.

"Where are we going? I don't even have my makeup here. I accidentally left it on my sink at home," she said suddenly horrified, thinking about having to face the public without her beauty mask.

"I just happen to have a bag here with a few items you may find appealing for such an outing as today. Not only do I have clothes, shoes, and socks, but makeup for my girl," he said climbing out of bed and reaching into the closet. He pulled out a blue travel bag. He opened the closet wider to display a few new dresses and a coat that hung neatly on hangers. Several things were on the top shelf.

"My gosh, Matt, where did you get all those clothes?" Ruby asked, not believing the trouble he had gone through to pick out clothes for her, not to mention everything was the right size, she noted walking over to look at the labels. "Are you sure you haven't bugged my apartment? Or have you broken into it before?" she questioned him curiously. "I wouldn't put anything past you."

"I figured you wore the same size you did two years ago. Remember when we went shopping together? Or did you forget?" he teased. "I hope the makeup is alright, though. That's not my best department," he smiled. "I personally don't think you need any. You're beautiful just as you are," Matt interjected looking at her stunned face. "Don't you like the clothes?" he asked timidly.

"Of course, Matt," Ruby said walking over to hug and kiss him. "I'm thrilled! Really, How did I ever get lucky enough to deserve a wonderful man like you?" she asked looking up at the ceiling as if God were there.

"Since you feel that way, maybe we should make love one more time before we shower!" he replied gently stroking her head and then the rest of her body. He sure was persuasive. But she wasn't exactly fighting him off either.

They showered and were drying each other off, when they heard a knock at the door. Matt quickly threw on his robe, closing the bathroom door behind him and answered it. He asked the waiter to leave their breakfast on the round table in front of the window. She could hear dishes and silverware being placed orderly. Ruby peaked out of a crack in the door to see Matt give him a few bills before he left.

"Hurry and dress. The eggs and the coffee are nice and hot," he said pouring two cups of coffee. Ruby could smell the rich aroma.

In the closet she found a tan pair of khaki pants and a white turtleneck sweater folded neatly on the top shelf. She discovered a navy blue button-up vest hanging between two dresses and slipped it on over her top.

She carried her coffee into the bathroom and began playing with her new makeup. The cream, mascara, and foundation were of the same brand and colors she always used. Matt did give her a new bright shade of lipstick and rouge. Ruby decided she liked it for a change. She braided her hair and tied it with a scrunchie.

"How about some breakfast?" he asked, taking the silver lids off of the eggs, bacon and toast dishes.

"I'm starving. I guess the morning activity has given me quite an appetite."

"I know what you mean. Here, have some fresh fruit," he said handing her the bowl. "Look at that ocean. Isn't it breathtaking? If it wasn't so cold outside, I'd open the door so we could hear the surf," he reflected, taking a sip of his coffee.

Matt was dressed in a blue and black plaid shirt and jeans. He looked incredibly handsome. He wore his wire rims.

Ruby didn't know how they did it, but they managed to meet Charles exactly at 10.

"Good Morning, folks. I trust you both slept well," said Charles opening the back doors for them.

"Yes, thank you, Charles. And I hope you did too. What a beautiful day! Could you take us to the airport, please?" Matt said. Then he winked, "And don't forget those other arrangements we talked about yesterday."

"You got it," replied Charles, tipping his hat.

"Just exactly where are we going now? What time are we coming back? Are we spending another night at the hotel?" Ruby inquired, peppering him with questions.

"Yes, we are going somewhere. We should be back around seven, and yes, we are spending another night if that is alright with you" he smiled remembering to answer them all.

The sun was bright and Ruby held her hand up to block the rays.

"You should have brought your blue sunglasses."

"How did you know that I've been wearing blue sunglasses?" Ruby asked, fearing her life was under a microscope. "Is my life an open book?" she said taking her hand and placing it on her heart. "Even if it is you, Bond, reading my book, a girl is entitled to some privacy," she said proudly holding up her nose and looking out the window.

"I told you, I have my sources. Actually, I had to come down near the beach area for some additional training last year, and I happened to see you a few times, from a distance," he replied casually looking at her shrugging his shoulders. "I needed to make sure you were OK."

"You beast," Ruby said feeling hurt. "Why didn't you come to see me?"

"Because you'd gotten on with your life, and I thought at the time, it was probably for the best. I was working and couldn't see you then, anyway. I wasn't going to tell you but you know I have to tell you the truth."

They arrived at the airport and Charles drove the limo to where the small planes and hangers were located. They thanked him, and Matt told him to pick them up at seven. They walked towards the last hanger facing the air traffic controller's tower. Matt's little yellow plane was parked inside. Ruby was happy to see it again.

"Hi, handsome," she said to it as if it was a long, lost friend. "How are you? You haven't been carrying any blonds around lately, have you?" she smiled saying it loud enough for Matt to hear.

"Good thing, he doesn't talk," said Matt.

The flight was as smooth as glass. Matt taught Ruby how to steer the plane and how the throttle worked. He explained the instrument panel and what each one meant. He said, "Flying is the easy part, it's the landing that's the hardest to master."

Ruby guessed they were going to Asheville. The plane lifted up over several mountains before she could see Matt's cabin. He flew around the lake then proceeded circling back to the airport. He lined up the plane to the landing strip while he slowly lost altitude. He explained the procedures for landing to Ruby. He made it seem easy, but she knew it wasn't. They floated down to the runway as if on a cloud. He parked on the yellow T and turned off the engine.

"I'm glad we're here because I need the bathroom. I'll be right back," Ruby said opening the door and stepping out. It felt good to straighten her legs. She clutched her purse and headed towards the store. She noticed Matt's jeep was parked by the fence.

"Ready to go?" he asked.

"Go? Where?"

"To the cabin. The jeep is heating up. It's a little chilly out here in the mountains today, even though the sun is out," he said pointing up to the sky. "I already threw my bag in the back."

"What cabin? I thought you sold it," Ruby said. "Did you buy another one?"

"Nope," he said winking at her. "I wanted to surprise you. Let's hurry and get there so we can get the fireplace going," he said holding her hand.

The house looked snug and happy surrounded by the pine and evergreen trees. The furniture had neatly been replaced on the porch. Ruby noticed curtains hanging in the window and the 'For Sale' sign was gone. The wooden letters spelling 'Connelly' were still sitting proudly on top of the mailbox. He parked the car and turned off the ignition. He walked around to open the door for her. He reached in the back seat for his bag. He had a grin on his face.

"I can't believe it!" Ruby exclaimed looking at the cabin.

They walked up to the front door holding hands. He took out his key and turned the lock. He opened the door. He put his bag on the porch and reached over to pick her up. "Can I do this one more time?"

"O.K., Bond, but if you get in the habit now, I'll expect it all the time," Ruby replied lifting her arms around him. He carried her over the threshold and kissed her. He walked across the room, carefully putting her in the rocking chair by the fireplace. The room was a little cold, but not as cold as she'd expected. It was obvious that someone had been here recently to turn on the heat. *Was it Matt?* He handed Ruby a quilt from the couch. Glancing around the room, it looked immaculate. Everything was the same. He took a box of matches off of the mantle and struck one. He lit the pre-stacked logs that had been placed, Ruby assumed, by him.

Matt put a jazz tape in the machine and pressed play. She listened to the soft music.

"Champagne?" he asked opening the refrigerator and retrieving the bottle.

"Yeah, that sounds wonderful. Thanks, Matt," Ruby replied looking into the fireplace and watching the fire starting to grow.

"Are you glad about the cabin, Ruby?" he asked cheerfully?

"Of course, I am. But I thought you sold it. Where's the lady that owns it?"

"I'm looking at her." Ruby looked shocked. "Matt what are you saying?"

"I didn't buy it only for me, silly" he said leaning over to kiss her

"Do you mind telling me what's going on, Matt? You drive a woman mad, you know? You disappear from the earth, sell your house and townhouse, know everything about me, and put money into my account. Then you send me and my daughter presents and beautiful flowers. Now you're buying me clothes that happen to fit me to a tee. I don't know how to get in touch with you, and you show up playing a saxophone and leave with a blond in New York City," Ruby said summing up his. She shook her head trying to understand the man she was in love with. "Now you tell me I own this cabin?"

"I brought you here because I want you. I always have," he said sincerely putting her hand in his. "I want you to be my wife. I don't expect you to say "yes" right away. I have no right to ask you to wait for me, especially with my foreign orders just days away. I've already told you too much about my job. I can't put you and Sarah in danger and that is why I choose not to discuss my work any further."

He reached under the couch and gave her a small wrapped present. "I want you to have this. I was planning to give it to you yesterday but I wanted to ask you here," he said softly.

Ruby opened the gift. The engagement ring was beautiful, so delicate and dainty. A simple gold band with a diamond held in a tiffany setting. She lifted it out of its velvet case. Matt removed the ruby and placed it on her right hand. "It was my mother's ring," he said softly. "I give this ring to you, so that you know the depth of my love for you. I want you to always have it. I can't think of anyone else that I'd rather have wearing it."

Tears welled up and began to spill down her cheeks. Matt gently wiped them with the thumbs of his hands. "Matt, I love you. I never thought I'd feel this way about another man until you came along. I'll wait for you as long as it takes," she whispered. "I'll treasure the time we can spend together." She held up her left hand for him. He placed the ring on her finger.

He took the glass out of her hand and set it on the table. He said, "Let's go upstairs and make love."

"Ruby, there's one more matter I want to discuss with you," said Matt when they came back down the stairs.'

"I don't know if I can take any more surprises, Matt."

"O.K. This is a legal one because you need to sign some papers."

"What kind of papers?"

"To make the cabin yours, I had to make it legit. It says on the 'Bill of Sale' that I sold you this place for one dollar. Is that a great deal or what?" he said raising his eyebrows smiling.

"Matt, why not keep it in both names? What are you thinking?" Ruby asked not understanding his reasoning.

"Let me explain. You're right about me not being able to visit as much as I'd like. That's where you come in. You and Sarah can come and go whenever you please. You can invite friends, relatives, etc. The boy that takes care of my jeep, David Smith, knows now that you're the owner and that he is at your beck and call. I still have him on my payroll. You can also use the jeep, but you'll probably want to drive your own car. I know you!" he laughed finishing the last bite of his roll.

"What's the other reason, Matt? I know there must be more to this."

"Yes, and the other reason is I was advised to relinquish all of my assets while living abroad, so that's what I'm doing. I have funds accumulating in a savings account and other investments with my corporation. I also have a life insurance policy that I want to add your name to. You can't change my mind about these matters so don't even try," he added looking at her surprised expression.

"I don't owe any money on the house. I'm paying the personal property tax each year for you. Everything has been arranged for payments to be taken care of through my work. Here are the papers. All you have to do is sign," he said pulling the papers out of a brown envelope. He handed Ruby a pen.

CHAPTER 20

Ruby's photograph graced the cover of the 'New Artist' magazine. She received a copy in the mail. She also had been invited to several elite private art shows in New York. She had to decline the ones that interfered with school but the others she definitely wanted to attend.

Matt had been gone for several weeks, but it seemed like years. She kept her engagement a secret because Matt wanted it that way. It was his way of protecting her.

John invited Ruby and Sarah to his retirement party in Jackson Hole, Wyoming during the Easter holidays. He had insisted on flying them himself. Ruby drove her car to the airport at six in the morning and met him carrying two suitcases. Sarah carried her bear.

"Hi. Do you have enough room for these?" she asked rolling the cases over to the plane.

"Sure, Doll. I always have room for anything that's yours," he said holding out his arms. Sarah ran around behind Ruby and into his arms. He bent over and patted her small back. "Hi Sarah, how's my girl?" he asked with a deep laugh. "How is school going?"

"It's fun," she replied grabbing his arm and rubbing up against him. "You should come meet some of my friends. You'd like Josh, but sometimes he pulls my hair," she added trying to get sympathy.

"Well, let me have a talk with him. He shouldn't be pulling your hair. We'll have to remedy that," he retorted with a frown.

"What does 'remedy' mean?" asked Sarah not sure what he was telling her.

"Oh, sugar, it just means we'll get him to stop pulling your hair."

The weather was perfect for takeoff, but John had informed Ruby there were several fronts in their flight pattern once they crossed the mountains. He promised to fly around them if he could or maybe land at a nearby airport if the weather turned unfriendly.

As John had predicted, the sky turned thick gray and visibility was difficult. The turbulence was quite rough and Sarah became frightened.

"I think we should land in Nashville and try to wait for the storm to pass," said John looking at Sarah's face and seeing the fear she was experiencing.

"It's alright, Doll. It's just a little wind," he smiled at her. He talked over the radio with an air traffic controller.

"Mommy, I'm scared. Can we go home?" Tears began to trickle down her face.

"Honey, it's only a small storm. We'll be fine. You know the wind has to go somewhere. Remember the story of the lightning and thunder dancers? Well the wind has to move them around so they can dance all over the world. It won't hurt us. You'll see." Ruby was trying to convince herself when an unexpected gust made the right wing dip. The wind seemed to treat the plane roughly as if it were a toy. She was afraid too.

They landed hard on one wheel on the Nashville Airstrip, but finally the plane balanced. Country music could be heard throughout the airport as they waited for the storm to pass. John treated them to an early lunch and he purchased a rag doll for Sarah. She named her Martha. Ruby didn't know why she picked that name but it took her mind off the uncomfortable plane ride she experienced hours before.

With the storm far away, they left Nashville and landed in Jackson

Hole later that night with Sarah hugging Martha in the backseat. A limo drove them to John's house. Since it was dark Ruby couldn't see the city or the outside of his house very well. White lantern lights outlined the long, wide driveway up to the front door steps. It appeared to be a two story, ski lodge surrounded by tall, bushy trees. There was a wrap-around porch with pillars and huge, ceramic flower-pots with purple and yellow pansies that greeted them by the front door.

"Come in the house!" said John allowing the servants to attend them. He said 'Hello' to his employees and then directed them to the rooms he wanted their bags to go. A tall blond maid came over to introduce herself as Alice and asked Ruby if she'd like to take a bath before retiring to bed. Ruby nodded with pleasure.

She bid John 'goodnight' and quietly followed the maid up the stairs to bathe and sleep. The rose colored drapes matched the bedspread and pillows of the sheets that had already been turned down and there was an adult robe with slippers, as well as a child one for Sarah. Ruby was expecting to see a chocolate on their pillows! After bathing Sarah, Ruby dressed her for bed. She hugged Martha tightly in her arms while Ruby tucked the two of them in their queen-sized bed and gave her a book to read to her doll.

The room had a high ceiling with a stone fireplace on the far wall. There were two, olive green, Queen Anne Chairs and a coffee table adorned with a basket of fresh fruit and water with two glasses. Ruby discovered the chocolates in a green candy dish next to the phone. Of course, she had to try one!

In between the two front windows, John's wife had painted a picture of the Buxton Lighthouse. It had been framed with a dark blue border, showing it off against the cream-colored wall. Ruby admired her detail of the tall lighthouse and the sea oats blowing in the familiar wind. Ruby could almost smell the salty air.

She ran a bubble bath in the Jacuzzi and soaked admiring the gold fixtures in the plush bathroom. The room was larger than her house! Oh the life of the rich and famous—so different from her own. Ruby set the timer and relaxed in the steaming whirlpool. It was just what the doctor ordered.

The next day was busy. Ruby and Sarah were scheduled to meet John's family for lunch in the dining room. His relatives were flying in on a private jet sometime that morning and John had sent his limo to retrieve them. Ruby was a little nervous about meeting them. She didn't really know why, except John had been such a great friend and she felt like they would frown upon their friendship because of their age difference and, of course, his millions.

The household employees were occupied with cleaning, preparing meals, pruning the gardens, sweeping walkways, and cutting grass. Ruby offered to help but John insisted they relax and enjoy breakfast in the sunroom. It was located in the back of the house with a breathtaking view of the mountains. Ruby could see why Matt had thought of moving here. She pictured him living in a log cabin on the side of the mountain with a cold stream trickling nearby. Ruby could paint and he could rescue people. *What a team!*

Ruby and Sarah waited for the relatives in the living room. Sarah wasn't feeling well so Ruby rocked her to sleep. She thought the bumpy ride in the plane and all the excitement had made Sarah tired. Ruby hoped she wasn't getting sick.

Ruby remained seated with Sarah asleep in her lap as they walked in to inspect her. John ushered an older, white haired man that she knew had to be Abe. Abe was taller and more muscular than his brother and had a rich, deep laugh. He quickly began to whisper when he saw Sarah sleeping. His daughters were close on the tail of their father wondering why he was whispering. John and Abe motioned to Ruby they would move on out to the terrace so they could visit. The rest of the family stayed with Ruby.

Sally and Tammy were only eighteen months apart, both with blond hair and blue eyes. Sally was very petite and was a hairdresser at a small shop on the corner of Main in Willow Springs.

Sally shook Ruby's hand limply. While smacking on a piece of chewing gum she said in her southern draw, "We've heard so much about you, Ruby, from Uncle John. You look about our age," she said sizing her up. "Just exactly how old are you?"

When Ruby told her, she rolled her eyes in Tammy's direction and started fussing with one of her bright red nails that matched her outfit.

Tammy seemed to have a somewhat higher intelligence than her sister and Ruby later found out that she sold real estate. She was a little more personable and demonstrated sincerity about her. She was dressed in a tailored black suit and a smart looking pair of high heels. Her husband, Leo, was quiet but appeared friendly. It looked like he and Tammy had dressed alike for the occasion. They could easily have been an advertisement for a fashion magazine.

"Sally, darling, you don't go asking people their ages. She and John are just good friends," Tammy replied scolding her sister.

"It's alright. I'm glad to finally meet you all. I've heard a lot about you too. Did you have a nice flight?" Ruby asked trying to change the subject.

"Yeah, we flew in Uncle John's private jet. It's so much better than taking those commercial airlines, you know," said Sally still working on her nails.

"As usual, Uncle John took care of us. He had a limo waiting when we landed. Uncle John is so thoughtful," bragged Tammy pointing in the direction of the terrace and blowing John a kiss with her hand. He smiled and waved at her gesture. It was making Ruby sick!

"Have you ever been here before?" she inquired looking back and forth between the two of them for an answer.

Sally was quick to respond. "Of course, we've been here many times with Aunt Ruth and Uncle John. They always said we were the children they never had."

She made it quite clear with her tone of voice that she was going to keep it that way.

"Oh, here are our brothers and Louise," said Tammy giving them the quiet signal. "Charlie, why don't you introduce yourself and everyone to Ruby? But speak softly because her daughter's sleeping."

"Hi, I'm Charlie and this is my wife, Louise," he said tipping his cowboy hat. "This here's Lester and Bob."

They also tipped their hats and said quiet 'Hellos'. Eventually they headed outside to join their dad and uncle. Louise stayed behind to socialize with us girls. Ruby learned that Charlie was a farmer on the old homestead where the Carlson Family had lived for six generations. Lester and Bob helped out during tobacco harvest time, but Lester taught middle school and Bob worked as a mechanic. Louise was a nurse at Asheville Memorial and knew Ruby's cousin, Bridgett. She was originally from Greenville. *What a small world.*

Ruby excused herself and carried Sarah upstairs to get ready for lunch. She realized Sarah was running a fever and gave her some aspirins. She informed John that she regretfully should stay with Sarah and miss lunch. He was disappointed, but understood. He wanted to call a doctor in to see Sarah, but Ruby knew she would be fine.

John had their lunches sent to the room. The tray had a vase of fresh flowers and a note attached. The note read:

> *Dear Doll and Doll Baby,*
> *I missed you both at lunch with my family. I look forward to seeing you ladies tonight. Get some rest. I'll wake you when it's time to get ready.*
> *Love,*
> *John*

How thoughtful and sweet John was to have lunch brought up to them. Ruby was convinced it tasted better alone in their bedroom than with his questioning relatives. She was relieved not to have to deal with his family right then. Ruby knew John sensed their greed and he suspected how attentive they were to him with Ruth gone. (John had confided to Ruby that Ruth didn't really care much for his family.) He was a smart man but also very lonely. Obviously he didn't get to be where he was from being naive. After all, they were his kin. Ruby was a serious threat to their bank accounts and she felt their daggers, at least the ones from the nieces. The men seemed to be less vicious.

Ruby tried to take a nap but was unsuccessful. She was ready to go home, but the girls had a big night ahead of them.

CHAPTER 21

"Come on, Ruby. We don't want to be late," said John tapping on her bedroom door.

"Hi John," she remarked opening it. He stood before her wearing a black tux and she couldn't take her eyes off of him. He was an extremely good looking man, especially all dressed up. "You look so handsome in your tux," Ruby said putting her arms around him and kissing him on the cheek. She could smell his familiar cologne.

"Ruby, stand back and let me look at my doll," he said whistling. "You are a picture I wish I had! I like you in gold. You should wear it more often," he remarked handing her a rectangle box wrapped in pink flowered paper.

"John, what is this?" Ruby said surprised.

"Go on, open it, Doll."

She unwrapped the package carefully, excited about its content. She lifted the cotton and saw a beautiful gold bracelet with small stones alternately embedded into a pattern. She noticed three different gems repeated four times.

"There are three different stones, Doll. There's amethyst, amber, and aquamarine. I bought it in Florence last month. Do you like it?" his twinkling eyes asked.

"John, this is exquisite!" Ruby expressed with surprise still in her voice. "It has a tricky catch, could you help me fasten it?" she inquired trying to hold in place around her wrist. "Thank you. I love it!" Ruby smiled when the clasps was secure. She put her arms around his neck. He took Ruby's face in his hands and kissed her. It caught Ruby a little off-guard. He whistled again walking over to see Sarah.

"How's my little 'Doll Baby'?" he said handing her a small gift, as well.

"For me?" she asked tearing the paper as fast as she could. Inside was a gold bracelet with a heart-shaped charm. "Mommy, look. It's a heart and bracelet. Hurry and put it on Me." she squealed in one outburst.

"What do you say to Mr. Carlson?" Ruby asked helping her with the bracelet.

"Thank you," she said hugging him shyly.

"I had something inscribed on the heart, Shug. Maybe your mom can read it to you," said John looking at Sarah.

Ruby examined the golden heart and turned it over. On the back it read, "To my Baby Doll, Love, JC". "Thanks, John. You are spoiling both of us. What a sweet, thoughtful man you are!"

He lifted Sarah and kissed her on the cheek. When he put her down she twirled around and asked, "Do you like my dress, Mr. Carlson?"

"Yes, mam. You are mighty pretty tonight. I'm the luckiest guy in the world to have two gorgeous dates for my retirement party. Are you ladies ready for this gala?" He led them both down the stairs holding their hands.

The relatives were gathered in the hallway watching in silence Ruby's every move. John escorted Sarah and Ruby into his limo and instructed his family to take the cars behind them. Ruby could tell that didn't set very well with them.

The party was at the Hatchet Resort. There were about five hundred of John's friends attending. Many had traveled long distances to wish the man they admired 'good luck' on his retirement. Sarah was the only child present, making another reason for the family not to like Ruby's relationship with their uncle. John never left her side. He introduced his dates to everyone, and his friends shared fond memories of working with John and how they were going to miss him. He always introduced Ruby as a new, upcoming artist and assured them she would earn a name for herself. She retained many business cards from his friends and appreciated their support. Many of his guests mentioned seeing some of her work in his office in New York. A few even mentioned seeing her on the cover of an artist magazine. John grinned at Ruby and was proud of her.

"I figured with all the art critics visiting my office daily, they could see my favorite artist preference, Doll."

"It's time for me to give you a break and take Sarah outside to enjoy the scenic view I've heard so much about. I'm sure you have some personal goodbyes to make with all of your friends." Ruby took Sarah's hand and led her out the back door.

Ruby was glad to finally acquire a little peace and quiet. She fixed Sarah a plate of food and picked up a glass of punch at the buffet table. She was too nervous to eat so she ordered a soft drink to settle her stomach. She located an isolated table. The band started playing big band tunes and people were dancing. Ruby could see their shadows swinging to the beat through the windows.

Suddenly Sally and Tammy appeared and sat down next to them. Ruby was disappointed about not having some time alone with Sarah, but smiled taking a sip of her drink. She observed their clothes and jewelry. Sally had a low-cut, bright pink gown with a rose sash and her nails had been re-polished to match. Her hair was up in a French twist. She wore pearls around her neck and on her ears.

Tammy was wearing black again. Diamonds drooped on both ear lobes and around her neck and wrist. She had curled her blond hair and clipped a gold barrette on one side to hold her bangs. The sisters were drinking flutes of champagne and each carried a dish piled with fruit and cheeses. Ruby wondered if the jewelry had been gifts from Uncle John.

"Would you like some of our appetizers?" asked Tammy holding out her plate for Ruby.

"Thanks," Ruby replied taking some cheese and grapes. She put them on a napkin.

"Where's Uncle John?" asked Sally nibbling on a chunk of cheese.

"He's inside visiting with his friends. Sarah and I thought we would come out here and enjoy the mountains and fresh air." Ruby looked out into the wilderness. "What about you two? Aren't you going to dance?" she inquired wondering why they were outside and not mingling with the guests. Surely they had to know more people than she did.

"I don't know anyone really and unfortunately, most of the men are here with dates," retorted Sally taking a pink nail and playing with her hair. "I thought Uncle John would dance with me, but I haven't seen him on the dance floor yet. He's a great dancer, don't you think?" she said trying to find out if Ruby had danced with him before.

"Yes, you're right. He's hotter than a hot tin roof," Ruby lied but couldn't help herself. The sisters exchanged wide-eyed glances.

Sally quickly changed the subject. "I love your gold dress. Did you buy it at the beach?"

"Yes, as a matter of fact I did. My boyfriend, Matt, bought it for me," Ruby added thinking of the extra money he had sent her last month.

"Did you say boyfriend?" asked Tammy perking up. "Do tell more!"

"He works overseas so I don't see him as much as I'd like to," Ruby answered wishing he were there dancing with her.

"What does he do overseas?" asked Sally.

"He's in the service," she quickly answered smiling to herself. *If only they knew.*

"Sarah," Ruby heard John's voice say. "Let's go dance. Do you think your mom wants to dance too?"

As they stood up to leave, he winked and asked his nieces if they were having a good time. They both nodded with fake smiles. Ruby left their empty glasses and plate on the table and took John's arm smiling.

John was an excellent dancer. He was extremely patient with Sarah. Suddenly Abe appeared on the platform and held a microphone in his hand. He asked everyone to gather around. Several presentations were made to John including several gag gifts that brought the audience into an uproar.

The most unexpected gift was from his company in DC. They gave him keys to a new green and white Learjet. He had always dreamed of having one to fly clients around on business trips. Now there was no one but him to fly. They showed him a picture of it, parked at the airport with a ribbon attached on top. He became emotional trying to fight back the grateful tears that had formed. He quickly wiped them away and gave a speech, thanking his family and friends for the wonderful gifts and a lifetime of fond memories.

The evening was a truly memorable one for Ruby despite his family's indifferences and jealousies. She was happy to share the special occasion with such an honorable, respected man.

When they finally returned to John's home, Ruby put Sarah to bed. John asked her to meet him in the sunroom. She changed into jeans and a sweatshirt. They laughed when they saw each other. He was also dressed more casual. He handed her a glass of sherry and they sat on the couch.

"I guess dressing up once in a while is fun, but doesn't it feel good to change back into more relaxing attire?" he said still laughing. "Did you have a good time tonight?"

"I had the best time," Ruby assured him. "And what about you? I'm sure it was a difficult evening for you giving up your lifetime business and maybe never seeing some of those friends again."

"Yes, it was emotional for me. But having you two ladies there was a great comfort. With Ruth gone, I can't think of anyone I'd rather have stand beside me," he added taking her hand.

Ruby could feel the energy between them as he suddenly kissed her. It was a deep, lustful kiss that made her aware of his power and unmistaken affections for her.

"Ruby, I think you know by now how serious I am about you. You've been a caring and loving friend but now I want more. I think you know I'm in love with you, don't you?" he questioned her as she nodded her head hesitantly up and down. "I want to ask you to consider marrying me," he said seriously. "I've thought about this for a long time, actually since that stormy night in Hatteras," he revealed slowly standing up and walking over to the fireplace. He took a sip of his sherry and continued, "I admit that we met shortly after Ruth's death, and I was on the rebound. But I went out on several dates to see if it was just that, but I fell in love with your innocence and honesty. The other women I've dated were only interested in where I keep my planes, where we could go in Europe, and staying in all the five star hotels or in the penthouses. I've told you before I know you would never love anyone because of money. You are a special lady, and I don't want to lose you.

As you know, I have a huge, empty house, actually seven empty houses that you could fill with Sarah and more children if you want. I think it was Ruth that couldn't have children, but as far as I've been told, I'm still fertile." He laughed suddenly and said moving his eyebrows up and down, "I may be old, but I'm still good!"

Ruby laughed with him and wiped away a tear.

"You don't have to answer me right away, Ruby. But I want you to know that I love you and am going to do everything in my power to have you. Put your shoes under my bed."

"John I'm confused. I love you too but in a different way. I've been in love with someone else for five years. I never thought our friendship would come to such a close relationship."

"Who and where is this man? You've never mentioned him before," asked John hurt by the news but wanting to listen to the explanation about Matt.

"He's in the CIA and travels all the time. I don't know of his whereabouts because of obvious reasons, but he previously worked with me in DC and that's when we fell in love. My marriage with Troy wasn't going well after he became involved with one of his female colleagues. Matt was my boss at the time and helped me believe in myself again. He encouraged me to paint and go on with my life," Ruby explained with tears in her eyes. John wiped them from her face with his fingers. She continued slowly, looking up at him, "Matt has also asked me to marry him. I'm waiting for him to come home for good, so I can."

"Is that why you work yourself to the bone and are determined to do everything all by yourself?" he questioned holding her chin in his hand. "Don't you get tired of not having someone to lean on?" he asked. "I can give you everything you've ever wanted and more. I'm a very rich man. We can travel anywhere in the world displaying your art, you can buy all the clothes you've looked at through glass store windows, I will pay for Sarah's college, I can pay off your student loans, and I will love you the rest of my life," he explained running his fingers through her hair. He kissed the top of her head. "Remember, I have a new plane now. We can fly to Hatteras anytime you like. I'll fix up my old house and turn it into a home if that's where you choose to live." He pulled her mouth to his but she pushed away.

"I'm sorry, John. I love Matt. If I didn't have him, I know my answer would be different. I hope you understand. Besides, I fear your family would be busy sharpening their knives at the thought of me and you together. They love you, I'm sure, but I'm not blood kin and they will never accept me into the family as Ruth once was. With all respect to your family, you've invested a lot of time with them and they know they'll inherit your fortune. A wife and child pose a threat to their share of your money. I don't want to be the cause of your family splitting apart. Not to mention a chance for us to have a child, would suggest an even larger concern."

"I don't care what my family thinks. If I love someone, I will be totally committed to that person, damn it! My money belongs to my wife and our family first," said John frowning. "If my family ever interfered to cause my wife unhappiness or to feel uncomfortable, I would take them out of my will so fast their head would spin!"

"I didn't mean to upset you, John. I just wanted to share my concerns and feelings. Let's say goodnight and sleep on it." Ruby drank the rest of her sherry and went upstairs to bed leaving him alone with his thoughts.

221

CHAPTER 22

John's relatives hovered and demanded his time and attention. They purposely avoided Ruby and Sarah's presence. It was difficult for Ruby to see his hurtful glances towards her as he made small talk with everyone. His proposal had caught her off guard. She struggled with the guilt of not telling him about Matt, but it had been Matt's idea to protect her while he worked undercover.

Once detached from his friends and relatives, John remained silent during the flight home. Ruby was convinced his silence stemmed from exhaustion, but she also understood he was dealing with her rejection.

Ruby observed the sun's rays sparkling on the water below. The Cessna landed in Wilmington ahead of schedule. She regretted not discussing their relationship but thought maybe more time was needed to let the healing process take place.

"I have to fly back to Wyoming tomorrow to sign the papers and retrieve my new plane," John explained with a grin. "I feel like a kid with a big, new toy. Hopefully the Lear is in the process of passing inspection and the transferal of ownership. I still can't believe the boys bought me a plane." He unloaded their luggage and hailed the girls a cab. "I'll call you next weekend, Doll".

'He's the 'Doll', not me', Ruby thought to herself.

Ruby's schedule was filled with Sarah, school, art, and the longing to see Matt. She started to feel sorry for herself, even though she had managed to sell several of her pictures in a small shop in Wrightsville Beach. Why did Matt have to stay in the CIA for five more years? Couldn't he quit and get a job in North Carolina or somewhere safe?

John was right about her needing a shoulder to lean on. Ruby admitted that *She* was notorious about keeping herself insanely busy, filling the emptiness that built up inside. John made her aware of the youth she was missing and the opportunity to promote her art in a world that was extremely competitive. He had clout and VIP connections with dealers and collectors. Ruby needed his contacts to introduce her work and to have his colleague's support.

John offered Ruby and Sarah a life of luxury for the rest of their lives. Was the love she felt for John only platonic or guilt? Was he her substitute for Matt until he returned? How could Ruby explain the energy that she felt when John kissed her? Was she a complete fool?

John was a powerful and possessive man. *Will I ever be able to handle having someone control my life the same way Troy did?* Ruby thought about that for a long time.

After a sleepless night, she concluded that there would never be anyone for her but Matt. He was her knight in shining armor. Matt supported her art and allowed Ruby to be herself. She had to be patient and wait for him, she promised him she would.

But Ruby loved John as a friend and she needed his love too. She cared about him deeply. She had to explain her feelings and gratitude.

Ruby was devastated by the news when Abe phoned and informed her of the accident. John died in a plane crash outside of Jackson Hole. It had been assumed that he had had a heart attack and collided into one of the mountains near the airport. It was also believed that when John understood what was happening, he veered off course to avoid hurting anyone. Ruby could picture him making the decision seconds before hitting the earth, while in agony from his coronary. She prayed to God that he had passed out before the impact.

The funeral was in Willow Springs at his family's church. Sarah wept softly in Ruby's lap while they sat in the sanctuary. Ruby wiped tears that slipped down her cheeks with a tissue she clutched in her hand. It seemed that the father figures in Sarah's life were always leaving.

Chris had insisted on accompanying the girls and gave them the support they needed. He became the rock they leaned against, to strengthen their emotional states.

Charlie thanked Ruby for the flowers. He helped his dad with the funeral arrangements because Abe was unable to function. Abe took John's death the hardest and Ruby felt sorry for him. Perhaps his children were numb, but she pictured them deciding what color sports car they were going to buy, which house they wanted, and how much money would be deposited in their bank accounts. They barely spoke a word to Ruby. It was almost as if they had never met her or Sarah. After the funeral service, Charlie took Ruby aside, revealing information about a recent will John had signed. He explained that she and Sarah were included as family and the lawyers would be contacting Ruby soon.

Before leaving, Sarah and Ruby walked over to the closed casket holding hands. They stood beside the tombstone with Carlson engraved in large letters. Ruth Elaine Carlson was finally beside her beloved John again. Ruby touched her lips with her fingertips and blew John a kiss. "Now you are with your true love," she whispered. Ruby looked up at the sun peaking through the trees. When her eyes followed the light, the shadow of the leaves seemed to make the shape of a plane on the casket. Ruby couldn't believe it. She thought John heard her and was saying 'goodbye'.

Charlie returned Ruby's art that John had in several houses, which he mailed through UPS. Ruby did not hear anything from his family or the lawyers. She never knew the details of John's final will, but that was OK with Ruby. John gave her his friendship and that was all she ever wanted in the first place. Ruby knew his greedy family would never understand.

CHAPTER 23

In May 1990 Ruby's friends had much to celebrate. Elizabeth graduated from nursing school, Chris and Kyle received engineering degrees, and Doc was in his first year of residency. Ruby graduated with honors in art history and had several one woman exhibitions approaching in the fall. She decided to apply for a job overseas teaching art. She had ambitions to see the world, while Matt was out saving it. Ruby hadn't heard from him in a long time. She was beginning to worry.

The group decided to have a beach luau on Memorial Day to celebrate their long awaited accomplishments. Dugray purchased several slabs of pork ribs, marinating them with a secret recipe. The party began with the limbo, accompanied by salsa music. Elizabeth and Theresa were tied for first place. After three more tries, Theresa fell over backwards laughing, making Elizabeth the winner. Her fiancé, John, congratulated her with a dramatic kiss, dipping her almost to the ground while she raised her leg high in the air. He held her there for such a long time that everyone started counting and clapping.

Teams gathered afterwards for a volleyball competition, The Hawaiian Desperados against The Hawaiian Surfers. The Surfers wore strips of Hawaiian material that actually came from one of Chris's old shirts that they placed around their arm. The Desperados tied red bandanas on their heads. The radio blasted oldies as they struggled to keep the ball on the other side of the net. The Desperados won two out of three games. After it was over, it didn't take long for everyone to sprint down to the water, cooling off and dunking each other. Dinner followed the game with Dugray's awesome ribs.

Gag gifts were distributed and each required individual attention. Elizabeth received a rubber chicken to bring back to life, a plastic Easter Egg filled with bright colored M&Ms with hand written labels reading: Stress Release Pills. Crazy instructions were added so that eventually if a really bad day was happening, the entire bottle was to be consumed. Ruby drew her as a cartoon caricature with a nurse's face holding a huge needle that said, "I promise you won't feel a thing!" and 'Nurse Elizabeth' written on her uniform.

Kyle and Chris were given a book with instructions on "How to Build Strong Relationships." Kyle got a motorcycle clock radio to go with his new bike and leather jacket.

Chris was handed a new, colorful Hawaiian shirt and a pair of blue flip-flops with the price tag still clinging to the straps. Sarah selected a green bucket and shovel for Chris to play with at the beach. Since she was absent from the party, he poured beer into it, refilling it quite often!

Doc received a decorated bedpan, red silk pajamas for all the ER parties that went on during long on-call weekends, and a book on advice from Dr. Phil. He also got a bucket, but he kept his with the other gifts. He was smarter than Chris! The night was filled with eating, drinking, and tons of merriment.

For Ruby they chose a toy plane for her tub and a book of lawyer jokes. They also gave her a picture of her as the first chili queen in a frame surrounded with hot tamales.

Ruby was proud of all of them for reaching their goals. They supported and loved each other as family. She knew their friendships would last forever.

John and Elizabeth were married in New Jersey. At the wedding, Chris's attention landed on an attractive blond with brown eyes named Marcia. They dated steadily after the wedding connection. Ruby was happy that Chris finally met someone, but she knew their relationship would never be the same.

Ruby's sister, Lizzy, and her husband, Alan, graduated from law school in June also. Ruby and Sarah drove to Wake Forest meeting the rest of her family. They reserved several rooms in a local hotel. It was an emotional ceremony probably because Ruby understood the dedication and pressure of exams and papers. Lizzy and Alan were hired by two different well-established firms in Denver, Colorado. They were excited about their location because they were both avid snowboarders and enjoyed various other winter sports. Ruby was scheduled to have an art exhibition in Colorado and promised to visit them within the year. Ruby kept her engagement to Matt to herself. She would introduce everyone when the time was right.

Ruby had a week's vacation at the Frisco house in July. She needed to paint new pictures for her upcoming shows in the fall. She had applied for a teaching position in Portugal and was expected to have an interview in DC when she returned. If she accepted the job, she would have to give careful consideration regarding her art. The public would not look upon her withdrawal with a friendly eye. She had been given an unbelievable introduction into the art world because of John Carlson and she didn't want to tarnish his name in any way. His friends had encouraged and supported Ruby, especially after John's passing. She had sold quite a large number of paintings, and she was making a nice profit from her creations. As a budding artist, it was quite a gamble, but Ruby was a risk taker. She decided 'she'd think about that tomorrow'.

John's house was boarded up and there was a 'For Sale' sign in the front window. It seemed like John's relatives didn't waste any time liquidating his assets. She wondered what he had written in his will.

Ruby and Sarah were on the beach building a sandcastle when a small plane flew over. It circled the pier and dipped its wings.

"Sarah, quick, we need to go to the airport."

Matt was leaning against the propeller with one foot crossed in front of the other. He was a sight for sore eyes. He grinned and waved as Ruby parked the car and walked towards him holding Sarah's hand. He was dressed in his usual jeans and a white tank top t-shirt revealing his tan, muscular build. Matt looked handsome, and she wondered where he had been with his darkened skin. Ruby realized she must look a mess. Her hair was windblown and sand was plastered to her feet. She was sweating with the hot sun beating down on the tarred pavement. She used a towel she carried to wipe away her perspiration.

Ruby didn't say a word, but looked into Matt's eyes as hers fought back tears. She hugged him tightly feeling the watery drops trickle down her face. He reached down to kiss Ruby lightly in front of Sarah. "Hi Ruby. I've missed you," he whispered running his fingers through her damp hair.

"When did you get back?"

"I flew into DC yesterday." He quickly changed the subject when he realized Sarah was tugging at his shirt. "This must be Sarah," he said leaning over to shake her hand. "I'm Matt. I knew you when you were much smaller, but I can see you're practically a young lady."

"Hi," she answered shyly.

"You flew in this plane with your mom years ago. Do you remember catching a fish named *Marty the Smarty?*" he asked hoping to spark her memory.

"No, I don't, but I have that book," Sarah answered shaking her head back and forth. "But I remember riding in Mr. Carlson's airplane, but he's gone to live with God in Heaven. He died in his plane," she added sadly.

"I'm sorry to hear that," Matt sympathized looking at Ruby. He squeezed her hand and said in a soft voice, "I know he was very close to you and your mother."

"Yes, he was. Sarah and I miss him terribly, don't we?" Ruby replied looking at Sarah. Another tear appeared and Matt pulled her close. Ruby buried her face in his shoulder for a few minutes to collect her emotions. She reached out to touch his plane. "How are you old friend? Got any stories to tell me?" Ruby laughed sarcastically looking up at Matt. "I'm ready for a ride, what about you?"

"I was hoping you would say that," he said, unchaining the plane and checking the fuel. "In fact, I've arranged for us to ride horses on the beach at Portsmouth Island one day this week. Would you like to go today? The weather couldn't be nicer."

"I've never been on a horse, Matt. Will you teach me how to ride?" Sarah asked excitedly.

"Not only will I teach you how to ride a horse, but how would you like to sit in the front of the airplane with me and help me fly her over there?" questioned Matt, raising his eyebrows up and down. Ruby could tell he was winning Sarah's heart, like he had won hers.

"Can I really sit in the front and fly?" she asked in disbelief. "Mommy, can I? Please?" she begged, looking at Ruby and then Matt.

"I guess I'm outnumbered on this one. OK. I'll sit in the back just this once," Ruby remarked finding her seat.

Sarah strapped herself in with Matt's assistance. "It's not going to be bumpy this time is it?" she asked a little nervous thinking about the storm they were in with Mr. Carlson.

"Planes have to have some bumps so that they can fly properly. It's quite smooth up there today though. Do you still want to help me fly it?" he inquired putting her right hand over the controls.

"OK," she answered excited again forgetting her fears. "I like your little man up there," she said pointing to the emblem Ruby was familiar with.

"That's a famous movie star. He's also a special agent and an excellent pilot. You're probably too young to see any of his movies yet though. But trust me, he's a good guy," said Matt reaching back to touch Ruby's hand.

As she grabbed it, Ruby smiled looking at her two loves in the front seats. She was relieved that Matt chose to tell Sarah his real name. Maybe his dangerous missions were over. She hoped that was the case.

Ruby could hear Matt giving Sarah simplified instructions as to how to fly the 'Bond' plane. She enjoyed watching Sarah hold the throttle in her tiny hands with his guidance. She laughed when they hit bumps. Ruby was pleased she was overcoming her fear of flying. She wanted her to love it as much as she did.

They landed on Portsmouth Island and paid for two horses and a pony to ride for the remainder of the day. They smeared sunscreen over their bodies and were off. Matt had a way of teaching Sarah to ride, just like he did with everything. They galloped along the coast, weaving in and out of the surf. They found a great place for a picnic and rest. Matt had brought along beach towels, bottles of water and peanut butter sandwiches. He also had pretzels and grapes in his book bag. Matt and Ruby jumped waves holding Sarah's hands. She screamed and clung to Matt for safety when the waves looked too intimidating.

He helped Sarah feed the horses some apples and water. She kissed her pony on the nose. "Mom, can we get a pony? I promise to take good care of it."

"Honey, we don't have a place to keep one. Sarah, isn't it just as fun to come here and ride when you can? That way you don't have to clean up their dirty stable,"

"I suppose. He's the sweetest little pony, mommy. Will you take a picture of us together so I can put it in my room?"

"I forgot my camera. Matt, did you bring one?"

"As a matter of fact," he said whipping it out of his backpack. He took several Polaroid's of the girls with their horses, and Sarah took a few of Ruby and Matt together. She was amazed as she watched each picture roll out waiting to develop in one minute. Sarah was ecstatic to see her pony so quickly on film.

Ruby noticed Matt limping and decided to ask him about it. She pointed to the dark, circular purple and black mark, "Where'd you get that nasty bruise on your leg, and why are you having a hard time walking?"

"I've been out in the Caribbean on some fishing boats and accidentally tripped on some of the gear," he answered. "I guess I'm just a klutz when it comes to commercial fishing. It's much different than fishing at the lake," he replied, pulling his cap down to shade his eyes. "I guess when I fell, I pulled a hamstring. It's a little tender, but it's on the mend. You know I'll do anything to fish," he added sarcastically.

"I know, but it's not all fun and games. Have you played in any bands lately?"

"Oh yeah, I'm still playing my sax when I get the chance. I've learned a few new tunes living on the islands. I relate well to their reggae rhythm on my guitar," he added snapping his fingers to a beat and humming a few notes.

"I noticed your guitar in the plane. Are you going to serenade us tonight?" Ruby asked leaning over to kiss him on the cheek.

"I guess I can be persuaded," he grinned. "Sarah, do you want to lead?"

She hesitated before she spoke. "I can't do it by myself. Will you help me, Matt?"

"Sure. I'd be glad to," he said, saddling up next to her.

They flew back to Frisco and stopped for dinner. They returned to the cottage and showered. The girls worked on a jigsaw puzzle while Matt played his guitar and sang to them. They sang the 'Mockingbird' song before Sarah eventually fell asleep on the couch. Matt carried her to bed.

"How long can you stay?" Ruby inquired. "It never seems long enough."

"I can be here all week, if that's alright with you. I'm sorry I didn't give you any advance notice about my coming. I didn't even know for sure until yesterday, which allowed me no time to call you. It was too risky for me to try to call where I was anyway. As soon as I found out where you were, I hopped in my plane and here I am," he explained grabbing her. He pulled Ruby down to the floor and started tickling her.

"Stop, Matt," she yelled as quietly as she could, trying to push him back. Ruby retaliated by charging his most vulnerable areas.

"Don't stop, Ruby!" he laughed before kissing her. "I love you," he whispered.

"OK, you can stay for the week."

CHAPTER 24

It was early when Ruby awoke in Matt's arms. She didn't know how she was going to let him leave again. Each time became more difficult for her. She longed for the day they would be man and wife, raising a family of their own. Ruby worried constantly for his safety. She knew the world he lived in was amongst terrorists and gangsters. She wondered how much of the story he fabricated about the fish incident was real.

Matt was resting peacefully, so she decided not to wake him. She gently slipped from under his clutch, prepared the coffee and headed towards the beach with Sarah. The sun was beginning to awaken over the dunes. Sandpipers were running back and forth avoiding the waves, searching for food, seagulls were skimming the ocean for their breakfast, and sand crabs were busy tunneling. Carpenter bees looked for bright movable objects, and Ruby was one of their targets. She used her hat to chase them away. Hatteras fishermen had been up for hours earning their living while vacationing fishermen were on the pier, surf fishing, or out in chartered boats, each hoping to bring in the biggest 'Catch of the Day.' To her, the throbbing of the surf was a symphony of nature.

The girls walked to the Frisco Pier and were in the process of returning to the cottage. Sarah had stopped to collect shells. Out of the blue, a cute jogger with a limp stopped beside Ruby and said tipping his cap, "Good morning, miss. Fine day." He was wearing a pair of black running shorts, a tank top, and sneakers.

"Yes, it is sir," Ruby replied looking out over the water.

"I was wondering if you could help me find my girl. She has red hair and the most beautiful green eyes I've ever seen. She left me this morning without waking me. It caught me totally off guard. I'm usually a very light sleeper," he said with a puzzled expression.

"I can only say that you must feel as relaxed here as I do. I can even sleep through the famous Hatteras thunderstorms, and they're not quiet by any means," she boasted.

He stopped jogging in place long enough to kiss her on the cheek and announced, "I'm going running, at least trying to with this leg. I'll be back in about an hour." Ruby watched him until she could only see an ant-sized man bobbing up and down.

Sarah rinsed off her feet and watched a film on TV, while Ruby showered and prepared a cup of coffee. She grabbed a towel to drape over the chair on the upper deck and sat down. Ruby soon fell asleep. Sarah tapped her on the shoulder and told her breakfast was ready. Sarah informed her mom that she and Matt had made omelets together.

Ruby helped carry the fresh fruit and bacon back up to the deck. Matt had the rest of the breakfast on a tray. Sarah carried a vase of wildflowers she had picked.

They used a small wooden table to hold beverages and Sarah's plate. She placed the flowers in the center. They ate mostly in silence. When Ruby looked over at Matt he smiled and winked.

"Well, what do you think?" he asked holding his fork up and inserting some melon into his mouth.

"This is excellent. I should fall asleep more often."

"Mom, I broke the eggs. Matt taught me how to do it without breaking shells into the bowl," she shared proudly.

"I can see that he is a very good teacher, and you are a good pupil."

Suddenly Matt changed the subject. "What are your plans now that you have graduated, Ruby?" he asked taking a bite of his egg creation.

"I've applied to teach in Portugal at an international school. Have you ever traveled there?" she asked wondering what assignment would have taken him there.

"Yes, it's a beautiful country, but then again, I haven't seen much of Europe that I didn't like. But, Ruby, why are you thinking of leaving the states? Don't you think Sarah should be near your family?" he inquired sipping his coffee.

"I've given it a lot of thought, Matt. I want to see the world like you, but by using my art. This is the only way I know how to do it on a teacher's salary. Besides, think what a great education and opportunity it will be for both of us." Ruby smiled giving Sarah a hug.

"I think you should do it. Depending where I'm located, it might be easier for me to see you. When will you find out whether you have the job?"

"I need to attend a job fair in DC next week. Sarah will stay with mom, and I will meet with several headmasters for positions they have advertised. I have to admit, I'm very excited about my prospects. Hopefully, I will know something by next Friday," Ruby informed him.

"Don't worry, I'll find you," he grinned.

The rest of the week was filled with laughter and love. They fished, swam, played games, listened to music and sang, and Ruby painted pictures of their nights together on canvas. They ferried to Ocracoke shopping, biking through the small fishing village, and climbing the lighthouse.

They drove to Manteo to see 'The Lost Colony." The outdoor play was the re-enactment of Virginia Dare's family and the mystery of what happened to them on Roanoke Island. The only clue about their disappearance was the word 'Croatoan' carved into a tree. Sarah was thrilled to see the children that participated in the show. Additionally, she liked the realistic ship that passed the fort, and, of course, the queen.

Matt bought a purple birdhouse with two green whales on it and gave it to Ruby. He also purchased a toe ring and two sun dresses for Sarah. Ruby selected a silver ring with a red stone for Matt and to remind him of her, when he was out with blonds.

Their last evening together was so vivid in Ruby's mind. She could still smell the tuna cooking over the open fire at the beach, and see flames from the marshmallows. Sarah reached around Matt's head giving him a great big hug. "Where will you go when you leave tomorrow, Matt?"

"I have to fly overseas for a while, but I'll be back here with you next summer. Sarah, you'll have to take lots of pictures of you in school. Will you do that for me?"

"Yeah," she answered nodding her head up and down. He started wrestling her to the ground, and she clung tighter. "I love you, Matt. And so does mom," she added as she tried to hold back the loud laughter outburst from the tickling. "We'll miss you when you're gone," she said hugging him tighter. She suddenly looked him in the eyes and said seriously, "Are you going to be my new daddy?"

Ruby could see that he was touched by her question. "Would you like that?"

"You know I would. Can I be in your wedding? I always wanted to be a flower girl."

"I know you'll be the prettiest one I've ever seen," he said lightly cupping her face in his hands and kissing her nose. I haven't talked to your mom yet about this," he said looking at Ruby, "but I think we should get married right here on the beach. What do you think, Ruby?"

"You have a date, Mr. Bond."

CHAPTER 25

Ruby accepted a teaching position in Lisbon, Portugal. She and Sarah moved into a snug, two bedroom flat, within walking distance of their school. Sarah was entering the third grade. She loved her Australian teacher and made new friends quickly. Sarah was required to take Portuguese, and she could communicate fluently after several months of lessons and conversations with her native classmates. Ruby was amazed at how fast Sarah learned the language.

Ruby taught art history at the international high school and was stimulated by her foreign students. Her classroom overlooked the city of Lisbon, providing her a view of the Rossio Square, the gateway to the river and Lisbon's avenues, and the Baixa, downtown. Ruby was impressed with the history and the culture of the Lisbon people. She loved the colorful tile buildings and began collecting tiles everywhere she went. One of her favorite buildings was the Casa dos Bicos. It was a house of diamond shaped stones, built in 1523. The black and white patterned structure was an architectural splendor.

Transportation was easy in the city because the trams ran on a strict schedule and were inexpensive. Ruby and Sarah were able to see many sites on weekend excursions, often teaming up with other foreign staff and families. One of their most enjoyable pastimes was to sit at an outside café and watch the people.

Ruby arranged for her fall art exhibits to be moved to the following summer. The museums seemed supportive of her new overseas job and connections. They promised to keep in touch.

It was the week before Christmas and the girls were scheduled to fly to Raleigh to visit family. Troy had phoned to find out when he could see Sarah over the holidays. They set up a time and place.

Ruby was worried about Matt because she hadn't heard from him since the summer. No money had been deposited into her account, which she didn't care about, but it made her uneasy about the situation. She didn't know where he was or how to contact him.

They landed in DC and switched flights for the final journey home. She learned that a snowstorm was on the way. Her parents were waiting at the airport with open arms. She was told her sisters had called to say the airports were closed so they wouldn't be able to come. They were all disappointed but knew it was better for them to stay put under the circumstances.

The twins had invited their new college girlfriends to the Christmas Eve dinner. It was interesting to see the differences in their choices of women. Brad dated Mary who was short and had brown hair to match her eyes. She was a history major from New York. Tamara, Liam's date, had long blond hair and blue eyes. She was studying psychology and was from Georgia. They were both interesting girls and Ruby enjoyed visiting with them. With their previous reputations, she wondered how long these girls would last!

Ruby's family heard by the church's phone chain and television news, that the Christmas Eve Service had been cancelled. They decided to have their own worship. Mr. Fraser read scripture from the Bible about the birth of Jesus. The boys played guitars, and Ruby played the piano as they sang their favorite Christmas songs. Sarah sang 'Away in a Manger' rocking her doll in her arms. She had draped a linen napkin over her head singing to her baby. She was serious with her role as Mary and a good singer. Everyone couldn't help but laugh with her dramatic performance. Ruby could see her on stage with Diane doing a Broadway play. She certainly didn't get her acting from Ruby!

Ruby made Sarah hot chocolate and fed her cookies before putting her to bed. Exhausted, Ruby finally tucked her in and went to work on stuffing her stocking and displaying her Santa items by the fireplace. It was after she finished with her Santa Claus duty that she shared everything about Matt to her family. They were happy about the engagement and anxious to meet him. They could tell Ruby was happy but concerned about his whereabouts. She kissed everyone goodnight and went upstairs.

Changing into her nightgown, Ruby's thoughts were about Matt. She lit a candle and said a prayer for his safe return. She distinctly remembered dreaming; Matt and she were flying over Hatteras and dancing in and out of the clouds.

Sarah woke up with excitement and shook Ruby's shoulder.

"Mommy, get up! Santa has come! Hurry up!" she insisted, kissing Ruby on the cheek and pulling her free hand.

Sarah didn't wait for Ruby to get ready. She knocked on her grandparents' door and woke them. They sent her in to get the twins. Ruby could hear them wrestling and tickling her for waking them up. Fortunately, they were both good sports and rolled out of bed, each holding one of her hands and swinging her down the hallway.

"Look who we found!" exclaimed Liam lifting Sarah and giving her a hug. "I don't think I see anything in the living room for you Sarah. It looks like all bricks and bags of coal to me," he teased, peering in the doorway and covering Sarah's eyes.

"Let me see," she replied wiggling to her freedom. She ran in and started shouting, "Mom, look at my new bike!" She climbed on the seat while Ruby held the bars keeping her from toppling into the Christmas tree.

She placed her feet on the pedals and turned the handles left and right several times. Then she spied some other presents on the fireplace that she wanted to open. She seemed pleased with all of her gifts.

Suddenly the phone rang.

"I'll get it" exclaimed Brian putting the receiver to his ear. "Merry Christmas!" he answered.

"Ruby, it's for you," he said, motioning his sister over and grinning. "Go girl, work it, own it!" he strutted.

"Hello," Ruby said anxiously running her hand through her hair.

"Merry Christmas, Ruby!" said a distant, familiar voice. He sounded so far away.

"Matt? Where are you?"

"I'm in South America. It's warm here, nothing like Christmas weather in North Carolina or Portugal for that matter. I've heard you have lots of snow there. As you can guess, I didn't make it to Maui this year but my brothers and dad are there. Maybe by this time next year, we'll be there together."

"I'm counting on it, Matt. I'm going there with or without you, just like I told you several years ago. Do you remember?" Ruby said, laughing trying to keep her voice from cracking. She was so emotional. It was such a relief to know he was alive. She missed him terribly.

"Are you coming to Lisbon to visit me?" Ruby asked hopefully.

"I hope to be there as soon as this project is wrapped up. It shouldn't be long now."

"What did you say?" Ruby asked straining to hear the sound of his voice.

"I said, yes, soon," he chuckled. "Say, can you speak up? I can hardly hear you. I think we have a bad connection," he announced. A machine gun began to pepper his surroundings.

"Are you OK?" Ruby asked concerned. She could hear static through the wires and loud popping sounds. Then the phone went dead.

CHAPTER 26

The noise had pierced her ears, but she dismissed any signs of danger because static was common, especially with international calls. Ruby was disappointed not to talk to him before she had to return to work. She had so much to share about Lisbon, and she wanted to hear about Matt's adventures as James Bond.

Ruby and Sarah returned to Lisbon for the 1991 New Years. They celebrated with several colleagues and their children. Fireworks lit up the sky above the Tegas River. Loud salsa music encouraged dancing and partying in the streets. It was a breathtaking, festive occasion displaying brightly, decorated costumes and historic architecture silhouetting the skyline. Ruby's party traveled closer to the water's edge. Vendors were set up along the streets and Ruby purchased two CDs. One of the merchants handed Sarah a flower from his shop. Sarah thanked him in Portuguese before smelling its fragrant aroma.

Ruby had found the Portuguese a proud race. They honored Portugal's notorious, brave seamen for their contributions of navigational maps of the seas and oceans around the world. Facing the Tegas River was the 'Monument of the Discoveries'. The marble statue was led by Magellan in the bow of a ship, followed by other famous sea explorers.

The school year went by quickly. Ruby and Sarah traveled throughout Portugal and Spain. They vacationed on the Canary Islands during Spring Break. The beach was a welcomed sight. The girls rode camels through a canyon, took a bus tour up to the volcano on Tenerife Island, and lounged at the pool or beach. They met interesting vacationers, mostly from England and Germany. Sarah painted also and wrote stories in her journal. Ruby snapped photographs or painted scenes of the picturesque surroundings. Ruby had received a call from the Museum of Art in D.C. and was asked to bring several of her pictures for consideration in June. Ruby was beside herself. Ruby corresponded with Chris and Doc frequently by mail. They reported the news from Wrightsville Beach and tried to answer her questions. Chris was planning to marry in the fall. Doc had met a young intern and was 'seriously involved' according to Chris. Everyone else was busy and doing fine. They wanted to know when she would visit, but she was unsure of her schedule once back home.

Ruby drove Sarah to the cabin when they returned to the states. She wanted to see if there were any calls from Matt. The phone had a blinking light and Ruby listened to the messages. The first one was from the boy taking care of Matt's truck announced he had joined the army. He left a name and number of a person who could take his place. Ruby wrote down the information.

She continued to hear the messages. There were a few hang-up calls, but the last one with an elderly man's voice, caught her attention. "Hi, Ruby. My name is Mr. Connery, Matt's dad. I haven't had the pleasure of meeting you, but thought it might be a good idea. I'm traveling to DC at the end of June. I'm worried about my boy and wondered if you'd heard anything from him. Please call me at your earliest convenience." Mr. Connery left his name and number where he could be reached. Ruby's stomach became knots.

She phoned him immediately and heard a pleasant voice on the other end. "Hi Ruby, I was hoping you would be calling soon. I left that message about a month ago now. Have you heard from Matt?" he asked anxiously.

"No sir. I was hoping I would before now. We had a terrible connection when he called on Christmas Day. When was the last time you spoke to him?"

"Matt also phoned me on Christmas Day, but the line was as clear as a bell. He must've called me first. He said he would make contact again within the week, but I've heard nothing, and that's not like Matt. His brothers are worried too."

"Sarah and I have recently returned home from Portugal for the summer. I assume Matt told you I teach art there. Anyway, I wanted to visit the cabin first, in case he left any messages. But there aren't any. My daughter and I love your son, Mr. Connery. What or where can we go to find him?" Ruby was hoping he had leads as to contacting his superiors for information.

"I think we should start in DC. That's why I'm flying out there next week. Is it possible we can meet?"

"Yes, of course." They set up a place and time. Ruby would make arrangements to stay in the same hotel. It would make things easier for both of them.

"Before I hang up, I wanted to inquire about your health." Ruby sincerely asked.

"I had another bypass surgery in February, but now I feel like a new buck," he chuckled. "It's amazing what surgeons can do nowadays."

"I'm glad to hear it. Well, I'll see you in DC."

Ruby believed in her heart, Matt was alright. At least she had to convince herself or she'd go crazy without sleeping. The cabin had been neglected during the year. It needed her attention and it gave her something to do while she waited for her trip to DC. One of the water pipes had broken, taking several days to repair. The girls used fans to cool off, and they cleaned the place until it shined. It helped her pass the time and she enjoyed fixing up the cabin, adding a woman's touch.

Sarah and Ruby found Matt's old boat and rowed around the lake. They didn't fish, but they had fun just being outdoors and soaking in the rays. Ruby called Paul Sawyer to take care of the cabin. He was friendly, and admitted he could use the extra money for his wife and newborn. He came by the last day to retreive the key.

The traffic in DC was congested as usual, and driving through the city brought back many memories. Ruby was excited about meeting Mr. Connery. She wondered if Matt's brothers were going to be there too. She located their hotel, and the girls checked into their room.

Ruby contacted the museum to announce her arrival in DC. She had chosen five pieces of her art to be reviewed by the Board while she was in Washington. They offered her a place to hang one or more of her paintings. The curator complimented Ruby on her style and choice of subjects and colors. He said he thought the Board would be pleased with her art. Ruby needed to meet with Mr. Connery before she could concentrate on the museum.

Mr. Connery was seated in the lobby when Ruby and Sarah stepped out of the elevator. He was an older version of Matt, with a little salt and pepper in his hair, wire rims, and woolen Scottish cap. He stood up to shake their hands.

"Hi Ruby," he said softly giving her a hug. "Matt described you perfectly. And this must be Sarah. I'm Mr. Connery, Matt's dad," he said with a grin.

"Mom and I miss him. Do you know when we will see him again? He's going to marry my mom," she said proudly.

"I know. I'm so glad he found both of you girls."

"Mr. Connery, how was your flight?" Ruby inquired.

"I flew in yesterday, and the weather couldn't have been smoother. I don't care much for long flights anymore though, because of my arthritis. I have to walk around to get the circulation going again. Old age, and all that," he mused. "Should we go into the dining room and have dinner?" he asked gesturing for the girls to lead the way.

Mr. Connery and Ruby made light conversation because Sarah was at the table. Sarah told him about living in Lisbon and about the friends she had made. She spoke in Portuguese for Mr. Connery, interpreting her words, "You are a nice man, and I can't wait until Matt comes home either." Mr. Connery and Ruby looked at each other with saddened eyes.

"You speak Portuguese so easily, Sarah. Don't worry, we'll find him."

"Do you have a plan?" Ruby asked excitedly.

"Yes, my dear. We'll tackle that problem tomorrow. I've arranged a meeting with Headquarters to see what they can tell me. They may not reveal anything, but I feel I have a right to ask," he said trying not to say too much for Sarah's sake. "Do you ladies have something to do until three?"

Ruby explained wanting to visit the Smithsonian. "Why don't you meet us at the zoo when you finish your meeting? I'll be anxious to find out what they tell you."

The next day, Mr. Connery rode the subway to the CIA Headquarters. He signed in at the main gate and was told to wait in a small office.

A young man entered the room. "Hello, I'm Nathan Bailey. Please follow me," he said leading Mr. Connery to an elevator. He was dressed in a dark suit and had dark features. He pressed a button and they were lifted up towards the sky, stopping on the tenth floor. Mr. Connery was ushered down the narrow hall into another tiny room. An elderly gentleman sat behind a desk. He motioned for him to sit.

"Hello, I'm Mike Murphy. How can I help you today?" he asked curious about their meeting.

Ruby met with Jack Parish, the curator of the Art Museum that morning. She had parked her car at the back entrance, so she could carry her art selections to the basement gallery. Jack was pleased with her work and commented on the frames Ruby chose. The art was carried into an observation room and hung on the bare walls. Display lights were aimed towards the pieces, to show off the artist's strokes and talent. The Board Members made a decision of a floral painting. Ruby was pleased with herself. She thanked them for including her work among those that had been an inspiration to her art. They took several photographs of Ruby and a few with Sarah beside her. Sarah beamed with the attention she received. Ruby suddenly realized with the recognition of her art by the museum, her paintings were worth thousands of dollars. She could decide later about continuing her job in Lisbon, but first Ruby was anxious to see what Mr. Connery had to tell her about Matt.

The girls toured the museum after their meeting and had lunch in the restaurant. Then they walked towards the Air and Space Museum. They watched two films in the downstairs theatre and visited the main attractions in the building. Sarah had fun climbing inside the space capsule and checking out the life of an astronaut. Ruby showed Sarah her favorite exhibit called *The Whimsical*. It looked like someone had made it from a garage full of junk. Ruby liked the music that played, as 'the junk' rotated on a machine. Sarah was mesmerized by the moving art also.

Sarah and Ruby drove to the zoo and were at the gate exactly at three o'clock. Sarah was playing with her cotton candy when Mr. Connery reached around and snatched a piece before she could protest. Sarah laughed at his playfulness. "You're just like Matt," she said offering him another bite.

"I'll take that as a compliment. But I think you have it backwards, he's just like me," he laughed.

"Let's go see the bears, Sarah," Ruby directed using her map to show the way.

They followed the paw prints and found the open cage. Sarah ran ahead to watch them.

"Mr. Connery, I can wait no longer. Please tell me what you found out," Ruby pleaded.

"Well, Mr. Murphy shared what he could. He informed me that

Matt was working in Colombia, South America on an assignment. He didn't reveal what assignment, but I assumed it had to do with drug trafficking. The CIA lost contact with him and several others on Christmas Day. There had been a confrontation. Matt's partners were killed. The bodies of his friends were found by other agents and sent home for burial. They haven't heard from Matt since that day," Mr. Connery said, with tears in his eyes.

"My theory is that if Matt is alive, he may be a prisoner of the Colombian Gorillas. But if that were true, the party responsible would demand a ransom. And right now, no one has made such a claim. I just don't know what to do at this point," Mr. Connery revealed.

"How is the CIA trying to find him?" Ruby inquired.

"They said they can't disclose their rescue tactics. However, they assured me that they're doing everything possible at this time. Since it's been six months now, I'm not sure I believe them. It's almost as if they've written him off as a MIA." Mr. Connery shook his head thinking about his son.

"If Matt is a prisoner with those terrorists, I shutter to think what they are doing to him," Ruby said, using a tissue to wipe her eyes. She had to keep the news from Sarah. Luckily, she was preoccupied with the animals, to notice the adult conversation taking place.

"I guess the only thing we can do now is pray and hope Matt will come home soon. It's in God's hands now. I refuse to believe he's dead. And I won't, not until they produce his body," Matt's father replied, refusing to accept the possibility of Matt's nonexistence.

Ruby put her arm in his, while they continued to walk the hills of the zoo. They needed each other's strength, to bear the possibility of the loss of a son and fiancé. They stopped in the shade often, to block the intense heat beating down on the paved walkways. That day, Ruby became the daughter Mr. Connery never had. They continued the tour in silence.

Out of the west, a storm was brewing. Sarah wanted to see the tigers before leaving, so they took a quick hike to the cave. By the time they reached Ruby's car, heavy raindrops formed a wall, making visibility almost impossible. They drove back to the hotel at a snail's pace. By the time they showered and changed clothes, the sun reappeared. The threesome dined at an outdoor café and said their goodbyes the following morning. Mr. Connery promised to phone, if he learned anything about Matt. He invited Ruby and Sarah to visit the family in Maui for Christmas. Ruby agreed with all her heart.

CHAPTER 27

Ruby had a show in New York to attend, before leaving for Lisbon. She knew that work was the only thing that kept her mind off of Matt. She would have to be patient. Ruby wasn't ready to believe he was dead. She knew in her heart, he was looking at the same sun and moon.

New York was a fantastic show for Ruby. She had twenty pictures displayed in two adjacent rooms. Ruby was one of three artists exhibiting their art. She loved meeting new people and reuniting with old acquaintances. Her hotel room was paid for by the museum and Sarah liked the idea of accompanying her mom for the first time. Ruby bought each of them a new dress for the special occasion.

During the evening reception, Ruby was approached by a dashing, young man full of charisma and charm.

"Hi Ruby, my name's David Harrison. I love your work," he said pointing to it with a champagne glass. "It is so vivacious."

"Thanks, I'm glad you like it. Are you an artist too?"

"No. I wish I had that talent. I'm the historian for the Art International Corporation. I remember meeting you at John Carlson's

250

retirement party. You had mentioned you had an art history degree. Does my memory serve me right?" he added with a grin.

"Yes, and I remember you too. It's great to see you again. Are you located here in New York?" she asked curiously. She observed his tall stature and blond/blue-eyed features.

"No, I'm in Dresden, Germany. In fact, I'm in need of an assistant in my international office there. Are you in a position to accept an offer for the job?" he questioned. "Or are you enjoying a life of leisure, working as an artist?" he mused.

"Well, as a matter of fact, I teach art in Lisbon, Portugal at an international school," Ruby replied. "I'm supposed to return in August. My daughter, Sarah, and I both love it," Ruby explained.

"What would it take to persuade you to think about it?" he questioned, handing her a new glass of champagne.

"May I ask what the job description entails?"

"My office is in downtown Dresden. In my opinion, it's the most beautiful city in Germany. Many have dubbed it as 'The Florence of the North' but you'd have to judge it for yourself. If you like opera, you'll see the most magnificent shows in the Sempreopera House. With your background, I'm sure you already know the history of the city, remembering it was gutted during World War II, and then occupied by the communists until 1991. The people speak German, of course, Russian being their second language."

"Do you speak German?" Ruby wanted to know.

"No, but I'm in the process of learning. It's a struggle, but I know enough to get by," he reassured her. "The Art Museums are some of the finest and the royal jewels in the Albertium are amongst the best collection in the world. I think a true artist, such as yourself, would absorb the art it has to offer," he said, looking at her for a response.

"So what would my job be? You still didn't answer my question." Ruby waited for his answer.

"You would work out of the office in Germany and travel to

European countries occasionally. You would organize exhibitions between the states and Europe.

You would live in the city, at the corporation's expense. And your daughter would attend the international school in Dresden also paid by the company. How is it sounding so far?" David asked, hoping he was convincing her of the job's opportunity of a lifetime.

Ruby thought of the Elton John song 'Someone Saved My Life Tonight' and knew her answer. She accepted it with excitement and surprise because she was that butterfly.

Ruby and Sarah moved to Dresden at the end of the summer. They found a flat on the top floor of a pink apartment building. It was located on Oehmestrasse, near Schillerplatz and the Elbe River. Sarah's school was an old three story house, built in 1901 by a wealthy businessman. After WWII, he sold it to the city.

The girls adjusted easily to living in Dresden. Ruby was given a Mercedes to drive, but she often rode on the trams, because they were efficient and accessible. Sarah made friends immediately at her new school, while Ruby learned the trade of the art world, corresponding daily with international colleagues, on the phone or by email. She arranged art exchanges in different cities and Ruby was taking German because she loved living in Dresden. Ruby painted pictures in her spare time, using the European architecture and subjects to cover her canvases. She was making a name for herself, and the fame was demanding at times.

David was an excellent partner to work with. Ruby felt at ease and learned the trade of being an efficient art dealer and historian. Of course, she made mistakes but that's how she managed to become skilled at her job. Her business trips were usually done in a day, so she didn't have to make alternative arrangements for Sarah.

Ruby heard periodically from Mr. Connery conveying no word of Matt's whereabouts had been discovered. She refused to give up hope. Ruby and Sarah spent Christmas in Maui with Matt's family. Ruby was thrilled to finally be on the beaches that Matt loved. They comforted each other under the difficult circumstances. Shortly after New Years, Mr. Connery received word from the CIA that Matt was presumed dead. They never found his body, which made it hard for the family to accept. Without the necessary closure and peace that needed to take place, the situation haunted them.

Ruby had a private ceremony on the Elbe to celebrate Matt's life, as she finally came to terms with her own. She was 'free to fly' as the seagulls soaring above the beaches. She loved meeting new artists and helping them as she had been, not so very long ago....

Ruby heard the hum of a plane again. She could smell the scent of a rose, but she couldn't quite place where she was. Suddenly, she realized she had fallen asleep and the hot sun was causing her to perspire. Ruby felt something at the end of her nose, causing it to tickle. She opened her eyes. It took her a few minutes to awaken from her dream. She obviously had dozed off, remembering the sound of the plane. A figure was leaning over her with a stem in his hand.

"I told you I'd find you." Matt bent down and kissed her.

EPILOGUE

Ruby worked in Dresden for the next ten years. She and Sarah learned fluent German, and they loved their exciting life in 'The Florence of the North'. They traveled around the world on holidays, but always returned to North Carolina spending time between Asheville and Frisco. Ruby continued collecting tiles and CDs wherever she went because music and art were her life. Her family visited Germany at least once a year. Ruby finally purchased her own house overlooking the Elbe River where she could see three castles from her bedroom window. Sarah graduated from the international school and attended college back in the States.

Matt had been living outside of Cali, South America when he and his partners were attacked on Christmas Day. Matt was shot in his abdomen but managed to escape during the massacre, by rolling under a thick-leafed bush. Through the foliage, he witnessed his colleagues being killed. He used his shirt to wrap around his wound and waited for the guerillas to disburse. The pain was excruciating, causing him to vomit. Breathing was difficult. He must have passed out from loss of blood, because when he awoke, he was inside a hut being attended to by an elderly woman. She had given him opium to relieve his pain, while she removed the bullet. The woman sewed the small hole and bandaged the wound with a rag. He had developed a fever which meant he had an infection. She used medicines from the woods to treat his condition, using a cold, wet cloth to wipe the perspiration from his face. A mosquito net was placed around his bed. Matt remained in the bed for several weeks, slowly regaining strength each day. The woman continued to give him the opium to sedate his pain. Eventually, he was hooked on the drug, unable to think clearly.

When he felt strong enough, Matt quietly escaped one night. He had no idea where he was and soon became disoriented in the woods. Without money or an ID, the only weapon he had was the Boy Scout knife and compass Ruby had given him. Matt used the knife to make a weapons out of bamboo and the compass to try to find the shore to freedom. He decided he had to find work to make money. Without it, he didn't stand a chance of leaving the country much less contacting the CIA. He also knew he had to get rid of his addiction.

Unfortunately, one evening before the sun went down, Matt was caught by guerillas. They beat him severely and threw him into a caved prison. They decided he was more useful to them alive. The men kept him prisoner in Covenas and forced him to perform hard labor. Matt only spoke English, hiding his language comprehension a secret from his captors. Eventually, he knew every person's name involved with the drug trafficking in their organization and how they managed to smuggle the illegal goods across the borders. Meanwhile, he was given Opium to maintain his dependency. The guerillas assumed he wouldn't try to escape, if he stayed near his drug source.

Time seemed to be endless in Matt's Opium world. He remained at their disposal for years. Finally, a CIA agent happened to hear of an American being held prisoner. It took months of preparation for the organization to manage his escape. They attended his skeletal and drug abused body. Matt had to undergo the Hell of Opium withdrawals. His body needed nourishment and exercise. They weren't sure he would heal as quickly as he did. The only thing that kept him focused and alive was Ruby.

With Matt's information, the CIA managed to confiscate large quantities of coca, opium poppy, cannabis, and heroin. Matt revealed names of major drug cartel members and where operations were taking place.

Matt left the CIA the summer of 2001 and traveled to North Carolina to find Sarah. He had to question her about Ruby. He didn't know for sure if her mother cared for him or if she had become involved with someone else. He had to know. Sarah relieved his mind when she hugged and kissed him tenderly saying, "I'm still waiting to be a flower girl."

That same day he flew to the Frisco Airport. He saw a lady lounging on the deck. He walked along the beach with a rose in his hand.

Matt and Ruby had a small wedding on the Frisco beach with family members and a few close friends. Sarah was their flower girl after all. She tossed rose pedals high into the air, while the spectators watched them fly around in the Hatteras trade winds....